ALL GONE

M. K. Jones

This story is a work of fiction. Names and characters are the product of the author's imagination and any resemblance to actual persons, living or dead, is entirely co-incidental. Where real historical persons, places and events are features, they appear only as the author imagined them to be.

Cover design: www.alicat-design.co.uk

ISBN (paperback): 978-1-80227-791-3

Chapter 1

Email

Sitting in her window seat, propped up with squashy cushions, reading the latest release by one of her favourite authors, Belle Harrington paused to pick up her mug and glance out at the bedraggled garden.

Soon she would transfer to one of the two settees in front of the roaring wood burner, but for now as the light faded, she put a finger on the window to trace the downward path of one of the fat globules of rain smashing into the glass. The forecast had said that the rain and wind would cease by mid-afternoon. The forecast was wrong. At lunchtime she had contemplated taking the short walk down to the harbour, but having lost the battle to force open the kitchen door, changed her mind and her clothes and settled for a quiet afternoon reading.

She stood, stretched, rolled her neck and closed the shutters. Maybe some dinner, maybe not. She had just reached the settee when a ping in the background announced an incoming email. She rolled her eyes and sighed. Read it now, or leave it 'til the morning? Nothing important pending.

A yawn stretched her jaw. Might as well check.

Her desk sat in an alcove at the back of the room. She opened the laptop and the single email. The sender was not a name she recognised: *lizzibird,* and the address a string of meaningless letters.com. Spam. The content held one sentence.

'Leave it alone, Penning'.

'What the hell ...?' A moment of bewilderment, then she jumped up and back from the desk. Who ...?

Calm down. Think. Her heart slowed as she sorted out thoughts from reaction. *lizzibird*? No-one she knew had that email name. She sat tentatively back down on the computer chair, staring at the words on the screen.

Think logically. This is hostile. Someone wants to stop me doing something. But I haven't done anything! No-one knows why I'm here.

'Leave it alone, Penning.'

Penning? She and Sam Harrington had married in her first year of university so she had been known as Harrington for over thirty years. The only people who knew her as 'Penning' were from her school days. What had happened to ...?

The reunion.

A month earlier, on a Saturday in mid-September, she had attended a school reunion, her first, feeling able at last to re-visit her past. She had recognised a few former schoolmates; one she had casually kept in touch with, most not. They had told stories of their lives, adventures, successes and tragedies. She hadn't shared, of course, just listened, smiled, nodded, sympathised where required, then moved on. Some she had expected to see had been missing, which took her back to the story – she couldn't recall who had told it – of one particular group, memorable for all the wrong reasons, none of whom were there, except for their group leader. Back home she had put it and them out of her mind. So, why the email? Why now? What had she done?

She closed her eyes, clasped her hands behind her head. The photograph? In one of the last moving boxes she had found an envelope of old black-and-white photos, that included one taken at the school, in their final year, of the now missing group. The day after the reunion she had posted the picture on its website, asking if anyone knew where they were now. There had been no replies.

Is that what this was about? Could there have been credence to the tale? Which meant, could her innocuous question have scared someone enough to send a threating message? She could just ignore it, of course, delete it. Pretend she hadn't seen it. There had been no response to her enquiry, after all.

No.

She took a deep breath and typed back. '*Who is this?*'

Five minutes. No reply. She tried again. '*What do you want?*'

Ping. '*Leave it alone, Penning. Or else.*'

Wow! Or else – what? Definitely intimidation. Anger replaced fear. How dare they, whoever they were.

She typed again. '*Not sure what you want. Is it about the photo?*'

No reply.

She glanced back at her novel, sitting on the settee, waiting for her, sighed, then turned her attention back to the laptop and began searching. For a group of girls, now women; six women, who, according to the story at the reunion, had died or disappeared at five-yearly intervals, in the December following each five-year reunion, over the course of twenty-five years. A group of six she had known. A group of out-of-control school bullies.

All gone.

Chapter 2

Co-incidence?

After a couple of hours' restless sleep interrupted at hourly intervals, Belle got out of bed and peeped through the curtains at the wreckage of the garden. This had been the first serious storm since her arrival at St Foy. The house agent had assured her that the south coast of Cornwall was far less exposed to the vagaries of the weather than the wild Atlantic north coast, but after last night – well, she'd definitely been bamboozled there. Estate agents, eh?

It wasn't as bad as she'd feared. The wind still howled but there was no serious destruction to plant life. Most looked bedraggled and stressed, but a dose of quiet and sunlight would ensure recovery. The cottage garden – unusually substantial for a small, historic hillside town – had attracted her as much as its size and location, just a five-minute walk from the town square on the estuary. And the fact that it had been available on a six-month rental, renewable for a further six months.

In the galley kitchen, she made herself a pot of strong coffee, donned a raincoat and wellies and went outside to take a closer look. At close range the damage was still minor, nothing that couldn't be quickly repaired.

She crossed the lawn to the half a dozen steps and the gate that led to a narrow back lane and walked down to the sea.

There were few visitors in the town. She had the harbour front to herself, and sat on the low wall, overlooking the turbulent waters as they swept in and up the estuary. She watched yachts bobbing and swaying on the opposite bank, where the new marina had been built a few years earlier, beneath the older settlement that crowned the summit of the hill. The tide was full and smashing waves against the wall, sending up showers of water that would have soaked any unsuspecting tourist sitting there to admire the view. She pulled her mass of auburn curly hair out of her face and tied it up with one of the flamboyant headbands she kept in her coat pockets.

This was her calm, go-to spot, at any time and in any weather, but today 'bracing' was more apt, as she fought against a sudden gust attempting to blow her over the wall into the water, forcing a retreat to a bench a few yards back.

On a milder day she would have walked along the esplanade to the small beach, the site of her final and happiest memory with her father in this place, just after her ninth birthday.

Gillian had stayed in the car, she remembered, *rigid and disapproving. In those days you could park on the side of the road and she and Dad had the beach to themselves. Gillian didn't like sand. Gillian didn't like anything, or anyone. They had had a lovely time, playing on the beach, building sandcastles, swimming in the calm, cold water. She should have been in school, but Gillian had insisted on a short break. The beach had been empty. Then, there was someone else there. Then, everything had changed. Her life had turned from happiness to misery. It was the boy, but what had really happened? Gillian's dying revelation had been shocking, told in revenge and spite. She wanted to believe it, but nothing Gillian ever said was trustworthy. Belle needed the truth. She had to find the boy, to be certain, but after almost six months in St Foy she had found nothing.*

Whatever the risk in following it up, this email would at least provide her with distraction from her lack of progress on the other thing. She opened her eyes and forced her thoughts back to the notes she had written last night about the school reunion and as much as she could remember of what had been said by people she had spoken to. '*Leave it alone.*' Had she heard something that someone didn't want revealed? Possibly, but what was it? Her scribblings had prompted nothing further, no sudden revelation, no dawning realisation of a major issue hiding in plain sight. Nothing, apart from the curious co-incidence of the dates.

Co-incidence; hadn't she had a discussion not long ago on that subject? She puzzled for a few moments, closed her eyes and squeezed her brain to bring the information forward. It was at the reunion. She'd had the discussion with her old classmate, Maggie Gilbert, the only person with whom she kept in touch from time to time. Maggie, now a genealogy investigator, had talked about her experience when exploring peoples' history. Maggie believed that, whilst there were random events in the world that occasionally clashed, parallels on this scale had meaning. Sometimes clear, other times hidden so well that you had to work hard to discover their relationship and significance.

In a perverse way, those six women had added to the direction Belle had chosen for a career, for her life. Not that she thanked them, not then, not now. She could only remember them as she had last encountered them, at eighteen – loud, brash, spiteful and vicious. She could recall her dismay when, at fifteen, she had been forcibly relocated yet again. The school chosen for her was small and religious, a girls' school. Belle, the new girl, had been singled out from her first day, but her silence, her refusal to rise to any of the baiting, had bored them eventually and they had turned their attention onto others less able to ignore them. Internally she had raged, but had kept herself cool and apart, determined that one day she would find a way to gain the satisfaction of annihilating this destructive, soul-destroying behaviour. And she had succeeded.

She took out a pen and notebook, but the wind whipped the pages making it impossible to write. She jumped to her feet, turned away from the sea and headed along the main street of shops to the ninety-degree corner where the street climbed in a dogleg uphill and into the maze of smaller streets and ancient lanes. Pushed on by gusts of wind, she climbed the half-dozen steps to the front door of a small café and flung it open. It was time to share.

Chapter 3

Curiosity

It had begun with Mavis. It was Mavis' fault, plus Belle's inability, despite her determination, to mind her own business in the face of a nemesis when she had first found the café.

Belle had come to live in St Foy by way of a mini mental breakdown. She had already bought an apartment in South Wales, although she wasn't sure why she had bought it, other than that she had to get out of London and away from everything to do with Gillian. Newport had just been somewhere she knew from the past, from her school days.

She had held in so much pent-up fear for so long, then rage. One day, standing on the balcony looking out over the river and the town, she had snapped, wept, picked up her car keys and driven for hours. It was a miracle she hadn't killed herself or anyone else before she reached St Foy. She had been living in fog since Gillian's death. As she parked in the centre of St Foy, the fog lifted and Belle knew what she had to do, why her subconscious brain had brought her to the town. She began to look for somewhere to live.

It was always meant to be a short term stay. Her husband and son were both gone: Sam dead, James working in Africa. She didn't want or need friendship, certainly did not want to become a member of any kind of group.

After a few months she was on friendly greeting terms with the proprietors of the local bookshop, a few art galleries and the deli.

Wanting to use local businesses instead of supermarket or high street brands, she had found everything she needed in neighbourhood establishments. One of these was the small café, an outlier, about five minutes' walk along the High Street and up into the alleyways that characterised the town and enchanted the tourists. This particular café was run by a woman whose name she had discovered was Posy, a tall, angular woman, with a short grey pixie cut, always dressed in jeans, tee-shirt and lefty-sloganned apron.

Posy Clements wasn't the kind of proprietor who thought it was hospitable to ask prying questions; she had realised after a couple of visits that Belle was not a tourist and had served her with a pleasant smile and silence.

Belle usually headed to the café after one of her long walks along the coast or into the countryside, once a week, sometimes twice, and had adopted a preferred table: in the smaller of the two window alcoves. A few times she had noticed a group of three women sitting in the opposite corner at the furthest table from the door – a table positioned well away from others. Sometimes it had a 'reserved' sign to stop other customers trying to use it.

On that particular day, as Belle entered, just one of the women sat at the corner table. Standing over her, haranguing her with a wagging finger was someone she hadn't come across before, an imposing character, short and solidly wide, wearing the ubiquitous two-piece suit and pearls of the wealthy, not-quite-elderly chair of many committees, her salt-and-pepper hair pulled into a tight bun with not a strand daring to escape. The sitting woman had backed as far into the corner as she could go and was now trying to push herself into the wall. *Like a trembling rabbit*, Belle thought. But it was the expression on the face of the lecturer that killed her momentary amusement and set her off. She had seen it so often in her career, and before, cruelty and malice combined with enjoyment at the ensuing reaction.

Don't get involved, Belle, she urged herself. *None of your business. This is not what you came here for.* The woman trying to blend into the wall began to cry. Posy Clements looked furious. That did it. A lightening flash of the past, a woman standing over a man, screaming abuse, lashing out as she watched, helpless. A cold, quiet rage surfaced. Most of the time she could control it, push it back down and out of reach, but in some situations it was beyond control.

She walked up to the counter and mouthed to Posy, '*What's her name?*', pulling an expression similar to the crying woman. '*Mavis,*' the café owner mouthed back.

Taking a deep breath, Belle turned around and slid past the lecturer and onto the bench, causing the wagging finger to pause in mid-air.

'Mavis! Sorry I'm late. My dear, what's the matter?' She looked up. 'Who are you and why is my friend crying?'

The woman stopped mid-sentence. 'Who do you think you are? This is a private conversation.'

'No, it isn't. It's being conducted in front of the entire café. Whatever it's about, please leave my friend and me alone. Remove yourself. Now. Please.' The entire café was a table of four other customers, who were staring at each other, heads to the side, trying to catch every word.

Mavis stopped crying and her mouth dropped open.

On the face of the other, outrage replaced malice. 'How dare you speak to me like that. I am an important person in this town.'

Belle shrugged and turned away, leaving the woman, finger still in the air, standing and uncertain what to do next as Belle whispered to Mavis. 'Don't worry. She'll go any minute. Trust me.'

And she did. As the woman marched to the door, its old-fashioned overhanging bell clanged and Mavis' friends entered. They stopped as Mrs Outrage passed them. They stared at her, then at Mavis and Belle, then rushed to the table.

'Mavis, oh my goodness, I'm so sorry we're late. The Fox got here before us.' This was spoken by the younger of the two, an attractive woman in her mid-forties, with long fair curling hair and beautiful large grey eyes.

Belle stood. 'I'll let you sit down with Mavis. That woman was haranguing her. I stepped in. Sorry if I overstepped the mark.'

'Not at all, thank you,' Mavis said, sniffing into a tissue.

Belle went to move back to her usual table, but the third member of the group stood in her way.

'Who might you be?'

'My name is Belle Harrington. I'm living in St Foy. Now, as the crisis is over, I'll just get back to my table.' She smiled at Posy, who said, 'Lucky dip on the cake?' Belle nodded.

'Not so fast,' said number three. 'What's gone on here, then?'

'You'll find that Mavis was being verbally assaulted by the woman you called The Fox. I stepped in. That's all, really. I'd like to go now, if that's OK with you.' She put her hands in her pockets, controlled her breathing.

'I suppose so. Um, I'm not sure if I should thank you or not.'

Belle summoned up a smile. 'Ask Mavis.'

'I will.' This one wasn't exactly belligerent, but was clearly the strongest member of the group, the one who might have done what Belle had done, if she'd been there in time.

'Sit down, Bette,' Posy said. She turned to Belle. 'Take your seat, and I'll bring your coffee and cake.'

The cake here was exceptional. Belle had tried three or four kinds and each one was outrageously good. Today Posy had decided on and served ginger. Belle was just finishing her notes, ignoring the bent heads and whispering from the corner, when a voice called her attention.

'Excuse me, Belle. We were just wondering how you knew Pearl Hawkesworth Fox would go, just like you said to Mavis. Would you mind coming over to our table?' It was the pretty one, whose name she hadn't picked up.

This was exactly what she didn't want, but given how she had pushed herself in earlier, it would be rude to refuse. She closed her book and nodded. 'I was about to leave, I only have a few minutes.'

'A few minutes will be enough.'

She joined them.

'Right, Belle, isn't it? I'm Bette Jones,' said number three. Mavis you know, and this is Rose. So, how did you know Pearl would leave? We're curious. We've never been able to get rid of her that fast.'

How much should she tell them? As little as possible, but enough to satisfy their curiosity, hopefully. 'The Hawkesworth Fox woman is a classic bully. Her reaction was predictable. I know that because it was part of my profession, to deal with bullies.'

'Funny profession,' Bette Jones replied, scowling.

'Not to me. I worked in "employee relations". It involves dealing with people who behave badly at work.'

'You must have been good at it,' the ethereal Rose remarked.

Belle smiled. 'I was; very good at it. Someone like Pearl Hawkesworth Fox must be seen to be in control. Once I pointed out she was being observed, then ignored her, she had two choices, either to continue and I would continue to ignore her, or walk away. I saved her making the decision by asking her to leave. She's not the kind of personality you can reason with long-term, though, but I guess you know that already. She'll be back. I'm sorry if that will cause you more hassle,' she said to Mavis.

'She always comes back and you've hit the nail right on the head,' Bette Jones said.

'Now, I have to go,' Belle said, standing up.

'We was discussing it, and we wondered if you'd like to join us for a chat, maybe tomorrow?'

Oh no, Belle thought. A group of gossiping nosy parkers with a problem was high on her list of people to avoid.

Before she could reply, Bette Jones said, 'We meet here once a week, sometimes more often. We're not just a bunch of gossips, which is what you're thinking. We aren't interested in goings-on, or affairs, or scandal, that kind of thing. There are certain matters catch our attention: peculiarities, oddnesses, surprises,' she paused, then added 'malignancy.' We're … a sort of club.'

Even worse. Definitely no clubs, groups or associations. Nothing with rules.

She began to shake her head and politely refuse, when Bette Jones spoke again.

'We,' she swept her arm back at the table, 'are the Curiosity Club of St Foy, and we think you're exactly what we need, right now.'

'I see. So, what are the rules?'

'Rules? Don't be daft. There aren't any rules.'

Chapter 4

Plans

It was the bullying that had drawn her in, with Bette's reference to "malignancy". Despite how little she knew or cared about this group, she had been unable to resist the opportunity to help deal with a bully. She had dedicated her life's work to confronting behaviour she found abhorrent, and the people who exhibited it. It was the way she had chosen to deal with her own demons and find a way to fight back, choosing a role that had been more vocation than profession, one that many Human Resources professionals avoided. She had embraced it. That had been welcome enough for the companies she had joined, and she had been so good at it that no-one had ever questioned her motivation. Just as well.

But this would be a one-off. No joining any group. She was there to help with one issue. Hers was a short stay.

Belle had joined them the following morning. They had been welcoming, friendly and, surprisingly, lacking in inquisitiveness about her personal life, or why she had come to the town. She had given them a few basic facts. Her former career they already knew about; she told them she was a widow with a son working abroad, and that her mother had died recently, in a care home in London, where the family had a large house in Kensington. She had sold the house, liquidated the remaining assets, bought an apartment in her original home town of Newport in South Wales, but come to St Foy to recuperate from the stress of the deaths of her husband

and her mother, which was fifty per cent true. They had accepted it without invasive probing.

Bette Jones had been forced by the others to admit that the 'Curiosity Club of St Foy' had been an on-the-spot invention.

'I knew right away you have skills we don't have, to deal with Pearl Hawkesworth Fox, but I didn't want you to think we're just a group of chattering, nosy busybodies. We do actually talk about problems we know about and how we might help.'

Belle had laughed, and never told them that was exactly what she had thought. Curiosity: not one of the seven deadly sins, but definitely one of the indented sub-headings.

She found she liked them and this was, against her instincts and resolve, the beginnings of friendship. Most importantly, they respected her privacy, didn't pry. Perhaps it would be OK, until she had to go.

* * *

At the top of the steps a strong gust at her back thrust her over the threshold and slammed her up against the counter. Posy had run to shut the door behind her.

'Sorry, it's bad out there.' Belle sat at her assigned chair at the back corner table, the first to arrive.

'They're probably on their way,' Posy said, bringing coffee and cake. 'I have a fresh Victoria sponge today, thought you'd like to try.'

Belle took a bite. 'Wonderful,' she sighed. 'You're a brilliant baker, Posy.'

'Not me. I have a local supplier. Ah, here comes the club,' she said, grinning.

The Curiosity Club of St Foy had remained a joke amongst them. They were five in all, Posy included and Belle making up the fifth and, as Bette assured her, the final member. 'Five is quite enough. The table's not big enough for more.'

Bette Jones was a local farmer's wife, Belle had learned. Approaching sixty-five and lifetime resident of St Foy. Her husband Bert the farmer was eight generations St Foy. Mavis Tregoss, a quiet, thoughtful woman in her late fifties, short and with a stoop, was also local, the wife of a solicitor whose expertise was in conveyancing. Rose Teague, to Belle's surprise, was the wife of the local vicar, Harry Teague. Rose hadn't struck her as religious and, since knowing her better, was now quite sure that she wasn't. She hadn't met Harry Teague yet, but had been told he was about ten years older than Rose, cheerful, popular and that they were a devoted couple. Posy, well, she was like Belle, a woman with a past who kept it to herself.

They sat down and spent five minutes discussing the storm, as Posy served drinks, then joined them.

Rose turned to Belle, smiled serenely and nodded. 'What's up with you, Belle?'

'Your spooky radar at work, Rose?' She pursed her lips for a moment and glanced at the four women. *Rose's radar*, as they referred to it, was never wrong.

'Something's come up. You remember I mentioned went to my old school reunion? A story was circulating that a group of women, who were close to each other at the time, had all either died or disappeared and at around the same time of year?'

'You didn't mention that story,' Mavis Tregoss said. 'You said you posted a photo that you found, on the site, but no-one replied.'

'Well, last night an email arrived from someone I don't know. All it said was, "*Leave it alone*".'

'So of course you replied and told them to clear off.'

'No, Bette. I asked for details. The response I got was "*Leave it alone, or else*".'

'That's not nice. Something for the Curiosity Club to get its teeth into,' Bette said, with a huge grin.

'It's not funny, Bette,' Mavis said.

Bette huffed.

'Listen, I wanted to tell you what's happened, but I didn't sleep well and I'm tired now. So, how about you come to supper this evening? I can pull notes together and we can talk it over. I'd appreciate your input. That OK with you too, Posy?'

'Love to,' Posy replied. 'What time? I'll be closing up at five.'

'Around six thirty suit you all?'

Another check and confirmation. 'Perfect.'

'Good. I'll see you all then. You know I'm vegetarian. Is that OK or should I cook something else for you?'

'No, let's give it a go,' Bette replied.

'Good.' She checked her watch. 'Mavis, is there any more news on Pearl Hawkesworth Fox?'

The initial issue, they had explained, had been that Pearl Hawkesworth Fox was trying to interfere with the living arrangements for Mavis' ninety-four-year-old Aunt Tessa.

'She's been to see Tessa again. This time she brought the social services woman with her. I don't like it at all, but Andrew says we shouldn't worry, not yet.'

Belle wasn't so sure that Andrew Tregoss was right, but they could discuss it later.

Outside the café Belle turned right and up the short flight of steps onto a narrow pedestrian lane that ran between the backs of houses on both sides. There were many of these short flights of six or seven steps and interconnecting lanes in the town. Some ran parallel to the estuary, others up the hillside to where the high ground levelled off and there was a magnificent view of where the estuary suddenly narrowed and road and train bridges ran across to the opposite bank.

Pearl Hawkesworth Fox, she thought as she walked, *is a bully dangerous enough to cause real harm.* Whatever the nasty piece of work was up to this time, in Belle's opinion Mavis should be worried.

Five minutes later she was home. Divesting herself of raincoat and wellies and donning comfy slippers Belle started up her laptop and was soon printing off reams of paper.

She checked her email again. No more messages from her mystery intimidator. She wondered briefly if one of the girls would know anything about how to trace the email. She could ask. You never knew. She began her summaries.

Chapter 5

Dinner

They arrived promptly at six thirty. Posy, Rose and Mavis had dressed up, but Bette was in the same clothes including the wellingtons. They removed coats and shoes and walked through the internal entrance porch into the main sitting room.

Belle had built up the fire in the log burning stove, which was now cracking and blazing in the wide stone hearth. Two settees formed an L-shape in front of the hearth and Belle gestured to them to sit, asking if anyone wanted a drink.

They were all laughing and joking as she brought out coffees and teas and a gin-and-tonic for Bette. 'What's the joke?'

'I was just remembering the first time, shortly after we met and I had to 'fess up about the Curiosity Club of St Foy. Like I said then, I didn't want you to think that we were just sniping and gossiping, and the name just sort of came to me. Curiosity Club of St Foy.' She grinned. 'Good, wasn't it?'

Belle couldn't help smiling back. 'Yes, it was. I thought it made you sound dynamic. Like you had purpose, in a fun sort of way, but with edginess. OK, you made it up. But, you know, things happen for a reason. Perhaps deep down …'

'Deep down, we needed a solution to a problem that's been cursing this town for some time now,' Posy interrupted, 'In the person of that fat bitch.'

'Posy, don't talk about her like that,' Rose chided. 'Yes, she's an unpleasant woman and she's blighting lives, but we mustn't get down to her level. Fighting fire with fire hasn't worked. We need a more sophisticated solution.' She looked directly at Belle. 'I believe you came along at the perfect moment in time. You may be the solution.'

Belle frowned, but turned it into a smile. 'OK. How about we break here and eat. I want to hear more but it may be easier at the table over a meal.'

Bette jumped to her feet. 'Good idea. I'm starved. Come on girls, let's lighten this up a bit.'

* * *

As Belle cleared crockery from the table into the kitchen, listening to the chat and laughter coming from the group now making themselves comfortable around the fire she was, against her initial determination, thankful to have people with whom she could share her concern about the emails.

'Penny for them.'

She glanced up to find Rose standing behind her, hands full of plates and cutlery. 'That was a lovely meal. Harry says we should all be thinking about eating more plant-based food, but he knows I'm a hopeless cook.'

'Nothing much. I was just pondering on friendship. How it can happen.'

Rose smiled. 'You wouldn't think we'd be such a group, would you? What we've found is that what we have in common brings us together and keeps us loyal to each other.'

'A belief in fairness and decency.'

Rose beamed. 'Quite right.' She glanced around the kitchen. 'Thank you so much for inviting us here. You have beautiful taste. I love the pale blues and greys. Did I see some of these things,' she waved at a couple of pictures and vases, 'in a shop off the square?'

'Yes. I thought I'd buy local.' Belle paused for a moment. 'Rose, can I ask you something?'

'Of course.'

'It's about a story I heard from the past, about a boy who fell off the rocks down at Cash Cove, and died. Do you remember that?'

Rose frowned. 'When was it?'

'In the nineteen seventies.'

'I wasn't here. Harry might know. I'll ask him, or you could ask Bette.'

'No,' Belle replied, quickly. 'Don't worry. It isn't important.'

Rose shrugged. 'OK, but if you want me to find out …'

Belle shook her head again. 'Forget I asked, please.'

Rose paused for a moment. 'Shall we get back to the others? Time for the business of the evening, I think.'

In the living room the conversation died as Belle and Rose took their seats and all faces turned to Belle.

'Lovely dinner,' Bette said. 'Never thought I'd like beans so much. Where do we start?'

'Before we get into mine, I'd like to update my thoughts on Pearl and thanks, Mavis, for the background information. My initial idea was to find out more about her, where she came from before she arrived here. Everyone has a history. I'm interested in hers, so I asked my friend who's an expert in family history to dig about a bit. Her name's Maggie Gilbert, of Maze Investigations. She's puzzled why she can't find much and thinks they may have changed their names. Her colleague, Zelah Trevear, is looking into it. They'll get back to me as soon as they have something. It's worrying for Tessa, though,'

'She's bearing up,' Mavis said. 'Aunty Tessa's a feisty old woman. Truth is, she ought to be looked after, but she wants to die in her own home, and I think that's her right. She's ninety-four, after all and she's made it this far.'

The others nodded.

'Any news about the ownership of her house?' Belle asked. 'I know Andrew confirmed there was no record of her husband inheriting it, but what about your friend Dan? You said he's a local historian, Bette. Could he take a shot at it?'

'If he gets back next week, like he's supposed to, we'll ask him.' She rolled her eyes at the others. 'Dan's not the most reliable. He likes to wander and this time he's been away much longer than usual. He did say when he left in April, he'd be back in time for my birthday next month. It's my sixty-fifth,' she added with a grimace. 'And I don't want no fuss.'

Belle caught a quick wink from Posy and bit down a grin. 'Fair enough. Your choice.' She suspected planning was already underway.

'Are you sure Mrs Fox is trying to get Tessa out because she wants the house?'

Bette snorted. 'We suspect it's for a relative of hers. A nephew, I think. Fancies himself a second-home-owner, on the cheap.'

'But surely if there's proof of ownership, he wouldn't be able to easily get his hands on it?'

'Fox has got something up her sleeve,' Posy muttered. 'Don't know what, but I've seen the look in her eyes when she's talking about it. Triumphant, like.'

'Well, that's our issue. Now what about yours?' Bette said.

Belle stood and crossed the room to her desk. 'I've written up a set of notes for you. Basically, it's this.' She handed them each a set as she spoke. 'At the reunion in September, there was a story I heard, about a group, a gang of bullies, led by a girl called Kat Harris. She had six followers. Kat Harris was at the reunion in September. The six were not. The reunions take place every five years. Well, we left the school in the summer of 1987, so the first reunion for us was in 1990. I didn't go, nor did Maggie or her best friend, Jude Crawley Winters. Same as me, they went for the first time this year.'

'Why only this year?' Posy asked. 'Is that important?'

'No. I received the usual email. I'd always ignored them before. I'm not one for going back over the past, but when I was moving, I brought down boxes from the loft of my mother's house. Amongst the stuff I found was a photograph of the bully gang.' She stopped again for a moment. 'After the reunion I put the photo on its Facebook page, asking if anyone knew the girls in this group and what they were doing now. I didn't get a response, and I'd forgotten about it, until the email yesterday. Last night I did internet searches. The reason none of the six were at the reunion is that three of them are dead and three are just … missing.'

Rose said, 'You said the reunion takes place every five years. When did these six women stop coming and is that related to their individual stories?'

'There has been one fewer every five years, in the year of the reunions; now there's only the leader left. She's the same age as me, early-fifties.'

Rose nodded and put her head back down.

They looked up one by one as they finished reading.

'So far, this *is* somewhat curious,' Bette said.

'I thought so,' Belle replied. 'And it gets more so. I've tried to tell myself that it's co-incidence, no more than that. But I'm not sure. Let me give you the quick summary, to give you the context of what to read next. The reunion group is on Facebook, that's where I put the picture. But the response came by email. I hadn't included my email in the info I put on the group chat. On the following pages you'll find a summary of each case. Are you all happy to go on reading?' They nodded. 'Good. Off you go, then.'

Chapter 6

Summaries

Before I begin these summaries, here are the basic facts about our time in school together. We were all born in the academic year 1968/69. We began this secondary level of education in September 1980. The incident I will finish with occurred in January 1987, the academic year in which they were due to leave following 'A' levels. All seven of the gang plus myself, Maggie Gilbert and Jude Crawley Winters were taking 'A' levels, in our second year of sixth form, now known as Year 13.

Case No 1: **Angela Stephenson**.
Died.
Date of death: 1990. December
Cause of death: Drug overdose.
Age at death: 22.
Status: Single.
After an office Christmas party Angela and members of her team, of which she was the supervisor, went on to a nightclub. Angela had drunk a great deal of alcohol and expressed an interest in 'trying something else'. Her team left her in the club. Her body was found the following morning, amongst the rubbish bins at the back of the club. The autopsy showed a massive overdose of heroin cut with another substance, which had been injected. The verdict was accidental death. There was no evidence of her being an addict, but she had been known to use cocaine and smoke dope.

Case No 2: **Bernadette (Bernie) Moloney**.

Died.

Date of death: 13 December 1995.

Cause of death: Hit-and-run.

Age at death: 26.

Status: Married, two daughters.

Officer in charge was Sergeant Maldwyn – known as Mal – Jenkins. Bernie told her family she had received poison pen letters but had not reported them to the police. She had burned the letters. Investigation was eventually dropped after car not found.

Case No 3: **Tina Lewis**.

Disappeared.

Year of Disappearance: 2000, December, three days before Christmas.

Age at disappearance: 31.

Status: Married, no children.

Tina went to Cardiff to do last-minute Christmas shopping. She was last seen in a coffee shop. When she didn't return home, her husband reported her missing. He told police in Newport, where they lived, that Tina was unhappy about having to go to his parents' home on Christmas day. They had argued. Neighbours reported that the couple had many rows and there was a suspicion of violence. Police don't seem to have done much to find her. Police officer following up was Detective Sergeant Mal Jenkins. He concluded that she had had enough and disappeared of her own accord.

Case No 4: **Denise Goodright**.

Died.

Date of death: 2 December 2005.

Cause of death: Drowned whilst on holiday in Australia.

Age: 36.

Status: Married, two children aged thirteen and nine.

Disappeared after telling family she was going for an early morning swim at their beach resort. Didn't return. Body washed up a day later. No evidence of animal attack, but some damage at first unexplained by drowning. Autopsy and coroner eventually ruled she had been swimming with scuba gear around rocks and had become snagged, unable to free herself. Outcome: accident, no suspicious circumstances.

Case No 5: **Lizzie Maynard**.

Disappeared.

Date of disappearance: mid-December 2010.

Age: 42.

Status: Divorced, one daughter aged seventeen.

Daughter reported her missing. She had gone to work and not returned home. She had been seen in a pub after work, drinking alone. Frequently at the same pub after work, known to have alcohol problems. Told landlord when leaving she had to 'sort someone out'. Police investigation (Inspector Mal Jenkins) decided she had left of her own accord.

Case No 6: **Faith Shepherd**.

Disappeared.

Date of disappearance: last seen around early December 2015.

Age: 47.

Status: Single.

Known to police for prostitution. Known drug user. Living on state benefits. Disappearance not reported until mid-January 2016. Investigation conducted nominally by Detective Inspector Mal Jenkins. Evidence of being seen in Bristol in February. Conclusion of case: she had moved away, despite most of her personal possessions remaining at her bedsit.

Following the summaries Belle had added notes about how she had found the information from internet and newspaper research. She could see frowns, small head shakes. Rose, who had brought a pencil, scribbled furiously in the margins. Posy was the first to finish, Bette the last. At the end, they sat in silence.

'So, thoughts, anyone?'

'Well, this Mal Jenkins looks like a right tosser,' Bette said, with a grimace. 'Did he even bother to go any further into their backgrounds?'

'I don't think so,' Belle replied, 'but bear in mind that we have the advantage of seeing these histories from a different viewpoint, and all at the same time.'

'Hmm. I suppose. But even so …'

'What do you want us to do, to help you?' Rose interrupted. She turned to Bette. 'Let's not make any assumptions until we've thought this through.' She paused and nodded, her eyes flickering away from Bette to the ceiling and back. 'I can see why no-one would have picked up any connection between these cases. Unless you knew they had all known each other at some point, why would you?'

'Why don't you chat amongst yourselves for a few minutes. I'm going to put on a fresh pot of coffee.'

The hum of conversation picked up as Belle headed into the kitchen. As she waited for the kettle to boil, she glanced into the room. Discussion was animated. Bette, Rose and Posy were all leaning back and forward in their chairs, hands gesticulating, engrossed. Mavis wasn't joining in, sitting upright, frowning, biting her lips. Belle had learned this was Mavis' way, not immediately getting into the subject, thinking it through before speaking. Or perhaps she was wondering what she had got into and was trying to work out the quickest way to extricate herself. Either way, Belle thought, as she tipped the boiling water into the cafetiere, brought more cream from the fridge and pressed down the plunger, she'd have to discuss their involvement sooner rather than later. The profiles and notes would either excite them or horrify them. Time to find out.

She put the tray down on the table and told them to help themselves.

'Mavis, I could see you weren't joining in. You know, if you don't want any part of this I won't be offended.'

The others stopped and turned to Mavis, who blushed. 'It's not that. I must admit, though, if we get involved in this, Belle, if you want us to, there's going to be dark times ahead.'

'What does that mean?' Bette demanded.

'It seems to me, there's been a hand at work here, the hand of a disturbed mind. I don't think it's co-incidence. It's the dates, you see.'

'They all happened in December, I agree,' Posy put in. 'But what you're saying, Mave, is this was all premeditated, isn't it? What makes you say that?'

'The dates,' Mavis repeated.

'OK, they were all in December,' Bette said, 'but how can someone drowning in Australia be connected to a hit-and-run in Wales, and a prozzie deciding to leg it to another town? And you don't even know that last one did disappear in December. Not really.'

'Do you believe that, or are you being a devil's advocate?' Belle asked. 'Not that I mind if you are.'

'So, you really want to pursue this? What are your reasons?' Posy asked.

Belle put her hand down to the side of her chair and picked up a cardboard wallet. She took out a black-and-white photograph and passed it over to Rose, who had asked the initial question. 'Two reasons. Take a look and pass this around.' She waited as the picture moved from hand to hand, then back to her. 'That's them. This is the photo I put on the school reunion internet site, the one I found when I was unpacking the last boxes.' She had removed another sheet of paper from the wallet, with the email chain and handed it to Rose, who read it and passed it on.

'You've got someone going,' Posy said. 'How many people saw the photograph?'

'I can check that on the group page. There are a lot of members, so I expect quite a few. So, you've seen what I have. Should I leave it alone? One minute I'm quite sure, the next, I'm not.' She tucked the photograph and email back in the wallet, adding, 'You probably shouldn't answer that now. Perhaps think on it overnight and we can meet in the café tomorrow.'

'But what is it you want from us?' Rose asked again.

'For now, just your thoughts. In the end, it'll be me who takes any further action. I wouldn't want to get you involved in something that might have ugly consequences.'

Bette was about to say something, but Mavis put a hand on her arm. 'Belle's right. We have a lot to think about. I for one would like to ponder on this overnight. I b'lieve I have an idea, but I'd like to keep it to myself for now. I'm happy to meet again tomorrow.'

'I agree,' Rose said. 'Can I keep your notes, Belle? I've scribbled in the margins. Sorry, not sure if I was supposed to do that.'

'Fine with me. I was going to take them back, but I trust you. But all of you, please keep this confidential. OK with you if we meet at the café, Posy, say around eleven if that suits? I'd like to speak to my friend Maggie in the morning, see if there's anything new on Pearl Hawkesworth Fox.'

They all nodded and Bette pushed herself up from the sofa with a groan. 'Knees aren't what they used to be,' she muttered. 'We should go now. That was a good dinner and I need a bit of a walk before I retire. Lots to think about.'

The next few minutes were taken up with finding and putting on coats and shoes, exchanges of thanks and other comments, until Belle closed the door and was left alone. She returned to the living room and began to gather coffee mugs and other detritus, straighten cushions, all the time thinking over what had happened and what might come next. Her uncertainty about sharing everything with them had gone. The women had confirmed the range of thoughts she'd had for the past twenty-four hours.

The small high-set kitchen window looked out over the lane where the pathway was higher than on the inside, and she hadn't yet closed the blind. As she did so, she noticed a figure, dressed in a black hooded raincoat striding past, head down, hands in pockets. A neighbour, returning home? The walk was purposeful in the dark lane. Someone who knew where they were going. There were potholes that needed watching out for in the dark, especially with a hood pulled right up. She rolled her eyes at herself. None of her business.

Turning away, she put out the remaining lights on the ground floor. The evening hadn't been without tension, for her. Now that was subsiding, she needed to sleep.

Outside, the hooded person stumbled on a small pothole, grunted and turned back to look at the high wall of the cottage. The doorway opposite had provided shelter and the opportunity, from time to time, to creep forward and look beyond the kitchen at the group of women, note what they were doing and then watch them looking through papers as they sat around the fire. But it had been cold and now it was time to get back to the warmth and comfort of another home. And decide what to do next.

Chapter 7

Decisions

'Good to hear from you, Belle. Send me the notes and I'll continue as we've discussed. Let's have a talk again in a couple of days.'

'Thanks, Maggie. I have to go now, or I'll be late.'

Belle pulled her coat on as the call finished. In the hallway she grabbed a pair of sensible shoes, locked the door, shoving the keys in her pocket and began to run along the back lane. She was already late; the call to Maggie Gilbert had taken longer than she had expected, but productive.

She had slept immediately on going to bed, but awoke after a couple of hours, her brain instantly alert. It was what Mavis had said about the dates. Mavis, she thought, staring at the ceiling, was not a woman given to impulsive comment. Something had occurred to Mavis that Belle hadn't seen, or to which she hadn't given significance. After an hour of not being able to get back to sleep she went down to her desk and began to make more notes, including everything said over dinner, adding her own thoughts and ideas. A sudden huge yawn prompted her to have another try at sleeping.

What seemed like five minutes later she awoke to the sound of her alarm going off.

Slightly out of breath, coat flapping open, she ran up the café steps to the front door, to find that the shade was down, a large *Closed* sign in the window and the door locked. She tried twisting the handle but the door didn't budge. Dismayed, she wondered if they had decided that they didn't want to meet after all, when the blind moved, and Posy's face appeared. Belle blew out a sigh of relief as the lock clicked and Posy opened the door, pulling her in, locking it behind her.

'Hawkesworth Fox was here just after the girls arrived. I told her I was closed for stock taking,' she said as Belle saw Bette, Mavis and Rose at the corner table. 'Go on over, I'll get you a black coffee.'

Bette signalled to her to sit. 'We need to get right down to business. Mavis has to go in ten minutes.'

Mavis was clasping her hands in her lap. 'Trouble?' Belle asked.

Mavis nodded. 'She's organised a social worker, for a formal meeting.'

'How is your aunt taking it?' Belle asked.

'Angry, planning to give them an earful. I've told her it's not the best thing to do. She should listen politely, then tell them she's capable of managing on her own, but she won't be told. If I wasn't going to be there, I reckon she'd throw them off the doorstep.'

'Why don't you just let her do that, Mavis? If she says it coherently, I can't see how a social worker could claim she's not in possession of her own mind.'

'Because no matter how coherent Tessa is, Hawkesworth Fox will claim it's dementia-related, her being unable to control her temper.'

'You have a point,' Belle said, as she took her coat off. 'Listen, how about I come with you? I do have a little experience, not that I'm saying your aunt has dementia,' she added quickly as Mavis was about to protest.

'Well, I suppose it's not a bad idea,' Mavis conceded. 'But that doesn't give us long here.'

'We can pick up again later,' Belle replied, 'that's assuming we have something to discuss?'

'Well of course we do,' Bette spluttered. 'If we weren't going to help you, we wouldn't all be here, would we.'

'That's what I was hoping you'd say. So, how about we meet later. If that's OK with Posy?'

'Better not be here,' Posy said. 'I need to be open this afternoon.'

'Back at my place, then. Five o'clock? That work for you, Posy?' The café owner nodded.

'And by that time I may have a fuller report from my friend Maggie. I spoke to her this morning. She's enthusiastic about uncovering the truth about the demon woman.'

Bette thumped the table, making them jump. 'Good job. You two had better get off, then. Get there before The Fox and the social worker and keep Tessa calm. We'll all see you at five.' She thrust Belle's coat at her, moved aside the coffee that Posy had delivered from which Belle had taken one mouthful and stood to shoo them out of the door.

'Come back with good news, Mavis. We'll see you here just before five and walk down to Belle's cottage together. Safety in numbers, eh?'

* * *

The knock came at five exactly, just as Belle had put down the phone. They rushed eagerly into the living room, and Belle indicated the dining table.

'Mavis has told us the tale of how you bested the dragon,' Bette began, her eyes shining.

'I wouldn't put it like that,' Belle replied. 'I just asked her questions she couldn't answer. It was Tessa who carried the day. She was magnificent.'

'Well, she didn't lose her temper and try to hit either of them with her stick, if that's what you mean,' Mavis said.

'And she spoke lucidly,' Belle said. 'I think she's convinced the social worker that, with the right amount of help she's capable of staying at home safely. The care package she suggested, with someone coming in three times a day, plus Mavis visiting, did the trick.'

'Tessa doesn't like it, as we'd expected,' Mavis explained, 'but when we told her it was that or a care home, and we did put it that bluntly' – a nod here to Belle – 'or at least Belle did, she decided to grit her teeth and bear it.' Mavis sat back in her chair. 'The look on Pearl's face was divine. I've never seen her so uptight.'

'That's when she'll be at her most dangerous, so don't think it's over yet,' Belle said. 'We'll have to keep an even more careful eye now.'

'Tessa liked you,' Mavis said.

'Well, I say "well done" to you,' Bette said with a fierce grin.

'Thanks. Now, shall we get back to where we were this morning? And I have news. My friend in Wales has been in touch with preliminary gen on Mrs Hawkesworth Fox.'

'That was quick,' Posy said. 'Is it good stuff?'

'Oh, yes. They're in a quiet patch. One of their clients has gone dark, so they have capacity. There's three researchers at Maze Investigations and they've all jumped in. I'll tell you in a minute what they found, but first of all, I want to know what you were about to say this morning, about my case, if that's OK with you.'

'It's OK with us,' Rose said. 'I've been designated spokeswoman. Here goes.' She gave a short cough. 'First of all, we are divided between thinking this is a co-incidence or not. Bette thinks it could be. So does Posy. I believe there's something in it, so does Mavis.' She went to speak again but shook her head. 'It's no good, Mavis. This was your thought. You're the best person to explain it, in your own words.'

Mavis, who had sunk back into her chair, sat up again, her hands fluttering on the table.' Well, if you insist.'

'Best coming from you, Mave. You said it good, and given us all something to think about,' Bette said, putting one of her red, work-roughened hands over Mavis' shaking fingers.

Mavis swallowed, then looked earnestly at Belle. 'Right then. Belle, first of all, thank you for sharing this with us. Rose says you are not a person given easily to sharing intimate and personal matters, so it's quite something that you've chosen to trust us.'

'As much you've chosen to trust me, I suppose,' Belle replied with a smile, thinking about how much she was hiding from them.

Mavis bit her lower lip. 'What you could be talking about here is… is six cases of murder. That's premeditated murder, not something done randomly. For these to have taken place in the same month, at five-year intervals, well, this isn't co-incidence, it's a lifetime of planning. That's the darkest thing I've ever heard.' She glanced around at the others, who were all nodding. 'Whoever it is, they see danger for themself, or themselves, and have warned you off. Now. You are a person who rises to a challenge. I saw that today with Pearl and you did it magnificently, I have to say, without any aggression, but firmly and steadfastly. But this – well – you're taking on someone with an evil mind. Possibly a deranged mind if this is no co-incidence.'

Again, she paused, taking a deep breath. 'So, my question, no, our question to you is: are you prepared for the danger you might put yourself in, if you carry on?'

Chapter 8
Revelations

Belle sat forward, elbows on the table, and exhaled a long, deep breath. 'Thank you, all of you. Mavis, you've just said exactly what my friend Maggie also said to me at the start of our discussion this morning, before I met up with you.' She sat back and folded her arms. 'I've been on the go all day since then, so I haven't had much time to think it through, but you're right, Mavis. The email was a threat to my safety, and I must take that seriously. But, at the same time, if it's right and six women have been murdered with planning and premeditation, that's serious too, beyond serious. So far, the police haven't picked this up. I sent my notes to Maggie. Her partner is a Chief Inspector of Police in South Wales. She's going to show him the notes, see what he thinks, and call me back tomorrow. If he decides there's something in it, then it's out of my hands. Somehow, though, I don't think he will.' She stopped and turned to Mavis. 'If I go ahead and keep on investigating, are you all willing to give me your thoughts and input?'

'Yes, of course, and I have something to say on that score,' Mavis replied. 'First of all, though, it's up to you.'

'Well, my gut reaction, I'm still in. I want to hear the rest of what you were going to say this morning, Mavis. Something more about the dates? Let me get us all tea. I need a break.'

In the kitchen Belle was deep in thought as she laid out mugs, a jug of milk and sugar. She knew the email was a threat. She had believed that nothing could surprise, upset or concern her but this was a whole new level. A person might actually have murdered six people, probably for the same excuses she had heard so many times, but had crossed a line of what they would do in retaliation. What could the motive have been? Hatred, revenge, an eye for an eye? The thought of murder terrified her. What might it bring back?

It came to her as she walked back in that, despite both her personal and practical experience, the psychology was beyond her grasp. Always had been. Apart from her husband, Sam, she had never told anyone about her childhood. She gave herself a shake. Push it all back down. This was different and she would have to find someone to talk to, to gain better insight. Perhaps Rose was right. What was it she had said, that Belle had come along at the perfect moment in time, to help them. Perhaps it was time for her too …

'You're looking pleased with yourself,' Bette said.

'I've been inside my own head, and I've concluded that I'm not going to back off.' She handed out mugs. 'Mavis helped me understand I'll have to watch my every step, take more note of what's going on around me. Now, Mavis. Can you please tell me what you're thinking?'

'It's the dates. All in December. Different days and circumstances, I know. But I thought about it from the perp's point of view.'

'Mave, you've been watching those American TV series again,' Posy said.

'Let her finish,' Rose interrupted.

Mavis blushed. 'I didn't want to say "murderer" but I suppose that's the legitimate word, maybe. Anyway, if someone chose December, it was for a reason. Actually, I have been watching a UK crime series, about a psychological profiler and a policewoman. He always looks from the "perpetrator's" point of view,' she said, with a scowl at Posy. 'So, I thought, why December? What happens or happened in December to make someone choose that month six times? Can you think of anything, Belle? Anything that might have started this off, given the first one died when she was twenty-two? Anything from your time at school? Was it about a Christmas event, perhaps?'

Belle squinted at her mug. 'Nothing that comes to mind immediately. It was a long time ago, mind.'

'Why don't you tell us about your convo with your friend Maggie, might help to change the subject for a few minutes?' Posy said.

Belle, who had sunk back in thought, snapped to attention. 'Sorry. Yes. There is something at the back of my mind, but it won't come out to play. Anyway, yes, Maggie and her colleagues. Pearl was born Ada Pearl Mary Fox in 1961 to a Dennis and Mary Fox. Dennis was a businessman, successful and when he died left everything to Pearl, not to his wife. Pearl was twenty-five at the time. She wasn't working. She lived with her parents and continued to stay with her mother after his death. Maggie doesn't think she was a kind person even back then, so the mother can't have had much of a life.'

'What makes her think that?' Rose asked.

'Apparently, Pearl changed school several times. It's a blank after that for some time, until she was in her thirties. There were only the beginnings of social media back then, no Facebook and the like, just chatrooms and forums, but Maggie's colleague got into a couple of sites on which someone had posted a comment about "that bitch, Ada Fox".'

'When was that?' Posy asked.

'Around the millennium, from what I remember Maggie saying. I do recall what it was like when we weren't dominated by social media, although it seems long ago now.'

'We have a church group online,' Rose said. 'But I don't like it either. Too much scamming these days.'

'Anything else from your friend?' Bette asked, sensing that they were about to get side-tracked.

'Yes. Her husband, Peter Hawkesworth Fox. They joined their names when they married. Before that he was plain Peter Hawkes, not Hawkesworth. And – here's the killer – he was never at the rank of major, as they're claiming. He was a captain. And,' she raised an eyebrow, 'there was something dodgy about the way he left the army. Covered up, of course. Unfortunately, Maggie doesn't think we'll get an answer to what happened, unless someone blows the whistle. She asked if we want to know. If we do, she'll give it a go.'

'Well of course we want to know!' Bette slapped a hand on the table. 'Surely anything we can get on the pair of them will be good for us, won't it?'

'I'll ask her to try, then. Before they came to St Foy they were in the Midlands, in another small village. There may be something there, too. Maggie's business partner, Zelah Trevear is going to pursue that one.'

'That's wonderful progress, Belle. Thank you, Aunt Tessa will want to know too. Can I tell her?'

'Of course you can, Mavis, but be sure to emphasise that she must keep it to herself.'

Mavis nodded. 'I'm sure she'll revel in knowing a secret. By the way, another secret. Tessa is going to be ninety-five soon and Andrew and I are organising a secret party for her. I'd like you all to be there.'

'Lovely idea,' Rose murmured. 'Of course. Harry will love that, too. You'll have to tell us what she'd like as a gift. Ninety-five is a great age, but I'm not sure there's many gifts she would appreciate and …' She broke off. 'Belle, are you OK? What's the matter?'

They all looked directly at Belle, who had slapped a hand to her mouth. 'Of course! That's it! The party. It was the party. Mavis, you're a bloody genius.'

Chapter 9

History

Mavis looked agog at Belle. 'I don't think so,' she muttered. 'I was just saying, that's all.'

'But you set something off for Belle; she's remembered something I think is crucial, isn't that right, Belle?' Rose said.

Belle nodded, gazing at the four expectant faces. 'I'd forgotten, it was so long ago. It was the school year we all reached eighteen. That was a big deal back then. She put her mug down. 'Give me a minute, will you. I need to think this through.' She stood up and walked back into the kitchen and stood, gazing out at the lane, her memory revealing details of the event that might have set off the subsequent train of events. She closed her eyes and tried to blot out the sounds of conversation coming from the dining table. How exactly had it occurred? After five minutes she was ready to return.

'It was an eighteenth birthday party,' she began, 'organised jointly by five girls. I'm going to tell you as I remember the details. They may not be exactly in the right order for now, but once I've told the story I'll write it down, later, when I'm on my own. So, all five of the girls had their birthday in December, on different days, but they decided to celebrate together. Now, these were not the "popular" girls, if you know what I mean. They were the timid ones, the nerds as they'd be called now. And they had all at some time been the butt of jokes and victims of the bullying and humiliations by Kat Harris and her group.

'They thought the rest of our year group would like them more if they organised a really good party. So they hired a hall and a DJ, all paid for by their families. They invited everyone in the school year and most of us agreed to go. There was going to be food and drinks – not alcohol although we suspected that someone might sneak in a bottle or two. One of the girls had a twin brother and he was going to invite boys along from his school. This may sound strange now, but a lot of us hadn't had much opportunity to interact with boys, so the prospect was quite exciting. They went out and bought new clothes, shoes, whatever, spend a couple of weeks discussing what music they wanted the DJ to play, what make-up they could get away with. I did notice Kat Harris not taking part in any of the chat, but I must have assumed she wouldn't be going, although she had been invited. Honestly, it would have been a relief if none of her nasty little group turned up. But no-one had anticipated what she was actually doing.'

She paused for a few seconds, grimacing with disgust. 'The big night arrived. Maggie, Jude and I had turned up early. The girls were there with their families. The DJ was warming up, Gwen's brother arrived with a couple of his mates. Everything looked good. It was just a case of waiting for the others to arrive. So, we waited. And waited. After an hour, the girls were nervous. So were we three. Gradually it became clear. No-one else was coming. Then, a message arrived, confirming Kat Harris had organised another party, at her house and everyone was there. Two of the girls began to cry.

'But that was when Jude Crawley Winters and Maggie Gilbert sprang into action. Maggie telephoned her sister and told her what was going on. I have to give Fiona Gilbert her due, she was horrified.

Within half an hour she had organised twelve of her friends, who were home from university, to turn up. Owen ran round and found another half-dozen of his mates. An hour later there were about thirty girls and boys in the hall, which filled it up a bit, although there should have been at least three times that number. A few had even managed to bring a gift and a card. I don't know how they did it, but they stopped the evening being a total failure. Of course, it couldn't alter the fact that, apart from the three of us no-one else from school had turned up. Their families were really, really upset.'

She paused again to take a long swig of tea.

Breaking the silence around the table, Rose said quietly, 'How spiteful and very humiliating. Those poor girls, on what must have been the biggest night of their lives.'

'Makes me want to find them and kill them, and I don't even know them,' Bette muttered, then stopped with her mouth forming an 'oh' as she realised what she'd said.

'That's a horrible story,' Rose said. 'But from that to killing six people is a very long stretch. I can't see it, myself.'

There's more,' Belle replied. 'Let me tell you what happened next, then you decide. You could have drawn a line down the middle of the sixth form common room from the following Monday for the week until the school broke up for Christmas. On one side, Kat Harris and the six, on the other side, the party-givers plus me, Maggie and Jude. And I mean literally. Jude re-arranged the armchairs and tables into two sides. It was an invitation to the rest of the year to decide which side they were on. It was interesting, watching the rest of Year 13 decide where to sit. A real "Mexican standoff". Quite a few were too scared of Kat Harris not to sit on her side. Others decided to join us.'

'What is that "Mexican thingy" you just said?' Mavis asked.

'It's where there's no way out without one side losing everything, no compromise possible,' Posy said. 'Now let her get on with the story.'

'We all went off for Christmas and when we came back two weeks later, it was easy to see that Kat Harris had decided that she was going to win, whatever the cost. The bullying became even worse, and physical. She must have really whipped up her six over the holidays, because after a week of it, everyone was tetchy and scared, going round in pairs or groups, never alone. Then, it broke. Kat Harris was discovered to have cornered one of the juniors, a girl named Josie McKenna. She was the sister of one of Fiona's friends. Maggie had to go down to the cloakroom, which you weren't allowed to do without permission, and found Josie unconscious on the bathroom floor, soaking wet. Maggie screamed for help. Josie had to be taken to hospital. The story was that Kat Harris had shoved Josie's head down the toilet, as revenge. But she went too far, and Josie passed out. Maggie, on her way down, had seen Kat Harris running up the steps and away from the bathroom. What followed was as you'd expect. Kat Harris was suspended, then excluded, which became permanent. The gang fell apart. The atmosphere changed once Kat Harris was gone. A lot of the girls turned on the group. They held their ground, but they were no longer a force to be reckoned with. That was our last year at the school. We sat our exams and left. And I never saw any of them again. I've kept loosely in touch with Maggie, Christmas cards, that kind of thing, until we met in person in September, at the reunion.' She sat back in her chair. 'That's the story.'

There were moments of silence, as each of the listeners absorbed what they had heard. Then a volley of questions began, and Belle held up her hand. 'One at a time, please.'

'Let me ask something,' Bette said. 'Were there any other incidents? Because, this was all horrible, but if the January incident was the end of it, surely it was over and done with?'

Belle sat forward and put her elbows on the table. 'There were a couple of shouting matches. The six didn't believe Kat Harris had done it, for a start. They all claimed that she had been with them around the time of the incident and couldn't have been the person who shoved Josie's head down the toilet. But Maggie was firm in her story of what occurred, and the school believed her. The six accused her, but she went straight to the Head and accused them of trying to bully her into changing her story. Maggie was a popular girl, so she was believed.'

'Luckily,' Rose murmured.

Belle's eyes shot towards her. 'They were a vile bunch who had gone much too far. Parents came forward, after the fact of course, saying their daughters had often not wanted to go to school because of the level of bullying they had either experienced or witnessed. It had been a toxic environment. I hated it, couldn't wait to get away. There was a good deal of criticism of the school hierarchy for not having picked up on it. They knew, of course, but had chosen to ignore it.'

'Do two wrongs make a right, then?' Rose asked.

Belle sighed. 'If you'd been there at the time, you'd have said, "*Yes, they do*". I can still remember my sense of utter relief when I knew Kat Harris was never going to set foot in the school again.'

Rose shook her head. 'I won't say any more, then.'

'What are you on about, Rose?' Bette said. 'Explain yourself, please.'

'Let me,' Belle said. 'Kat Harris was set up, which Rose has figured out. Maggie and Josie McKenna, who was a feisty little thing, did it together. Maggie was a bit over-enthusiastic when she put Josie's head down the toilet and the girl almost passed out, but not quite. However, they pulled it off. And they got the result they were hoping for. Maggie didn't even tell Jude what she was planning. I think Jude guessed but she never said anything.'

'Well, I say good on them,' Bette replied.

'Me too,' Posy added. 'But I still can't see how it could have led to murder. It's not enough, unless one of those party girls experienced something else, or was a budding psychopath. And nothing happened to the first of them until three years later.'

'That's where I become unstuck, Posy,' Belle replied. 'So, why the threatening email in response to a photo?'

'So what are you going to do now?' Bette asked.

Belle took a second to respond. 'I don't know. I want to think on this. Rose, you said I've set someone off. I have, and Mavis' words about what that could mean, tells me it might be something huge, a beast released. I want to think about it overnight, OK?'

Bette pulled herself up out of her chair. 'Fine by me. It's been quite a day and I need to get home. The boys will need me. Come on, girls, let's leave Belle to her thoughts.'

If they had arrived in good spirits, they were now leaving in deep solemnity. Each with a head full of questions, uncertain about what to say or do.

Once they'd gone and Belle was left alone, she threw herself onto the largest settee, put her hands behind her head and closed her eyes. No arrangement had been made to meet up the following day and she wondered if this was too much. The Curiosity Club of St Foy had become embroiled in something beyond curious. How they were all going to deal with what they had learned in the past twenty-four hours concerned her. Was it too much? Were they all thinking about how to find a way out? Was she thinking about how to find a way out? After an hour of thoughts bouncing around, nothing helped. She gave up and fell asleep, exhausted.

Chapter 10
Q&A

Belle awoke to a hammering on her front door, glanced at the clock and saw it was eight o'clock. She must have nodded off for a couple of hours. The hammering went on. One of the group must have left something, she thought, and staggered over to the door. To her amazement it was light outside. Surely, she couldn't have slept through the night. The combination of the bright sky and the pain in her back told her she had. Mavis stood on the doorstep, a questioning smile directed at Belle.

'You look like Quasimodo. Are you OK? Can I come in?'

Belle stood aside as Mavis walked into the living room. She turned to Belle, who was still peering around as if she had woken up in a stranger's house.

'I'll put the kettle on, make us strong coffee. You sit down, get your bearings.'

Belle did as she was told. She could hear Mavis humming in the kitchen. She still couldn't get her brain to accept that she had slept for over twelve hours. Hopefully, the brain cells would catch up with the eyes, ASAP.

When Mavis came back in with a tray of steaming coffee Belle grabbed a mug. Mavis sat quietly until, after a few minutes, Belle said, 'Thanks. That's helped. Why are you here so early? It really is morning, isn't it?'

'So I'm right in thinking you've slept in those clothes, on that settee?'

Belle nodded. 'I was exhausted when you all left last night so I lay down on the settee and closed my eyes to see if I could get clarity and then … here you are.'

She shivered. 'Hang on a minute, I'll get the fire going.'

'No time,' Mavis replied. 'I'm off to see Aunt Tessa. What are you planning to do?'

'Well, I didn't get far last night, and I really need space so I'm going to get showered and dressed and go for a walk. Thanks for the coffee. You get on now. Give my love to Tessa.'

'I will. You asked me why I came here. It was to deliver a message. We went round to the vicarage after we left here. We were all troubled by what came out of your revelations last night and Rose suggested we talk it through with Harry.' She held up her hand as Belle's head shot up. 'Harry Teague is the most trustworthy person we know. He won't say anything, but his insights are always useful, and last night was no exception. Long story short, we're with you one hundred per cent. But it's your decision whatever you decide to do.' She stood up. 'There's more, but you look like you need that walk. How about we meet up later, at the café?'

Belle nodded. 'Thank you. I'd like to hear about Harry but I do need to do some deep thinking myself.'

'Four o'clock. Posy will be quiet then and she'll close. Don't get up. I'll see myself out. And Belle …' She smiled gently. 'You've become our friend in a short space of time and sometimes people get second thoughts. Well, don't even think about shutting us out. That's all.'

Belle sat for five minutes after Mavis' departure, then jumped up, coffee in hand, put on shoes and let herself out through the back door into the garden. She wandered round checking all of the plants. Orange and pink echinacea heads were still strong, white tobacco plants that she had grown from seed when she arrived waved in the occasional breath of breeze and the last few roses, pink and yellow held their heads high. She would have to deal with them soon, but she couldn't bring herself to chop them down yet; they gave her a sense of peace. As she walked, she made a mental plan to get stuck into the garden as soon as she returned from Wales. One thought that had occurred to her before she slept was that she would have to go to Newport, to her apartment in the new block on the riverside and pick up again. Pick up what, though? Time for the walk.

* * *

Over the summer Belle had explored the countryside around St Foy, both on foot and by car and was becoming more intimate with her surroundings. Today she chose a coastal route. Throwing on a coat over the clothes she was wearing – a shower could wait until she returned – and walking boots, she headed out of the cottage, down to join the road that would take her to the coastal path to the cove. She had overcome her reluctance to visit the intimate little beach. In better weather she had swum most days. She paused for five minutes to buy a hot chocolate from the refreshment shack, which was open for its last week before the winter shutdown, then walked down onto the beach, across the sand to a set of steep steps and joined the coastal path edging the wood up to the castle on the headland.

The view out to sea was magnificent. The gentle breeze was stronger here, blowing hair into her eyes, which she swept back and secured with one of her headbands, then began her walk across and around the cliffs. This walk, which she knew well, was four miles, and refreshing. A few ups and downs, which at first had caused her to puff and cough. Now, after six months, she barely noticed the inclines and descents. After a couple of miles she reached a bench which sat a few yards back from the path. She hadn't done too much thinking so far, concentrating on negotiating the path which was muddy and slippery after the rain. As she sat down on the bench and sipped at the chocolate, it was time to decide exactly where she was in her thoughts and make a plan.

The sea was calm and clear, a magnificent cerulean blue, on its surface just two container ships on the horizon and one yacht, sails unfurled, making its way towards St Foy harbour. The sun came in and out between scudding clouds. This had been a peaceful spot during those summer walks, but now, her mind was uneasy. She closed her eyes, took a dozen slow, deep breaths until a sense of calmness relaxed her shoulders and her mind settled clearly enough to consider her options.

Question one: what she was facing? Three possibilities. The first: total co-incidence. A set of random events that looked like something but were just random. The second: there was a suspicious death, but just the one. Perhaps that was what the '*it*' in '*Leave it alone*' meant. Someone was worried she knew something and wanted to scare her off whatever it was they had done. The third: potentially six murders. Which had to mean dark psychopathy, somehow related to those past school events.

She could pretty much rule out the first. If there really had been nothing untoward then there was no need for the anonymous emailer to warn her off. What then? Either a single suspicious death, or as many as six. If just the one, the killer had been lucky, or careful enough, to get away with it. If six, the planning was admirably breath-taking, albeit horrifying. What lengths would such a person go to, to ensure they achieved what they set out to do and never be caught. Did she want to take on such a person? Because that was what she would be doing.

After half an hour of going back and forth over the various arguments for and against, Belle had her answer. She made her decision in the knowledge that her 'curious' friends had her back. Bette Jones may have pulled her remark like a rabbit out of a hat, but it had struck a chord. She herself was blessed, or cursed, with inquisitiveness, curiosity, about people, situations and events, but in the past, this had been from a safe professional distance. This was close up and personal. She stood and instead of continuing the circular walk, made her way back along the cliffside to the beach and the road to the cottage. By four she was ready to share what she was going to do next. She was caught up, sucked in, unable to extricate herself. What would be, would be.

Chapter 11

Biographies

I have put these notes together based on my memory and what I have been able to discover so far. There will be more, after I have spoken to each of them in South Wales. Five girls worked together to organise the party, on Saturday 13th December 1986. They were bound together by their 'nerd' status. None of them was interested in fashion, make-up, magazines, etc. In general they didn't attend parties or go out together (they were usually not invited to any parties and/or other gatherings). They preferred to organise study evenings together. To describe their group – they were all modern-day versions of Jane Austen's Miss Mary Bennett. It came as a shock when they announced their combined eighteenth birthday party. These are preliminary notes. I will add more when I have spoken to each of them.

No. 1: Gwen Williams now Morgan

Birthday: 10th December. Gwen had a twin brother, Owen. No siblings in school. An outstanding musician, played piano and oboe. Also a brilliant mathematician. Short dark hair, spotty face. Never looked at anyone when she spoke to them.

No. 2: Mary Conroy

Birthday: 24th December. Quiet and intensely religious to the point of fanaticism. We expected she would follow a religious vocation when she left school.

No. 3: Susan Jones

Birthday: 13th December. Very tall, almost six foot. Anxious. At one time lost tufts of hair, leaving bald patches. Was mercilessly teased by Kat Harris' group, who referred to her as 'baldy bigfoot'.

No. 4: Helena Parry

Birthday: 9th December. The academically most brilliant of the group, and of the year group. Destined for Oxford/Cambridge. Didn't communicate much outside the 'nerds'. Gave the impression she was above others, but in fact, when you got closer to her, was intensely shy.

No. 5: Jane Perry

Birthday: 30th December. Shortest person in the year, just reaching five feet. Nervous, tried to please everyone. Many jokes played on her by Kat Harris group. Called her 'midget', 'dwarfy', 'stinky Jane', other names. Poor background. Mother didn't seem to care too much. Often smelled, and clothes not washed (this improved somewhat after first two years at school when she became able to take more care of herself, but the name-calling didn't change).

Chapter 12
Logistics

'When are you going?'

'First thing tomorrow morning,' Belle replied to Mavis. 'I sent a message to Jane Perry and to Gwen Morgan and Sue Jones on the social media accounts. Jane and I are going to meet up mid-afternoon at my flat. I've asked her to talk me through what she knows. Jane confirmed for me she was the person who told the story at the reunion.'

'I bet she was excited to hear from you,' Mavis said.

Belle, about to carry on with her plan, paused. 'What makes you think she was excited, Mavis?'

'Was she?'

'Yes, she was.'

'She was one of them, Belle, the girls who gave the party. You should be careful what you discuss with her.'

Belle nodded. 'OK, she was, but she was also the person who noticed the co-incidence of the dates. She's still a funny little stick, is Jane, but she wasn't capable of hurting a fly then, and the impression I got at the reunion is that she hasn't changed in that respect. I did think she was making something out of nothing at the time, but since that email arrived, well, I'm more certain now that something happened, and Jane is the person who began to put the clues together.'

Mavis shrugged. 'Fair enough, but still, caution.'

'I will be careful, Mavis. Now, what do you think of the plan?'

Before announcing her imminent departure for South Wales, Belle had given out her set of notes on the party-givers, based on what she remembered about each of them and whatever she had been able to glean from social media during the day. As Mavis was delivering her advice, Bette, Rose and Posy were heads down, reading.

Bette looked up first. 'Five of them. Interesting. You've done a decent job here. How many were there altogether in your year group?'

'Umm, about sixty, maybe seventy in all, I think,' Belle replied.

'How many wanted to kill this coven of bitches?'

Belle laughed, despite herself. 'All of us. Although, they didn't pick on everyone.'

'Did anyone stand up to them, or defend those they did target?' Rose asked.

'Yes. Maggie and Jude and a few others. They stepped in when it became particularly gross. Jude even reported them to the Head on one occasion.'

'And?' Bette asked.

'They were "spoken to" and they, like the good girls they were, were tremendously sorry and promised never to do it again. Then sniggered as soon as they were out of her office.'

'And presumably became adept at being less obvious and more devious,' Posy said, her eyes blazing.

'Exactly,' Belle replied. 'But as soon as Kat Harris disappeared, everything changed. A few even started to bully them, but of course, they complained to the Head.' She closed her eyes. 'It wasn't a good school, from the pastoral point of view. Anyway, it's long gone now.'

'As are they,' Bette remarked.

Belle grimaced, then pulled her face into a serious expression. 'It doesn't matter what we think of them. If their lives were cut short unlawfully, then, if we believe in fairness and decency, we have to take the moral high ground. Despite how vile they were.'

'Just like Harry said,' Rose murmured.

'Mavis told me you'd been to speak to him. Is that really what he said?'

'It was,' Mavis replied. 'He doesn't think it's co-incidence and he does agree it should be looked into further.

'But he did urge caution,' Rose said. 'He wants us to keep in close touch with you, be a sounding board for whatever information you find out and what you plan to do about it, before you do it.'

'Has he been surprised that we're friends at all?'

Rose smiled. 'Not in the least. Harry is a man of strong religion, but he also believes that many things happen for a purpose and that you were sent to us at a time when we all needed each other. And he loves the idea of the "Curiosity Club of St Foy".'

'I'm looking forward to meeting him,' Belle replied. 'Now, I need to go home and pack. I have my apartment in Newport, so I won't be mixing too much. My biggest concern is that I may only have a short window for moving around. Covid cases are increasing, so there may be another lockdown looming. Any more questions?'

'How are you planning to reach them?' Bette asked.

'Three ways. I've already heard back from Jane. I've sent friend requests to Gwen and Sue. The other two, I'm not sure yet. The second option I have is to ask the organisers of the reunions if I can have contact details – that's if they're members – but I don't know if they'll give the information out. Data protection, et cetera. And then there's Maggie's partner. He's a Detective Chief Inspector. I'm going to ask him if I can speak to that policeman, Mal Jenkins.'

'The lazy knob?' Bette said.

'Yes, him. He may not have done the best job, but he'll have basic information, I hope. At this stage, everything is useful. Right, I have to go.' She turned to Mavis. 'How's Tessa today?'

'Cracking,' Mavis replied with a smile. 'She's so happy we got one over on The Fox. So much so, she's agreed to move her bed downstairs. I always fear so much about her falling, up and down those rickety old stairs. Her dining room hasn't been used for years, so Andrew and I are going to move her down at the weekend.'

'That's excellent,' Belle replied, smiling, but surprised to see a scowl on Bette's face, which was turned away from Mavis.

'I'll come with you to the door,' Bette said.

Mavis, Posy and Rose returned to the notes, as Belle and Bette stepped outside.

'What's up, Bette?'

'I won't beat about the bush. Andrew Tregoss is a bastard. He hits her. She thinks we don't know.'

'Wow. That's bad. The way she's describes him, he seems like a timid sort of man.'

'In public, yes. That's the face he likes to put on, the way he puts his clients at ease. Timid but smart. Don't be fooled.'

'Thanks for telling me.'

She turned and walked up the steps to the back lane, wishing that Bette hadn't told her. Then, chided herself. This was not how you reacted to a revelation from a friend, and if they were to continue in friendship, she would have to deal with it.

The weather had changed. Belle was finding out just how mercurial it could be in St Foy. The earlier sunshine had disappeared, blotted out by a heavy mist that had rolled in from the sea during the afternoon. Now, it was foggy and damp. Her footsteps echoed on the cobbles as the misty rain seeped through her damp mackintosh. Once, she thought she heard footsteps behind her. She speeded up, then slowed down, twice. Each time the footsteps stopped. Unnerved, she broke into a trot and was glad to get home to the warmth of her cottage and prepare for whatever was coming next. Inside, with the door locked, she shook herself. *Imagination, Belle Harrington. Get a grip.*

When she checked her email, Gwen Williams Morgan had already accepted her friend request. She messaged her back, asking to meet up, saying there was something she would like to discuss. Nothing from Sue Jones. Then she messaged Jane Perry to confirm their meeting, at her apartment at three, the day after her arrival. She intended to call Maggie back tomorrow once she was installed in her flat and ask to speak to Bob Pugh, Maggie's partner.

Although she felt anxiety about speaking to the police, there was no possibility that they knew anything about her past. She was ready.

Chapter 13

Meetings

Just after midday Belle let herself into her fifth-floor apartment, left her suitcase in the hall and flung herself onto the armchair in front of the window for a few moments of rest before checking her food situation. The apartment block sat on the east bank of the river Usk, in the town centre, one of a line of new builds on what had previously been docks and wharves and pills on the tidal river. Hers was the closest block to the footbridge across to the main shopping area of the town. She had asked a neighbour, who kept a key, to get in basic supplies: milk, tea, bread and so on, and was relieved to find them ready and waiting.

As she made herself a cup of tea, she wondered if this flat was really going to be her permanent home, having barely visited throughout the summer. The longer she stayed in Cornwall the more she grew fond of the town and surroundings, something she had never anticipated. The apartment held no such feelings. It was a good buy, though, and would increase in value for her. Being the penthouse, it had a stunning view over the town and beyond, down to the Bristol Channel and as far as Twmbarlwm mountain with its medieval mound, sharply clear under a sparkling blue sky, unlike the weather she had left behind in Cornwall.

When she had driven away just after eight that morning the thick fog that had rolled in the previous afternoon was still there and persisted over Bodmin Moor. It had hampered and slowed her drive. It was the first one she had experienced; it wouldn't be the last. She had heard about these sea 'frets' and had expected a mist that would dissipate after a couple of hours. What she had not been prepared for was air so thick it felt like she had to push it aside to move, having to put a scarf around her mouth to stop the feeling of choking on it. And the unsettling sensation of being alone. She had not been able to see or hear anyone else on her lane, just the dull echo of footsteps that could have been far away, or right next to her. She had reached her car and locked the door with a sigh of relief.

She shook her head; this was foolish. 'Gotta get used to it, Belle,' she'd muttered. *You've just contracted to stay another six months.* She finished the tea and jumped up, unpacked her suitcase and sat down to plan who she was going to try to contact first. The list was long. Apart from the remaining party-givers there were the families of the dead and disappeared women to be traced, contact to be made with the reunion organisers and with Bob Pugh, to see if he was prepared to help. If he would, at the very least, introduce her to Mal Jenkins, that would be a good leap forward. It was time to check in with Mavis. She had promised to let them know she had arrived, and what she was planning to do for the remainder of the day.

Mavis' number went straight to voicemail. 'Mavis, it's Belle. I'm at my apartment in Newport. All good. Just going over the bridge to buy supplies then home again. I'll check in with Bette same time tomorrow.' She ended the call, surprised Mavis hadn't been waiting. She hoped there was nothing wrong. Well, if there was, someone would let her know. Bette, Rose and Posy had her mobile number.

She put on her coat and shoes and made her way down to the riverbank and across the footbridge to a food-only branch of

Marks & Spencer in the middle of the new shopping mall, all the time thinking about her plan, but with a frisson of concern about Mavis' lack of response, hoping it was nothing to do with Tessa.

Back in the apartment she worked into the evening, making calls then developing a detailed plan of the people she should contact in the time she had available, what she could – and couldn't – say to them, and what it might mean once she had the information. Then, just after midnight, as she was about to pack up and go to bed, she found a piece of information that shocked and devastated her. And gave her a whole new line of thinking.

* * *

The next day she was due to meet Jane at the apartment at three, which gave her the morning to meet Mal Jenkins, an event she was not looking forward to since speaking to Bob Pugh the previous evening.

At Maggie's request he had looked at Belle's notes before he called her.

'I agree about the co-incidence of the dates. Me, I don't believe in co-incidence, but the rest of this … well, can't say I'm convinced, Belle, sorry. Too long between each one and over such a long period of time. Your average psychopath escalates once they step up to murder. What you've outlined here doesn't fit any pattern I've ever come across.' He paused. 'But, there's something here. It could be one suspicious death hidden amongst them. That seems to me a more likely scenario than six murders. My money would be on the hit-and-run.'

'But what if it was six?' Belle persisted. 'You've read about the party?'

'Yes, but the notion that someone would plan revenge in the first place is a stretch, let alone that it would involve killing six women, it's, well, it's just not feasible. And there's no proof that the three who disappeared aren't alive and well, somewhere. Sorry, but I can't give it any more credence, nor any help. We're stretched enough. You'd have to bring me something solid to open up a formal investigation.'

'What about Mal Jenkins? Could you arrange for me to speak to him?'

Another pause. 'I suppose so. Mal is due to retire in a couple of weeks. I doubt you'll get much out of him. He's not the helpful sort.'

His tone hinted at a requirement to read between the lines. 'OK, but if I could just speak to him unofficially?'

He paused, then said, 'Come into the Newport station tomorrow morning at ten. I'll have him meet you there.'

Maggie had called her back shortly afterwards. 'Mal Jenkins is not on our Christmas card list. He and Bob have had a number of run-ins over the years. He's lazy and careless and now just waiting to get his pension. And he has a temper. Be careful, Belle.'

* * *

Standing outside the entrance to the station, her fingers shaking slightly after too much coffee to counteract too little sleep, Belle wondered if this was worth the effort she was putting in, given the concern she felt about the threats. She gave her head a shake to force the thought aside, pushed open the heavy entrance doors with unnecessary force, marched up to the reception and asked for Mal Jenkins.

'He's expecting me.'

The policeman on duty rolled his eyes, but said nothing and punched a few buttons on a phone next to his desk. 'He'll be with you shortly. Wait over there.' He nodded to a row of hard plastic chairs.

Twenty minutes later, eyes closed, fizzing with anger, shuffling on the chair to ease the pain in her spine, she looked up as the whoosh of opening electronic doors provided her first sight of Mal Jenkins. He was heading towards her at speed, head and neck first, arms swinging. He stopped to button up a scruffy jacket over an extended stomach beneath which hung stained trousers secured by a thick belt, and jerked his head at her in a gesture to follow him. He turned and headed back through the doors without waiting to see if she was following. Belle stood slowly. The anger this performance invoked in her made her want to march straight out of the station, but experience told her that was what he hoped she'd do. So she walked slowly towards the doors, which closed before she reached them, turned her head to the desk sergeant, who grinned and pressed a button below his countertop and mouthed, '*Sorry*'. She shrugged and walked into the inner sanctum. Mal Jenkins was nowhere to be seen.

She paused in the corridor. He would eventually have to come out of whichever closed door he had entered. At least this gave her a moment to calm herself and decide not to rise to whatever bait was to be placed in front of her. One thing she knew from her years of experience, anyone this keen to get the upper hand so soon was, in reality, nervous of what might be coming. Mal Jenkins might be thinking he was in charge of this conversation. Mal Jenkins was wrong.

She stood and waited until, after a long minute, his aggressively crew-cut head appeared out of an open door. 'In here.' No please, no welcome. As calmly as she could, Belle walked into the office. There was one desk, with a huge chair behind it, a smaller and lower one in front, which made her smile. Classic tactics to give the person in the lower chair a sense of his power. Too obvious. A filing cabinet had two drawers open. It and the desk were strewn with papers and files.

Jenkins sat back in his chair, arms folded over his protruding gut. 'Well, Pugh says you have questions for me, about a couple of my old cases.'

'Detective Chief Inspector Pugh,' she emphasised the title, 'has been kind enough to arrange this meeting for us to discuss information I have on a number of cases, some of which came under your jurisdiction. I have questions.'

He sneered. 'Off you go, then. As you can see,' he swept his arm over the mounds of paper, 'I've nothing else to do, apart from fighting real crime.'

Bait number one, Belle thought. She reached into her bag, taking her time to take out a file that she had stacked with paper, most of it irrelevant, but he wasn't to know that. Next, she extracted a pad and pen. She watched him surreptitiously as she put the file up on her lap, making sure he couldn't see the contents, and was gratified to catch him squirming in his seat, before unfolding his arms and putting his hands on the desk. Realising that might appear too aggressive, he leaned back again and put his hands behind his head. *Too late, Mal Jenkins*, Belle thought, keeping her expression neutral as she looked straight at him across the desk, allowing a few seconds of silence before she began to speak. He shuffled again.

'Six women, dead or disappeared over a period of twenty-five years, the first in 1990, the most recent in 2015. You participated in three of the cases that I know of, perhaps others I don't know. I want to ask about—'

He snorted. 'Twenty-five years? You're having a laugh if you think there's something smoky about that.'

'If I may continue,' she said impassively. 'Each died or disappeared in the same month each time, at dates close to mid-December.'

He cocked his head to one side and grinned. 'So?'

'So, they all knew each other, all had been to school together, in the same class. And,' here she paused and leaned forward, 'they were a gang of bullies who tormented other girls on and off during their time at school. This included a particularly nasty incident, which took place on the thirteenth of December 1986.'

The grin had disappeared. He blinked several times, then put his hands down on the desk. 'Are you trying to tell me these "incidents" are related, just because they all took place in the same month, but five years apart? That's the stupidest thing I've heard in a long time. Co-incidence.' His tone was mocking, but his eyes darted from Belle to her folder.

'I'm suggesting that it's worth another look at each "incident", as you call them. Those women had families, parents, husbands, children. Someone told me about the "co-incidence",' she used the same mocking tone. 'I thought it was worth checking. As I said, there are questions.'

'Like what?'

She took a few pages out of her file, glanced down at them, then back again.

'The first one, in 1990, was Angela Stephenson. She was twenty-two years old. She died of a massive heroin overdose. She'd been known to use occasional cocaine and smoke dope, but ...' She stopped. 'Are you going to write any of this down?'

With a grunt he pulled a pad and pen towards him and slowly wrote the name and the year, then looked up at her.

'Chief Inspector Pugh is expecting a report from you later, so you may want to write more. However, up to you.'

His lip curled, but he didn't comment.

'I believe you might have been a detective constable on that case. Perhaps you'd like to check how much background checking was done. The next one, Bernie Moloney in 1995. Hit-and-run. Neither car nor driver found. Yours, definitely. The third one, again an investigation in which you were involved, was in December 2000, a disappearance. She was Tina Lewis. You headed up this investigation. You concluded that she walked away from her family. Again, how much background did you do?'

'The next one was in Australia. Denise Goodright. December 2005. She drowned whilst swimming, in a cove away from her family.'

He slammed the pen down on the desk. 'You expect me to know about some random woman who died on the other side of the world fifteen years ago?' he snapped.

'No, I don't,' Belle said, returning his stare eyeball for eyeball. 'The fifth was another disappearance. Liz Maynard. December 2010. You decided she had also walked away. The final one, in December 2015, Faith Shepherd ...'

This time he snapped the pad shut. 'That old slag. She went over to Bristol.' He smiled and folded his arms. 'Is this all you've got?'

'There's more. But first, whatever you may have thought about these women, they had lives and people who cared about them. Now, I went to school with them. They weren't nice people to say the least. They were a gang of bullies, led by another woman, who is still alive, but, if my theory is correct, won't be for long. It's coming up to five years since the last one went.'

'What do you expect me to do about it?'

'I am hoping you will go back into the files and check out what exactly you did to assure yourself that you did all you could, each time.'

'Well, sod that. On the evidence of this lot,' he swept the pad off the table, 'I'm not wasting my time.'

'There's more,' Belle said, maintaining her calm stare, although it was costing a huge effort not to scream out at him the news she had discovered the previous evening. 'They bullied a particular group of women, or the girls they were then, made their lives a misery. In 1987, one of them, who had suffered psychologically following that bullying, committed suicide. She was nineteen years old. She named the bullying by this group as the reason for the misery and despair she had never been able to shake off. Now do you think there's nothing to it?'

Chapter 14
Shock

Mal Jenkins remained silent at her revelation. She stood up, packed up her notes into her briefcase and left the room. He didn't follow her out. At the security doors the sergeant buzzed her out with a puzzled look.

Once she was outside Belle's legs turned to jelly and she had to hold onto a railing, bending over, fighting nausea, taking deep breaths, until she heard a footstep beside her, a discreet cough and a hand on her shoulder. Summoning up her anger to turn on Mal Jenkins, she looked up to find a man standing over her, a worried expression on his face. 'Are you alright, Belle?'

He was a stranger, but she recognised his voice. 'Bob Pugh, I presume?'

He nodded. 'The sarge let me know you'd walked out looking like a corpse. Do you want to come back in and sit down for a minute? I'd like to know what happened with Mal Jenkins.'

Belle shook her head. 'Hell will freeze over before I'm ever again under the same roof with him,' she muttered. 'I'm feeling better, now. It was just tension. He's not helpful, is he?'

Bob gave a bark of laughter. 'That's the nicest anyone has been about him in years. He's a bloody nightmare. But, if you tell me that he's been obstructive, I can still give him hell and make his life difficult.'

She shook her head. 'I want him to look back into the cases. I'm not just upset about him and his stinky attitude. I learned yesterday that one of the party girls – I'm presuming Maggie has told you the story of the party?' He nodded. 'Her name was Susan Jones. I say "was" because she killed herself back in 1987. I spoke to her sister yesterday. She told me Sue had been depressed since leaving school and had never got over the bullying.' She wiped away a tear. 'It destroyed her life. She hadn't been able to do anything, couldn't even leave her house.'

'Look, I think I should take you home.'

'That's kind, but I'm OK. It's walkable and I need the walk. But there is something you can do. Please make sure that lazy git does check out those cases.'

'My pleasure.' He put a hand on her arm. 'I do have one immediate thought, though.'

'Probably the same as mine. Was revenge for Sue responsible for what happened to the gang members?'

He nodded. 'Could be. Maybe the hit-and-run?'

'It can't be ruled out, can it?' Belle replied. 'One of my friends in Cornwall said that there might be one murder hiding amongst what is otherwise just co-incidence.'

'Well, it gives me the opportunity to put someone on it. Not Mal Jenkins. He'll be under scrutiny for what he did at the time, which will be uncomfortable for him. Sure I can't walk you home?'

She shook her head. 'Thanks, but no. I'd prefer to make my own way. I have thinking to do, plus I'm meeting up with someone this afternoon.'

* * *

Ten minutes later she reached the footbridge and looked up at her apartment but didn't feel inclined to go inside just yet. She stood in the middle of the bridge, looking down at the receding river. The tide had turned and the muddy brown water was beginning to flow downstream to the Bristol Channel. This river had the second highest tidal reach in the world. Sitting entirely on a bed of mud, the water was never anything but impenetrable, torpid brown, always flowing, never still. The mud, she knew, was deep, so much so that almost twenty years earlier the husk of a medieval merchant ship had been discovered at the bottom of a small wharf near to the ancient castle on the riverbank, a few hundred yards upstream from where she was standing. This discovery would one day make Newport a major tourist attraction, the ship being one of the oldest of its kind ever discovered. A search for investment was underway, to give it a permanent home. Its skeleton was regularly on display in temporary accommodation. Belle had never seen it. *I must do that*, she thought. *But not this time*. Which brought her back to why she was here, today, standing on this bridge.

The news about Sue Jones had been a shock. Belle had twice before been close to a person who had committed suicide, one of whom was in her workplace: a woman she had been dealing with about a redundancy. Her stomach churned as she remembered. She had been the last person to speak to the poor woman before she hanged herself. Over twenty years had passed but it was still raw, and she wiped away tears at the profound sadness the memory still evoked, wondering as always if there was anything she could have done to prevent it. Hindsight, of course. But now this. Someone she had gone through school with, a tall, awkward, gawky girl who was developing a permanent stoop out of embarrassment about her height. The bully gang had tormented her.

She had come across petty bullies during her years of employment and had developed a thick skin against the ways in which they tried to prevent her from recommending either disciplinary action or dismissal. Although she had listened with professional interest and had learned about the ways of bullying, as well as gaining the ability to instantly recognise the trait, she had only superficially studied the psychology. There was a huge amount of literature on the subject, but she didn't have time to read. She needed a consultation with a professional. Did she know anyone? Somewhere in the back of her head was a name, someone she had met recently. She pushed away from the railing and began to walk to the apartment building. A puff of wind squalled into her face, smacking her with a smell of sea and something rotting in the mud. The name would come to her.

* * *

Jane Perry rang the apartment bell at exactly three o'clock and Belle stood back as Jane scuttled in, her small, dark, sharp eyes sweeping around, taking everything in.

'What a lovely room,' she said, eyes and smile wide, with the tiniest hint of resentment. 'Oh, you have a balcony. Can I take a look?' She trotted forward to stand at the glass doors, which Belle opened for her. The wind had sharpened, but Jane didn't appear to notice, closing her eyes and turning her head up towards the sky. After a minute or so she turned back to Belle, smiled again and walked back inside.

'Where shall I sit? I know people have their favourite place and it's so annoying when someone just walks in and sits there, isn't it?'

'Wherever you like, Jane.' She put up a hand against the oncoming protest. 'Really, in the daytime I sit near the window, at night, opposite the TV. Treat yourself to whichever you prefer.'

Jane took the armchair with the view. 'My bedsit is in a basement; I don't have a view. This is heaven,' and she smiled again, her head tipped to one side. This time the smile was perfunctory. 'Well, you can't imagine how surprised I was to hear from you, Belle. Pleased, of course. You said you've been doing a follow up on my peculiar tale. Can you tell me what you've found?' Jane sat up and moved to the edge of her seat, staring expectantly at Belle.

'Jane, if what you've described is correct, there are three potentially suspicious deaths and three more suspicious disappearances. Is that what you thought? Had you already come to that conclusion when you told us back in September?'

Jane nodded her head. 'It took a long time to notice, if that makes sense. It … it sort of struck me, if you know what I mean, when Faith Shepherd didn't turn up last time. That they were all gone, I mean.'

'So had they been attending the reunions up to 2015?'

'Not all of them, no. But two or three of them were there, usually, sometimes with Kat Harris.' Her head shuddered as she spoke the name. 'I always tried to keep away from her. She's still not nice, is she?'

'That's quite an understatement, Jane. She's as unpleasant as she ever was, from what I saw. But was this the first time that none of them was there?'

'Yes, last time it was just Faith. This time, not her either. I spoke to her at that reunion, and she told me that Liz had walked out on her family and her job, shortly after the last reunion. Then, she told me about how Denise had drowned in Australia, which I didn't think too much about, but when she said that Bernie had been killed in a hit-and-run accident, I just thought it began to sound odd. I don't know about Liz, only that she wasn't there. Sometimes I'd pass her in town, but I hadn't seen her for a long time. So, I did a bit of checking. It seemed odd.'

'But you didn't have any suspicions about foul play?'

Jane opened her eyes wide. 'No, I couldn't bring myself to believe that. Anyway, I'd known for a long time that Angie Stephenson – she was the first to go – was accidental, because a dealer or whatever, had given her bad drugs. She was crazy on the night she died.'

'How do you know that?'

'Oh, sorry. I haven't told you. I was there.'

Chapter 15

Distaste

Jane had hardly stopped for breath as she spoke, her head pecking and turning like a small bird, hands jerking in her lap. Now she looked up at Belle, who had made a pot of coffee, but paused as she crossed the living room.

'What? Can you explain that, where were you?'

'I was working at the big government office, down on Cardiff Road. Angie worked there too. A few from school did. She was a supervisor, not the same department as me, so I hardly ever came across her. It was a Christmas party, with three departments together. After dinner a group had gone to a local nightclub. I went along, too. It was quite early and I didn't want to just go home on my own.'

Belle could imagine Jane tagging onto the group, probably unwanted, but tolerated, as she had been at school. 'So what happened?' she asked as she put the coffee pot on the table and nodded to Jane to help herself.

'Well, apparently,' Jane said, pouring coffee and lowering her voice to a conspiratorial whisper, 'she was known to try out drugs, if you know what I mean. She kept disappearing out to the ladies, and I actually saw her once, taking something from a bloke who was standing in the corridor when I went to the loo. Then she was all excited, dancing by herself, waving her arms around like a crazy woman, shouting at the others to join in. I thought her team looked a bit embarrassed, but they got up and joined her. Not me. Anyway, soon after, just after midnight it was, a couple of the team went home and I noticed that Angie wasn't there, either. The club had filled up and it was really crowded and noisy; lots of people Christmas partying. Anyway she'd been at the table next to mine and her coat and bag had gone, too, so I supposed she'd gone home, or off with someone.'

'When you say, "gone off with someone", do you mean a man?'

Jane nodded. 'There'd been a few around her. She'd been snogging one of them, pretty heavy stuff in public, so I presumed she'd gone with him. I'd had enough by then, so I went home.' She paused, took a long gulp of coffee, then said, 'She didn't turn up for work the next day. I saw her team at lunchtime in the dining room and they were heads down and sniggering. But at the end of the day the police arrived.' She shook her head again. 'It was shocking to hear she was dead. All of us who'd been in the club had to give a statement. I told them what I'd seen. I even had to prove I'd gone home, which wasn't difficult for me, as I'd taken a taxi and the driver remembered me. They thought she'd died between one and three in the morning, outside, next to the bins, sticking something into her arm with a needle.' She rubbed one forearm against the other, with a shudder of disgust.

'That must have been upsetting for you,' Belle said quietly.

Jane nodded. 'Yes, it was. Thank you for understanding that. Because … you know, I'd never liked her. But hearing that, well, no matter what someone's done, you don't want them to die like that, do you?' She picked up her cup again with a shaking hand, spilling a little into the saucer and onto the glass table. 'Oh, I'm so sorry,' she gasped, jumping up.

Belle stood and walked over to the kitchen. 'No worries. Sit down, Jane. It'll wipe up.' She returned with a handful of kitchen towel. 'Tell me, was there anyone else there who you knew from school?'

'In the nightclub, you mean?'

'Yes, and working at the government offices.'

'No, I mean, I think Gwen Williams might have been there at one time, when she was at university, just a holiday job, summer I think, or Easter. The same with Helena Parry. They used to take on extra staff to cover holiday periods, students usually. But as far as I can remember no-one else in work and for sure no-one I recognised in the club. Why do you ask?'

Belle didn't answer. 'Did you think at the time it was odd she'd died from a heroin overdose? I thought she was just a recreational user.'

Jane shook her head. 'I hardly saw anything of her in work; I don't know much about drugs. I've never used them, so I don't know how they affect your behaviour. Do you?' She looked up directly at Belle.

'I've had experience of dealing with addicts, not much, but eventually it catches up with them. It's hard to manage an addiction and a job.'

Neither spoke. Jane sipped at her coffee. Belle watched her and was thinking about who she could speak to for more information on Angie Stephenson, when Jane put her cup down and said, 'What do we do now?'

Belle was nonplussed. She had invited Jane for information. She wasn't planning on forming a team, but Jane was sitting forward, eager, one foot jiggling. She hoped she hadn't given Jane the idea that this was more than just a one-off meeting, but with mounting dismay, saw from Jane's widening eyes and pressed together half-smiling lips, that she was indeed anticipating some kind of follow-up. She'd better put a stop to that expectation, immediately, leaving no room for doubt.

'There's no "*we*", Jane. I'm interested, that's all. I'm not an investigator nor do I have any right to go poking about in people's lives.' Not true and she was indeed going to poke about but she had no intention of having Jane at her shoulder. She certainly wasn't going to tell her about the meeting she'd already arranged with Gwen Williams.

'But you invited me here to talk about them. And it was me who gave you the idea that something was odd.'

'Yes, that's true,' Belle conceded.

Before she could say more, Jane interrupted. 'I don't think you're being honest with me, Belle. You said there were three potentially suspicious deaths and three suspicious disappearances. Now you're trying to cut me out.'

'It's not a game, Jane.'

'But I can help. Please, let me help?'

Belle was torn, reluctant to involve Jane because she was one of the party-givers, but also because Jane was still annoying.

'I don't need help. Do you have any more information you think is relevant?'

Jane got rapidly to her feet. 'If I'm not worth bothering with, then neither is what I know.'

'So you do know something. Please, sit down. And try to understand. I'm not cutting you out, because there isn't anything to cut you out of.' *Again, not honest.* 'I've been to speak to one of the police detectives involved in certain cases.'

Jane stopped with one arm in a coat sleeve. 'You mean Maggie Gilbert's partner?'

'No, someone else. He's going to look up information. Look, the police don't believe there's anything to this, other than co-incidence. I'm not trying to prove there is but there is something that makes me reluctant to just leave it. That's all, at the moment. So, there's nothing to help me with.' She smiled, hoping this would be enough. Then, she remembered. 'Jane, did you know that Sue Jones killed herself the end of the year we left school?'

Jane rocked on her feet, her face draining of colour. Belle thought she was going to faint. She grabbed Jane by the arm and sat her back down. 'You didn't know?'

Jane shook her head. 'What happened to her?'

'I tried contacting her, via social media, but I must have had the wrong person. It's a common enough name. I tried a few other people, but didn't get a reply until last night I had a message from her sister, who told me what had happened.' Jane had put her head in her hands as Belle spoke. Now she looked up, dry-eyed, colour rushing back into her face, turning it puce. 'Kat Harris has a lot to answer for,' she hissed.

'Yes, she does. The nasty girl didn't change. She's become a nasty woman. I suspect she has a narcissistic personality disorder, not that I'm a psychologist.' She was still struggling for the name of the person she had met somewhere.

'No. Leonora Maginnis would know all about that.' *Of course*, Belle thought, keeping her face neutral. Lennie Maginnis. They'd met, briefly, at the reunion. Lennie the psychologist.

Jane was saying something, but Belle had tuned out. 'Sorry, Jane. My mind just went elsewhere. Nothing important.'

'I said, "poor Sue". I didn't know. Really, I didn't. I never kept in touch with her after we left school. How terrible.'

'I can see it's been quite a shock. Look, you get off now. Take some time. If there's anything else you think I need to know, give me a call. You have my number.'

Jane nodded, put on her coat and walked to the door. She gave Belle a weak smile as she headed over to the lift.

From the balcony Belle watched Jane make her way across the bridge. She walked purposefully, head up, back straight. She wondered if the news about Sue Jones had really come as a surprise. Jane had seemed completely shocked, but she had remained in Newport all her life and had attended all of the school reunions. Surely she would have heard something. Her impression from today was that Jane hadn't changed from the timid creature of their schooldays, a follower, not a leader. She had also shown just a tiny hint of enjoyment at being present when Angie Stephenson had died. Then again, she had had a solid alibi.

She went back to her desk and took out her file. Time to get on with contacting her list. At least she'd managed to convey to Jane that she was not going to play Robin to Belle's Batman and hoping that was the last she'd see of Jane Perry.

Chapter 16

Fear

There was one meeting that Belle wanted, needed, but had been putting off. Kat Harris. Convinced as she was that the woman had a damaging psychological condition, she had nevertheless been disgusted at Kat's arrogance and conceit at the reunion. She had overheard how Kat tried to belittle and insult Maggie Gilbert and Jude Crawley Winters, and how Maggie's response had shut Kat up. What Maggie and Jude hadn't seen, as they gave each other a quick grin, was the flash of rage on Kat Harris' face as she turned and walked away from them. Still, it had to be done, if she was to carry on. *If* she was to carry on.

How, exactly, was she feeling? Nervous, but unwilling to stop – yet. Glancing at her watch, it was past five and almost dark outside. She walked to the window to close the curtains, stood for a moment looking at the lights spreading out beneath her and into the distance. They looked sparklingly pretty in the heavy dusk, hiding the grey and black human cesspit that sat churning beneath them. She shut them off, returned to her notes and began to map out an agenda for the following day.

* * *

She caught up with Cornwall on a conference call at seven thirty. Bette, Mavis, Rose and Posy were ready and waiting in the back room of the café. As the call began the four were crowded in front of the extra-large screen Posy used for her marketing, that sometimes sat in the front window of the café, displaying her cakes and sandwiches.

'There she is,' said a smiling Bette. 'Must say, we're keen to know how you're getting on. Any progress?'

She brought them up to date, their smiles disappearing as she described the meeting with Mal Jenkins, then ranging from angry to upset when she told them about Sue Jones' suicide.

'That's shocking,' Rose said. 'How are you coping?'

'It was a shock,' Belle replied.' I have been wondering if I should go any further. I was worried about what else I might find out. But,' she paused and shrugged, 'I don't think I can stop now, if only to find justice for Sue.'

There was an exchange of comments and suggestions. Then Belle, noticing Rose hadn't joined in, asked her if she had any advice.

'Be careful,' Rose said. 'That's all for now. Keep your questions calm and friendly. Don't go poking sticks into anyone's psyche. People can react in strange ways, even people you think of as friendly. If something has lain dormant for years, it can be immensely stressful to have it brought up, even if the reaction seems innocuous.'

'Thank you, Rose. I've never lost my temper; I always kept aloof and in control, although that was in a professional setting. I was never involved in whatever had caused the individuals to end up sitting in front of me. This is different, it's my past, too, and I feel emotion that I hadn't expected, particularly about Sue Jones. I watched that bullying happen. Last night I didn't sleep well, kept asking myself why I didn't do something about it at the time. Could I have prevented it, been more helpful to her?' She sat back, closing her fingers into fists and opening them, closing and opening, closing and opening.

'No, you could not. Don't conflate the person you are now with the girl you were then.' This sharply from Bette. 'The adults, those teachers, didn't step in. It was their job to look after those girls, and they failed. Don't forget, bullying wasn't viewed then as it is now. There's still too much of it, though. My Joanna, she went through it when she was in school. It affected her. Mind you, I went to the school and they dealt OK with it. But many don't. Stop blaming yourself.'

'I'll give it a go,' Belle replied, managing a weak smile, imagining an unsuspecting schoolteacher being confronted by Bette in full battle dress and in 'take no prisoners' mode.

'What next, then?' Posy asked.

'I'm going to meet Gwen Williams in the morning. There should also be news from Bob Pugh about the investigations into the cases.' She took a deep breath. 'Then I'm going to contact Kat Harris, see if she'll speak to me.'

There was an immediate protest, from Posy, Bette and Rose. Belle had been expecting this and bit her lips together.

'I have a suggestion,' Mavis said, when the protesting died down. 'Put that one on the back burner for now. Concentrate on what you get back from the first one, the drug overdose. There was a police investigation, an autopsy, an inquest and a coroner's report. See what they all say. You'll get something definitive, one way or the other. If it was an accident, then it's possible so were the others. If there's any hint of suspicion, then it will be up to the police to decide what to do next, not you.'

'That's sensible, Mavis, thank you. I hope Bob Pugh will come back to me sometime tomorrow.'

'And you're right to put distance between you and Jane Perry. Although she does sound like a silly little sparrow desperate to stalk with the raptors, she's still one of the party-givers, so you can't entirely discount her, particularly as she was in the nightclub with the girl, Angela.'

'Jane would need a personality transplant to be capable of anything sinister,' Belle replied. 'She just wants to be noticed, by someone, for something. She hasn't changed.'

'Well, you know best,' Mavis said.

'How's your Aunt Tessa? How's the situation with The Fox?' Belle asked, keen to change the subject.

'Quiet, thank the Lord,' Mavis replied.

'We've not seen anything of her since you left,' Bette added. 'And we're all the better for that.'

'We're moving Tessa downstairs tomorrow,' Mavis added. 'I'll be greatly relieved once that's happened. And she has a carer, starting tomorrow, too. Three times a day. I think she's looking forward to it, although she's grumbling about having a stranger in her house.'

Belle smiled. 'Give her my best wishes. Good that Pearl's gone quiet but I suspect it won't be for long. Right. I'm done and our time slot is up. Anything more?'

They shook their heads. 'In that case, shall we re-convene on Sunday? I may have some progress, or this might even be over, with any luck, and me still in one piece.'

'Amen to that,' Bette said. They wished her goodnight and Belle ended the call. She felt in need of fresh air and let herself out onto the balcony. The night was fully black now, the city lit up below and into the far distance. She would go ahead with setting up more meetings, but put them a day back, to give her time to consider the reports on Angie Stephenson's death. Rose had made a good point.

Her stomach growled and Belle remembered she hadn't eaten since breakfast. Not wanting to be bothered with cooking, she ordered a takeaway, waited for it to be delivered, then fell asleep on the settee in front of a detective series.

She awoke suddenly from a dream about being caught on an incoming tide and trying to frantically flee from the rushing water along a narrow corridor with doors that wouldn't open; the glowing time on the microwave in the kitchen showed three in the morning and she was fully clothed and still on the settee. She stumbled to her feet and was heading to the bedroom, when she thought she heard a noise in the hallway outside her door. Her neighbour, most likely, coming home after a Friday night out. She stopped still, breathing in sharply, as something dropped through her letterbox. As it fell onto the floor she crept forward and picked it up. An envelope. Probably nothing, probably nothing. Inside, a single piece of paper. *NO MORE WARNINGS. WATCH YOUR BACK. I'M COMING FOR YOU.*

Without thinking she pulled the door open. No-one there, but in the silence of the night she made out light footsteps running down the stairs, already close to the ground floor. She slammed the door shut and ran to the balcony. A tall, well-built figure in black appeared from the lobby, glanced around and walked steadily to the footbridge, crossing to the main shopping square where it disappeared from view. She thought about shouting out but couldn't find her voice. She locked the balcony door, went back to the hall and picked up the paper and envelope. *NO MORE WARNINGS. WATCH YOUR BACK. I'M COMING FOR YOU.*

Written in black ink, in capitals, in the centre of the sheet.

She needed coffee. No sleeping now. Her hands had stopped shaking, but fear was infiltrating her body. What had she done? What sleeping monster had she awakened? It wasn't too late to back out. She could just pack her suitcase now, run down to her car, drive back to Cornwall.

Give yourself a good shake, Belle Harrington. You can show this to Bob Pugh, then decide what to do. Three in the morning is the wrong time to make important decisions.

She turned the TV back on, found another box set, and waited for dawn.

Just after eight, her phone rang. She hesitated for a few seconds, not recognising the number, but decided she couldn't ignore it, whatever it was. She breathed a sigh of relief when Bob Pugh introduced himself.

'Can you come to the station in an hour or so?' he said without preamble.

'Of course. Bob, something has happened that I need to show you and discuss with you.'

He grunted. 'Same here. Seems you've opened a can of worms. See you in an hour.'

Not just me, then, Belle thought. *Don't see how I can leave it alone now*. She showered and dressed, feeling weary, but with a dash of anticipation. At nine she was sitting in the foyer of the police station, fresher after the walk along the riverbank and through the town, glancing at anyone who came close. At least Covid was good for something – social distancing, making everyone aware of keeping their distance.

She had been there five minutes when Bob Pugh, bull neck jutting forward, burst through the electronic doors.

'Come with me.' He marched off. Over his shoulder he said, 'Looks like Angela Stephenson's death wasn't accidental, after all.'

Chapter 17

Concealment

Belle sat opposite Bob, eyes squeezed shut for a moment, hands clenched on the desk. As he began to speak, she looked up and saw he was holding up a fistful of dog-eared pages.

'They wanted to put it to bed quickly.'

'They?'

'An inspector, retired now, doesn't matter you don't know who he was. Mal Jenkins was his bag man.' He sat back. 'Can't really tell from these reports, but either they missed the significance of aspects of the autopsy and inquest findings, or deliberately didn't follow up.'

'Can I know what the findings were?'

He hesitated, then stuck out his bottom lip. 'Don't see why not. There was no evidence of hard drug use. No other needle marks anywhere on the body. She had taken drugs, no doubt about that, but there was signs of a sedative. Then, there were the bruises on her wrist and the pathologist noted she might have been restrained, a rope mark possibly.'

'Why would they not have followed up, if it was deliberate?'

He shook his head. 'I'm guessing because of the other drugs in her system. Easy enough to mark it down to a self-administered overdose. Sad and stupid. Case solved and closed. Tick in the box. Move on.'

'So, you're telling me whilst it seems clear that she was sedated, restrained and injected, which led to her death, they just let it go?' She could hardly believe what she was hearing.

'There's more,' he growled. 'A witness said she heard Angela arguing with another woman around one-ish or just before, in the ladies' toilets. The club was heaving at that point, she couldn't hear much, but Angela was drunk, as she thought, and slurring. This woman led her out into the corridor, holding her up, and propped her up against the wall next to the emergency exit, the one that leads into the back lane where she was found. The woman was supporting Angela with one hand. The other held Angela's drink, that the witness saw Angela pass over to her.'

'Did they follow up this woman?'

'Hardly. Mal Jenkins said the description given was vague, tall, long hair, sturdy, kind of, and they didn't attach importance to it. Their minds were set on the story that Angela went from the corridor to the outside lane to meet a dealer.'

'Could she have done?'

'Possible, but they should have checked more rigorously. Then, there's something else. They found her fingerprints on the discarded needle, but it was the wrong hand.'

Belle jumped up from her chair. 'Surely they recognised that was completely mistaken?' She stood glaring at him, her hands planted on the desk.

'Jenkins won't answer that one. Mind you, I had to read the reports carefully, a couple of times, to spot it. Hidden in the way they wrote it. They knew something was off.' He grimaced. 'I've told Mal Jenkins I'm considering opening a murder enquiry, but I'm flying a kite. I won't get the funding, thirty years on, to make it an active enquiry and he knows that. But I can hand it over to the cold case squad, which I'll probably do.' He grunted again. 'Not that they'll get to it for some time.'

'Can I ask a question?'

'Shoot.'

'A girl called Jane Perry had been in the club with Angie Stephenson's group. She says she went home shortly after midnight. Was that checked out?'

He flicked through pages. 'Uh, yes, here it is, with the other witness statements. She ordered a cab, was picked up at twelve thirty, dropped off at twelve forty-five, out on the Caerleon Road.' He looked up. 'Do you know different?'

'No, Bob. So, she couldn't have been the woman in the corridor with Angie? Not that she physically fits the description. Jane is five feet in height.'

'No, I'd say not. From this report, the woman in the corridor was at least six or eight inches taller than that.'

Belle sat down again. 'Good. I wanted to be certain. So, I had a call with my friends in Cornwall last night. One suggested that I wait for the outcome of your investigation. If it really was accidental, then she didn't think it was worth going any further. But, if not, well, then I should talk to you about what to do next, especially in light of this.' She reached down into her bag, brought out the anonymous note and handed it over to him, told him what few details she had about the incident.

'This is serious.' He rubbed his chin. 'Going to need thinking about. I don't have the other reports yet. I want to read all of them, then I'll give you a call. Please, go home, lock the door and wait for me to call.'

Belle was conflicted. She had arranged to meet Gwen Williams. It was now nine thirty. They were due to meet at ten, in the centre of town in a café in the square across the road from her apartment. That should be safe enough; she decided not to tell him. 'OK, I need to shop for food, but I can do that on the way.'

'I'll be in touch before the end of the day.'

* * *

As she reached the square Belle realised she had no idea what Gwen Williams looked like. She hadn't seen her for over thirty years. She remembered the girl, average height, short dark hair, intense, nervy, never looking directly at anyone. Gwen had chosen the location. Most cafés still hadn't opened, others only if they could serve customers outdoors. Fortunately, there was only one customer sitting at a table for two outside the selected chain store café, a large white cup on the table. The woman stood as Belle approached, smiled and beckoned her over.

'Belle Harrington,' she said. 'I'd love to shake hands, but we can't do that, can we. Never mind, do sit down.'

Belle sat, thinking that Gwen had certainly overcome whatever had caused the shyness of her youth. She was an inch or two shorter than Belle's five feet eight. Her dark hair, once hacked and shapeless, was cut in a fashionable messy style. She wore a smart black short jacket over grey trousers, a cleverly tied woollen scarf and leather gloves. She exuded energy. Belle ordered an Earl Grey tea from the barista who eagerly approached them.

'Gwen, thanks so much for coming to meet me,' she said, taking her seat.

'How could I do otherwise? Someone I haven't seen or heard from for over thirty years suddenly wants to meet me to discuss something she couldn't say over the phone. Let's do a quick catch-up and you can tell me whatever it is we're going to talk about.' The speech was disarming, accompanied by a warm, wide-eyed, seemingly genuine smile.

Belle's tea arrived, giving her time to compose her thoughts. For the next ten minutes they exchanged brief histories. Gwen sat with her elbows on the table, a hand cupping each side of her face, taking the occasional sip of coffee, as Belle told the story she had now perfected.

'Cornwall, eh? St Foy. I love it there. Lucky you. And retired, too. Mind you, I'm not far off. Five more years. I teach, back at the old place.'

Belle's head jerked back in surprise. 'Really? What subject?'

'Maths. It was always my first love. My second is Roger, but don't tell him I said that. We've been together for coming up thirty years. Met at Uni. Never looked back. He teaches too, not at the same school; that would be too much of a good thing.' She laughed, then gave Belle a quick update. She had gained a first-class honours degree at Bristol University, followed by a Master's at Cardiff, done her teaching qualification, then moved back to Newport.

'Simples, that's me,' she said.

'And quite content with life,' Belle replied, smiling.

Gwen nodded. 'Yes, I am. I moved on.'

For a moment Belle thought about not revealing what she knew about their other school acquaintances. On the surface this woman seemed innocent and happy. Did she have the right to upset that? She took a deep breath, deciding to proceed slowly, pull back if necessary.

'I didn't see you at the reunion back in September. Have you been to many of them since we left?'

'All of them. I teach there. I feel obliged each time, but honestly, I'm not one for rose-tinted spectacles. It wasn't that memorable, was it?' For the first time, Gwen frowned.

'No, it wasn't.'

'Am I guessing correctly that our meeting is something to do with our happy - not - schooldays?'

'Yes, Gwen. Do you remember Jane Perry?'

'Of course. She always attends the reunions.' She paused for a moment, folded her arms. 'This isn't about that story she was telling back in September, about Kat Harris' lot not being around any longer?'

'Yes, it is. Why do you ask?'

'I suppose ... because it's Jane. If you remember, she used to make up a load of stuff.' She raised her eyebrows and Belle grinned.

'Thing is, I've been taking a look. And today I've found out that at least one of the Kat Harris gang, Angie Stephenson, who was supposed to have died of a self-inflicted drug overdose, didn't.'

She watched for Gwen's reaction. Gwen's face remained blank. 'What do you mean, Belle?'

'She may have been deliberately killed.' Again, she watched for a sign of reserve, or fear. There was none, just a cold, hard stare. Then Gwen shivered and pulled her scarf further up her neck, almost covering her mouth. 'It's cold this morning. Winter will be here before we know it. That's pretty shocking.' She paused for a moment, turning her face away. Processing, Belle thought. Gwen turned back to face her.

'Do you think there might be truth in the story?'

'Honestly, I don't know. Of the six, three died accidentally and three have just disappeared. Now, one of the accidents probably wasn't.'

'Why are you telling me?'

Now came the crunch. 'Do you remember the eighteenth birthday party?'

For the first time, Gwen grimaced. 'Of course I do. Maggie Jones and Jude Crawley Winters managed to retrieve an iota of dignity for us, so it wasn't total humiliation. But it was still humiliating. And shameful. My mother cried for me, for us.' Now she spoke with anger. 'Kat Harris was an evil girl, truly evil. I think she still is.' Then her eyes widened. 'You think one of the girls who gave the party might have done something to them.' It was a statement, not a question.

'I'm not saying that,' Belle interrupted, seeing a flash of fury in Gwen's eyes. 'I've been trying to think about everything they did, that might make someone hate them enough to kill any one of them. There were enough episodes of cruelty to fill a book, apart from your party. I had to start somewhere.'

'I hated them, yes, but kill any of them? No, not even Kat Harris. I might have said "I'd like to kill her", as you do. But it was just an expression, spoken in anger. Lucky for me, when I got to Uni, I met Roger and thanks to him I was able to let it all go. This has upset me.'

She started to stand up, but Belle said, 'Just another few minutes, Gwen, please.'

Gwen nodded. 'Just a few.'

'Did you know Sue Jones killed herself the year after we left school?'

'Yes. I went to her funeral.'

'Do you recall who was there, from school?'

'Just a few: me, Helena, Mary Conroy. That was it, I think.'

'I spoke to her sister. She told me Sue never recovered from the bullying at school.'

'I know. I see a lot of it, you know, in school. Girls.' She pulled a disgusted face. 'I've been able to use my own experience to talk to a few of them, help them to understand they are not to blame. They do blame themselves, as I think Sue must have done. I also talk to the bullies, try to get them to understand the consequences of their actions. We've had one suicide in school.' Her eyes filmed over.

'Gwen, I'm so sorry. I didn't want to upset you, but I think something is wrong.'

To her surprise, Gwen nodded. 'You may be right.' She stood. 'I must go.' She turned to walk away, then turned back to face Belle, who had also stood and was putting her coat on. Her eyes were cold. 'I hated them and you've made me see I've never lost those feelings. Am I still angry? No, I am enraged. I don't care if someone hurt them. They destroyed Sue. They deserved what they got, if someone did it to them.' She walked away, body held stiff, shoulders hunched, fists clenched inside her leather gloves.

Belle leaned against the table, devastated. *Enough*, she thought. *Enough. I'm doing more damage than good. I'm going home. Let the police take care of it.*

Then, her phone rang.

Chapter 18

Distaste

'I'm guessing I have the right number for Belle Harrington?' The voice had a slight American inflection, the tone hinted at sarcastic.

'Yes. Who is this?'

'Someone you need to speak to.'

'I have a number of people I need to speak to. You think you might be on my list?' She was in no mood for games. 'Tell me who you are or I'm ending this call right now.'

'I am Kathryn Francois.'

'Why would I need to speak to you, Ms Francois?'

'You can call me Kat.'

Belle said in a low voice, 'Kat Harris?'

'You got there. Congratulations.'

Belle tried for calm and uninterested. 'I suppose it wouldn't do any harm for us to meet. Are you proposing we meet or speak by phone?'

'Oh, I think a meeting would be best. Somewhere public. I'm safe enough, for the time being, aren't I, Belle Harrington.'

'Where are you?'

'About thirty feet away from you. I watched you speak to Gwen Williams. You upset her.'

Belle spun around. She couldn't see another woman near her with a phone to her ear. She had to make a quick decision. She sat down again. 'OK.' She ended the call. Her heart was thumping.

She wasn't prepared for this; she'd have to play it by ear. From across the square a tall, thin woman in a long beige overcoat walked slowly in her direction. As the woman ambled up to the table Belle felt it first in her gut, as she had at the reunion, the clenching sensation, the stiffening shoulders. The tightening jaw. She gripped the arms of her chair. The woman smiled, but there was no warmth in the smile. She sat down, put her bag on the floor, then looked up and stared at Belle with a hard, unblinking gaze.

She's challenging me, Belle thought. *Who's going to be first to speak. Well, that won't work.* 'It's been a long time, Kat. How are you?' She smiled back, equally false.

Kat Harris said nothing, continuing to stare.

'Look, I'm busy. If you're trying to faze me, it isn't working and it won't. Tell me why you're here, and why you're stalking me.' She saw the merest flash of anger before the features composed themselves back to neutral., *That got her going.*

'I've been watching, over the years. I've seen when each of the girls met their end. It was interesting. Angie's death seemed stupid on her part. Unnecessary. When Bernie was killed in the hit-and-run five years later, I was intrigued when it wasn't solved. Hit-and-run accidents usually are. It was after Tina disappeared that I noticed the similarity in the dates with Angie's and Bernie's deaths. I've been watching ever since. Denise, Liz and Faith confirmed it for me.' She leaned forward, and whispered, 'There is no co-incidence. And you think so too, although you're trying not to.' She sat back. 'The longer you try to put a square peg in a round hole, the more you'll convince yourself there's a simple explanation. There isn't, and you know it. But are you prepared to admit it?'

'Why are you telling me this?'

'Good, answer a question with a question. Diversion. I like it.' She reached into her bag, took out a pack of cigarettes and a lighter, put one in the corner of mouth and lit it with a snap of the lighter.

Belle laughed. 'Who do you think you are, Dick Tracey?'

Kat took a long drag on the cigarette, blew the smoke out to the side of her mouth. 'Yes,' she said.' That's exactly who I am. But more V. I. Warshawski.'

'Never heard of him or her, whatever.'

'Then you should read more. Good books; if you like that kind of thing. I'm a PI. That's a—'

'Private Investigator,' Belle interrupted. 'So, you've been watching from a distance and now you've come to me. Again, why?'

Kat stubbed out the cigarette, as the barista approached. She waved the girl away without looking at her. 'I have a proposal for you. We work together.'

Belle laughed and stood up.

'Sit down,' Kat barked. 'Please.' She glared at Belle. 'We need each other. I know I'm next. I know stuff you don't know.'

'I very much doubt it. I have good contacts.' She wasn't ever going to tell this woman who they were, or do anything that hinted of co-operation. Breathing the same air was repulsive.

'Mags Jones' partner, the Chief Inspector. I know about him. I have a better one.'

'I doubt it,' Belle replied.

'It was one of the useless nerds, because I destroyed their party,' Kat Harris said in a flat voice. 'The dates of my girls' deaths and disappearances, each one three months after a reunion and around the anniversary party date, well, only an idiot wouldn't have been able to put that together. And now we know Angie's death wasn't accidental …' She left the words hanging in the air. Belle had taken a step away from her, but stopped. How could she possibly have known that? Bob Pugh had told her just over an hour ago. She winced and closed her eyes. Only one other person knew. Mal Jenkins had seriously overshot the mark this time. At least she could put a stop to him. She turned back to Kat Harris.

'Too much information, Kat. He must have forgotten to tell you he'd handed over the file to the Chief Inspector. Maybe he didn't believe Bob Pugh would tell me. After all, Bob plays by the rules and I'm just a nosy civilian.'

She could see from the flicker of surprise that crossed Kat Harris' face that what she had thought of as a trump card had turned out to be a dud.

'I have more,' Kat said. She stood up now, held out her hand, thrusting a business card into Belle's palm. 'Take this. If you change your mind, let me know.' She walked away across the square and into the library.

Belle dived into her bag, took out her phone and dialled Bob Pugh's number. To her relief, it didn't go to answerphone.

'Did you go home, Belle?'

'No. I had someone to meet. But it was outdoors, in the main square. Now, before you tell me off, I have something urgent to tell you.' She relayed the information about Kat Harris. He didn't have to be told where her information had come from.

'Right. Leave it with me. And go home and lock yourself in. Now.' He ended the call.

Belle had to control herself not to run across the road and over the footbridge. She was panting when she reached the front door to her block. She hadn't taken out her keys and began to fish in her bag, when a wave of fear and anxiety hit her as she fished out the entry door tag.

The main door to the apartment block could only be opened with the electronic tag. Sometimes during the day people would tailgate in and out. She had done it herself. But at three in the morning? Whoever had pushed the note under her door had been able to let themselves in. With a key tag. Which meant they could reach her front door with ease at any time. Could be waiting for her now, on the top floor. She let herself in, approaching the lift with trepidation. On the top floor, as the doors opened, she inched forward, checking to left and right, holding them open with one hand as she leaned forward until she could see her own front door. With keys in her other hand she ran across the foyer, pushed the key into her door, let herself in and locked the door behind her.

Her heart was hammering like a booming bass, a pulse throbbing in her neck. She threw herself onto the settee, put her head back and closed her eyes.

This apartment was no longer a safe refuge. She had to get out. Today.

Chapter 19
Psychology

Pushing aside all thoughts of what she had learned during the morning, she went into the bedroom and began to throw clothes into her suitcase, breathing heavily, but as her breath slowed down, she sat on the bed and allowed herself to consider her choices.

If she left right now her role as chief inquisitor would be taken over by Kat Harris. Did she want that? No question – she did not. It also meant she would be giving up. No way could she continue to investigate from Cornwall. Did she want to give up? Again – instinctively, no. Her heart had returned to its normal rate and she felt better able to analyse what she had learned, and consider if she wanted to find out what Kat Harris knew, if there really was anything that hadn't come from Mal Jenkins. Thinking through her list of potential interviewees, she definitely wanted to talk to Leonora Maginnis, the psychologist. She wanted to know if teenage experience of bullying could lead to psychopathy so intense it could make an adult murderer out of a bullied child. It seemed far-fetched, but what did she know?

There were still two of the party-givers she hadn't managed to find: Mary Conroy and Helena Parry. And then there was Jane Perry, who had sent a text message, as yet unread. Finally, the families. Perhaps that was Kat Harris' 'extra information'.

No, she couldn't give up. From the table in the sitting room she picked up Kat Harris' business card. Could she? No, absolutely not.

She went to put the card in the bin, but stopped, not sure why, and put it on the breakfast bar, shrugged and went back to thinking about where she could go, away from her apartment, but close enough to keep investigating. There was a hotel she had stayed at before lockdown began. Hospitality was in play again. They might have a room. It was a large, modern hotel on the outskirts of the city, close to her old school. She rang immediately and booked herself in for a week. The receptionist sounded delighted to have the business.

Back in the bedroom she finished packing and, with a mixture of reluctance and relief, locked up her apartment and headed down to the hotel.

* * *

The room had a desk and good free Wi-Fi. As soon as she was settled in Belle set up her laptop and notebooks and re-started her attempts to find Mary Conroy and Helena Parry. Her stomach growled. It was past one already and she hadn't eaten since the early hours when she was waiting for dawn. The hotel had a reasonable small restaurant where they served breakfast and dinner and a bar menu was available in the foyer area for lunch. It would do. She went down and installed herself in a comfortable armchair and waited for her sandwich and fries.

Jane's text was still waiting. She unlocked the phone, expecting another cringing exhortation not to exclude her. Instead, Jane had provided the information she needed.

Mary Conroy went to Australia, but she's back in Newport, visited family and is stuck because of Covid restrictions. I know where Helena lives.

Belle's first thought was: *fantastic*. Her second: *how did she know I was looking for them*? Her third: *I'm getting paranoid. Or am I?*

A plate of hot chicken and bacon sandwiches and sweet potato fries arrived on the table, delivered by a smiling teenager in a smart uniform. The short pause, as she tucked in, gave her time to think back over her conversations with Jane.

Had she told Jane she wanted to speak to the other party-givers? No, she hadn't. She had deliberately not told her she had lined up a meeting with Gwen Williams. Of course Jane wouldn't just drop out. Perhaps she had been watching the apartment. This was her way of letting Belle know she had no intention of being excluded. But what to do? Asking for the information about Mary Conroy and Helena Parry would bring Jane back to hang around her neck like a dead weight. Same for Kat Harris, who might also have useful information. She had a vision of being the pivot on a seesaw, keeping the two ends balanced at an equal height but at a sufficient distance to ensure neither had sight of the other. Nightmare scenario. On the other hand, how much further could she get without them? She probably could manage some progress on her own, but not fast enough and that was going to become a problem, given the ramping up of the threat. The lunchtime TV news had said another lockdown was inevitable in Wales. One thing Belle was sure of: she didn't want to get stuck here, like Mary Conroy. It was only a couple of hundred miles to Cornwall, unlike Mary's dilemma of a family on the other side of the planet. Still, this was not where she wanted to be for more than a week or so. The news item didn't say when the proposed lockdown would begin but hinted that it might be imminent. A firebreak, they called it, just a short, sharp period to halt the increase in Covid infections. Belle suspected that wasn't where it would stop. She might be stuck in Newport until Christmas. That decided it. She would have to ask for Jane's information, now, today. Kat Harris she could hold back on until she found out if she could prise anything helpful or useful from Mary Conroy and Helena Parry. At least neither Jane nor Kat could be the person who had sent or delivered the threats. Neither fitted the build of the figure she had glimpsed and were both invested in working with her, not in stopping her. She texted Jane back to meet her later in town.

* * *

By the time she set off heavy rain was falling. 'Typical Welsh weather', Belle muttered. *Sunny in the morning, soaking in the afternoon.* She parked her car in the reserved space in her apartment block. No point paying for parking. If Jane saw her walking across the bridge, she would think Belle was still staying there. No reason to tell her otherwise.

Just the one café was open serving indoors. Jane was already there, her eyes lighting up with excited anticipation when Belle entered and took off her raincoat.

'I've ordered you a black coffee, that's what you like, isn't it? Did I remember that right?'

'Yes, thanks, Jane.' Belle was irritated already and she'd hardly sat down. She hoped her response didn't sound too snappy. She forced out a smile. 'You've been doing more homework. Well done.'

Jane's smile of gratification made Belle want to shake her. 'I've found out where Mary is. It wasn't hard, you know,' she said, leaning across the table. 'Her family still lives in the same house as when we were in school. And Helena Parry – would you believe it – is a nun! She's out in the convent towards Cwmbran.'

'That is a surprise,' Belle replied. 'She wasn't the particularly religious one. I always thought that would be Mary Conroy. Helena was the brilliant one. I'd have expected her to be a rocket scientist, or something similar. Mary was the religious fanatic.'

Jane shrugged. 'People change. You have, me too.'

Belle held back a grin. You're exactly what you were back then, she thought. 'How have I changed, Jane?' Not that she cared for Jane's opinion, but still ...

'You were always the strong and silent type, but now you're deep, too. You hide a lot, don't you?'

Belle sat back, arms folded. 'We've all had experiences in life that we prefer to keep to ourselves, Jane.' For a second, she worried that Jane had been fishing. 'Haven't you?'

Jane smiled and shook her head. 'I wish.'

'Right, do you have an address for Mary? I can contact the convent myself to speak to Helena.'

'I have a phone number. Would you like it?' Jane spoke with a challenge in her voice, which said 'you'll have to give, to get'.

'Of course I'd like it.'

Jane handed over a piece of ragged edged paper. 'Will you arrange for us to meet her?' There it was. Belle had her answer ready.

'No, I don't think so, unless she prefers to meet. But if she does, it can only be two people, not three. Covid rules, Jane.'

Jane had been outwitted. She opened her mouth, then closed it again, scowling in frustration. 'You'll tell me what she says?'

'Of course, if she has anything to add. If she doesn't, I'll let you know that, too. Same for Helena, or whatever her name is now.' She gave Jane a gentle smile.

Jane got to her feet. 'Well, I can see there's nothing more for me here.' She pulled her arms into her coat. 'Enjoy your coffee.'

'Jane, please ...I didn't mean ...' Belle began, but Jane was already at the door and didn't look back. Belle felt a touch of shame, although this was what she'd hoped for. She had intended to fool Jane and drop her once she had the information. The coffee arrived and she shrugged. In a few days she'd have to head back to Cornwall. She had to gather as much information as she could. She'd think faster without Jane's twittering.

She'd tracked down Lennie Maginnis via the internet and discovered she was at the local hospital. A quick call had been enough. Lennie had been delighted to hear from her and happy to meet. She was at work today, finishing at three. With a sigh of relief, Belle had set up the two meetings far enough apart, but still hoping that Jane would leave before Lennie arrived.

Belle had been upfront with Lennie about the intended subject of their conversation. Of course, she wouldn't ask for a professional opinion, just an insider's insight to how a bullied teenage girl might become a killer. Lennie was the person to give her what she needed.

She didn't recognise Lennie when she arrived, running across the square from the direction of the car park and launching herself through the café door. The tubby, medium height girl with frizzy hair and acne was a different woman. The frizzy hair had become platinum white, cut short and snappy, no frizz, emphasising the startling blue eyes and the oval face. She was dressed in jeans and jumper with a figure that wouldn't have been out of place on a catalogue model. Other customers stopped to look at her. Unaware of their interest, Lennie made a beeline for Belle, arms extended, to which Belle put up a hand laughing.

'Damn, I just cannot remember that we aren't supposed to hug any more,' Lennie said, looking at the seat vacated by Jane and throwing herself into it. 'Someone has been here before me.'

'Jane Perry,' Belle replied.

'Well, well.' Lennie raised her eyebrows. She looked up at the barista, who was hovering in the background, pointed to the table and mouthed, 'Flat white, please,' her mouth widening into a huge toothy grin. The girl laughed.

'So, Belle Harrington. You haven't changed.'

'You have,' Belle replied, sipping at her drink.

'Thank God, yes I have. No more frizz and several stone lighter.'

'And looking good on it.'

'Thank you. Now, what's this all about. Tell me everything. We can catch up later.'

No small talk, Belle thought, with relief. She took a deep breath and ran through the story, watching Lennie's facial expressions alter between questioning, amazement and horror. As she came to the end, Belle said, 'That's about it, in a nutshell. What do you think?'

'What's the question, Belle? I have many thoughts, but what exactly is it you want me to give my opinion on?'

Belle paused for a moment, put her cup down.' I want to know if someone who suffered bullying and humiliation of the kind Kat Harris dished out for that eighteenth birthday party could become a killer.'

The barista arrived, giving Lennie a pause. 'Interesting question,' she said once the girl had gone. 'There's no way I can give you a formal professional opinion.'

'I know that. I want your insight into bullying, Lennie. Don't be influenced by our both knowing the characters involved. Just the psychology of bullying and the bullied.'

'OK. From my work I know that the after-effects of child bullying don't necessarily go away. But individuals deal with them differently, depending on the life experiences that follow. Let's start with the victims. Some can put it behind them, can shake it off, not allow their judgement to be influenced by it. Others, if they don't have good experiences in relationships or interactions with other people and better opportunities, will be dominated by what happened to them, either physically or mentally, or both. It will affect how they believe they are seen and judged. It can affect their mental health, reduce their opportunities and their family relationships. They can struggle to hold down a job and may be more likely than others to be bullied at work, too. They're more likely to suffer from depression and can become suicidal.'

'Like Sue Jones?' Belle interrupted.

'Yes, but I don't know anything about Sue's case, so I can't say definitively that the bullying she suffered led to her suicide.'

'It did, according to what her sister told me about her suicide note. But indirectly?'

Lennie sat back in her chair. 'It's likely to have been a factor, especially as her sister mentioned it to you, yes.'

Belle took a deep breath. 'What about the opposite? What about anger and the need for revenge?'

Lennie nodded. 'Many people who suffered bullying that wasn't dealt with by those in authority who should have dealt with it, will harbour such feelings. But …' she help up a hand. 'I cannot say that person would turn to murder – to several murders, if that's what you're telling me. There would have to be something else, some other event, or multiple events.' She paused, grimacing, a finger tapping the side of her head. 'There was a study, around 2012 or 2013, that found a fourfold likelihood of girls who had been bullied developing a personality disorder. However severe that might become, could it lead to a move from wanting to kill the person, or in this case, persons, who bullied you to actually doing away with them? Sorry, Belle, again I can't give you a definitive answer on that. I can do research for you, if that would help?'

'It would, thanks, Lennie.'

'Now, the bullies. They are likely to have had an upbringing of being bullied themselves, usually in their home situation. And, contrary to popular belief, they aren't stupid oafish thugs. We know that. Kat Harris was popular, alluring, almost; she could get others to do whatever she wanted, to get in with her. Remember, Jane Perry was desperate to be part of her group. To her, they were glamorous.'

Belle nodded. 'What about when they grow up?'

'Yeah, that's when the trouble starts. If they weren't given guidance to understand their own behaviour when they were children, or adolescents, they become difficult to deal with later on. Workplaces often won't tolerate such behaviour.'

'That I know. I spent years heading teams that dealt with employee behaviour. I never met a bully who could convince me they really didn't mean it, that it was all a joke or just banter, although many did try.'

Lennie's eyes widened. 'That's interesting. We need to talk more.' She glanced at her watch. 'Let's exchange details. I'd love to hear more about your experiences. Now, I have children to collect and re-distribute around the town.'

'One more question, Lennie, and yes, I'd be pleased to speak to you further. My question is: where should I start to look for evidence of a bullied teenager being pushed over the edge?'

'I'd try work,' Lennie replied. 'If you can find evidence, if you're right, it continued after school, one way or another. I really must go, but I have a question for you first.'

'OK.'

'Why are you pursuing this? What's in it for you?'

'That's two questions.'

'Are you going to answer either of them?'

'It's two different things, I think. The first, Lennie, is about Sue Jones. There was no justice, natural or otherwise for her, no regret, no care, from the people whose behaviour drove her into submission. The second is because of me.' She paused and breathed deeply. 'When I saw Kat Harris coming toward me across this square, I knew the pure unadulterated hate I felt like bile rising up in me, that could have consumed me when I watched her in school, still needed some kind of release. I thought I had it under control, but I don't, still. If I can find out what happened to those women, at least I can give myself healing. Does that make sense?'

'If it makes sense to you, then it makes sense,' Lennie replied quietly. 'Someone hasn't dealt with it so carefully, though.'

'And as much as I hate her,' Belle continued, 'I don't want her dead. That would make me no better, would it? I think Gwen feels the same.'

'The feelings that come from the assault on a person's self-esteem in the way it was delivered by Kat and her crew never goes away. But I understand and support what you're doing. Right, I really must go now.'

'I'll walk with you,' Belle said. 'My car is over in the car park. Thank you for listening to that rant.'

'No problem,' Lennie smiled.

They let themselves out of the café into the unremitting rain, sheltering under Belle's umbrella. At the car park entrance they stopped.

'Belle, be careful. I don't like what you've told me. Whatever this is, again I'll say – if you're right – it's been planned over twenty-five years. That's so bizarre and rare. It's definitely sociopathic, but incredibly restrained, for a serial killer. They usually escalate. This one doesn't fit the pattern. No, what I'm concerned about is the threats to you. If this person knows they've been sussed, and they have this ongoing plan, Kat Harris isn't the only one whose life may be threatened. Someone who may have killed multiple times, even if there is a plan, I don't think would hesitate to remove anyone who got in their way of achieving the plan. Look, would it be OK with you if I discuss this with a colleague, in greatest confidence, of course? I know someone who is more expert than I am. He might have better insights than mine.'

'All help appreciated,' Belle replied. 'Thank you, Lennie. I know there's danger, but I have to keep going. I've tried to walk away, but I can't.'

'Let's hope those aren't famous last words,' Lennie replied. She gave Belle a quick hug, then walked to her car.

Belle felt a shiver down her spine. She turned and hurried back across the square to the footbridge to her car, glanced around before letting herself in, and drove away and back to the hotel.

With their heads together, talking and laughing as they had fought the wind, neither had noticed another umbrella user, who had stood on the opposite side of the square to the café, then followed at an inconspicuous distance to the car park entrance, ducking into a shop doorway as they stopped.

As Belle ran over the footbridge, the watcher waited for the apartment lights to come on and was puzzled when it remained in darkness. But deciding it was probably too early, turned away and left the square.

* * *

As soon as she reached the safety of her room, Belle checked her phone and found two texts waiting, one from Mavis, the other from Bob Pugh. Both asked her to call urgently. This didn't sound good.

She decided to call Mavis first, but the call went to voicemail. She left a quick message, then called Bob Pugh. He answered his phone on the first ring.

'What's up Bob?'

'Something you're not going to like. There's been a death, a suicide, accompanied by a note. The note says the individual could no longer deal with their guilt about having killed someone years ago, in a hit-and-run.'

Belle held her breath. 'Which one of them is it?'

'That's the thing, Belle. It's none of them. You must – absolutely must – keep this confidential, until the name is released. Do I have that promise?'

'Of course, Bob.' Belle held her breath.

'OK. It was a woman, but not one of the names you gave me. She's admitted to running down Bernie Moloney on the thirteenth of December 1995. Says it was an accident. She is – was – called Monica Smith. Does that name mean anything to you?'

Belle shook her head. 'I've never heard of her,' she whispered.

Chapter 20

Accident?

Bob couldn't give her any further detail, and she didn't want to hear it anyway. The shock was too great. Did this mean she'd been wrong, right from the start? Had been led on by Jane's story? What an idiot she'd made of herself if that was the case. But was it?

For the next ten minutes she wandered around the room, making tea, looking for her notes, discarding them. Who was Monica Smith? The name didn't ring any bells, but then again, there were over sixty girls in the year group, divided into various subject groups. Maybe she wasn't in Belle's groups. Maybe she wasn't in the same year, or even in the same school. She tried a couple of search engines for Monica Smith, then a Facebook profile. There were too many of that name, even in the UK, and without more detail there was no chance of pinning down the right one. Bob had said it was an accident but if so, why only admit to it now, twenty-five years later? And – was this the one murder? And if it was, who had been protecting Monica Smith and who had sent the threating email and note?

Too many questions. Bob had said he would be back in touch once the autopsy had been carried out. She knew he shouldn't be talking to her in this much detail. Was he telling her to give up on the idea of multiple murders? No point speculating. She'd have to wait for the autopsy results. At least he had said it would be given priority, due to the confession in the suicide note.

A sudden thrash of rain against the window turned her head in that direction. She moved across and closed the curtains against the darkness. It was almost six already. She didn't feel like eating but pacing round the room wasn't helping. Perhaps sitting in one of the comfortable armchairs in the bright, warm foyer would allow her to assemble her thoughts into a more coherent order. She picked up her notebook and made her way downstairs.

She was the only person there, which helped, with no distractions from nearby conversations. After the unavoidable hot drink brought over by a bored waitress desperate for customers, she settled back, closed her eyes and began to think through the events of the day, and what she should do next. It didn't help. Her head was whirling, ideas rising up and pushing each other out of the way. The only two that might help she immediately rejected: speaking again to Jane Perry or Kat Harris. Or both. She needed distraction, which arrived with her phone ringing: Mavis answering her call.

She knew as soon as Mavis began to speak that something was wrong.

'It's Tessa, Belle. She's had an accident, fallen down the stairs. Except, I don't think it was an accident.'

'How is she?' Belle gasped.

'Not too bad, under the circumstances. She's fractured one of her fingers. Problem is, for someone her age fractures don't heal easily. She was lucky, though. She fell about three or four steps.'

'Why wasn't this an accident, Mavis?'

'She says she tripped on something on the stairs, something that wasn't there when she went up. And, she heard something in the night, called out "Who's there?", but there was no answer.'

'Could there have been someone there? Was there a break-in?'

'No sign of one, no. Only people who have access to a key is Andrew and me and the carer who's looking after her. She knows the number of the combination to the key safe next to the front door. I've spoken to her. She's promised she's told no-one else.' Mavis stopped, a sob in her voice.

'Where is Tessa now, Mavis?'

'The hospital insisted on keeping her in overnight. She's insisting on coming home tomorrow, when we're moving her bed down. It was lucky we went in this morning first thing, to finish off moving the furniture and take her clothes down. Andrew and I found her. We called an ambulance at once. She couldn't get up.'

'Do you think she'd been there long? Had she been unconscious?'

'No, thank the Lord. Only about half an hour. It was cold, but not enough to cause her hypothermia. She was quite lucid, too. Only thing is, Belle, I checked the stairs and the hallway. There was nothing there she could have tripped on.'

'She was quite sure she tripped on something?'

'Positive. She said it was something hard, round she thought, small enough to dig in underneath her foot.'

'Any sign of "you know who"?'

'Oh, yes. She was round my house this afternoon. Told me she was going back to social services, because it was clear now that Tessa is a danger to herself at home and has to be moved from the hospital into a home.' Mavis started to cry. 'I don't know what to do for the best. Tessa is determined to come home tomorrow. She's giving them hell at the hospital.'

Belle laughed. 'She's a tough old girl.' She waited until Mavis had stopped sobbing. 'Mavis, what do you really think? Are you worried about her being at home, even though she'll be on the ground floor? At least she can't fall down the stairs, but the broken finger will be restrictive and she may need more support. What does the hospital say? I assume she's been seen by a geriatric specialist?'

'He says he'll assess her tomorrow. Really, I think if he's willing to discharge her to home, I'd prefer that. I can't bear the idea of her being in an elderly care home any more than she can.'

'You know, Mavis, that might have to be a longer-term solution.'

'Yes, but in the meantime, if I can get her home, I'm thinking I might be able to bring in more help. Don't know where I'll get the money from, though. Andrew thinks it's time for her to go into a home, even if that means risking losing the house.'

'Hmm. Just an idea, Mavis. Do you think Tessa would put up with visits from one of us, during the day? Between us, we could organise a timetable for the next few weeks. I include myself as I'll be back by next Friday. That might put Hawkesworth Fox off for a while, and convince the hospital that she'll be well cared for. What do you think?'

'Belle, that would be wonderful. I did try to call Bette and Posy. Rose will be in church at Saturday evensong.' After a few seconds' pause she said, 'Could you talk to Bette for me? Let her know what's happened and ask her if she might help out?'

'Of course. I'll call her. Where are you now, Mavis?'

'At the hospital. We have a meeting with the doctor any minute.'

'Right, leave it with me. I'll call you back as soon as I've talked to Bette.'

By the time she had tracked down and spoken to Bette Jones, who had been horrified at the news about Tessa, fully approved the visiting plan and taken over its organisation, Belle was reeling. She had been on the go since meeting with Bob Pugh and had now reached the point where information overload was going to fry her brain if she didn't stop. After bolting down a meal she returned to her room, lay down on the bed and was asleep within minutes.

Chapter 21
Lunch

This time she slept well, not waking up until after nine. As it was Sunday, breakfast in the hotel was extended until ten. A shower and a change of clothes woke her up, but she still couldn't bring herself to process everything she had learned the previous day. A good breakfast would restore energy and, hopefully, clear her head. An hour later, revived with protein and caffeine, she was ready with her notes and phone, deciding who to try to contact first. Before getting stuck in, she gave Bette a quick call and was pleased to hear the hospital consultant had agreed that, so long as there was plenty of help for the next couple of weeks, there was no reason Tessa shouldn't go home.

'Mavis is so relieved,' she said. 'I got hold of Posy and Rose last night. Posy is stuck with café opening hours but she'll work around them. And Rose, of course, can't wait.'

They had agreed to speak again, later in the day. Belle hadn't felt ready to share what had been happening to her investigation and Bette didn't ask, so she left it for later. She had already planned to speak to Mary Conroy and Helena Parry. Mary first. The convent would be busy first thing Sunday morning, she guessed, as she dialled Mary's number.

She remembered Mary Conroy as a girl of medium height, from a Welsh family. She had been bilingual, but had used only English in school, although her family spoke only Welsh at home.

The person who answered the phone had an instantly recognisable Australian accent.

'Is this Mary Conroy?' Belle asked.

'It's Mary Conroy. Who wants to know?'

Belle introduced herself.

'Really, from school? Boy, was that a long time ago. How did you find me here?'

'Jane Perry gave me your number and told me that you're stuck until restrictions are lifted and you can get back to Australia.'

'Jane Perry, eh? She was at the reunion, back in September. So, is this a social call?'

'Not really, Mary. I'd like to talk to you about …'

'Please, not about Kat Harris' gang all dead or missing and not by accident?'

'I'm afraid so, Mary. It's turning out it may not be entirely wrong, which is what I thought, but now, I'm not so sure.'

There was a short silence at the other end of the line, then, 'You'd better tell me why you're thinking this, but not over the phone. Where are you? Still in Newport?'

Belle hesitated for a moment, but decided the hotel lobby was safe enough, if it continued to be quiet. 'I'm close to the Vacation Stop hotel, down near Knyghton House. Could you come down, any time today?'

'Yes, I could. How about lunchtime. You can treat me.'

'Fair enough,' Belle grinned. 'See you around twelve, in the lobby. By the way, Mary, does the name Monica Smith sound familiar to you?'

'Uh, not immediately. Was she one of us, from school, I mean?'

'Could be.'

'Well, I've still got old school papers and photos here I can check. Does this matter much?'

'Yes, it's important.'

'OK, I'll take a look. I must say, this has livened up my week.' She ended the call.

The convent didn't answer the phone until almost midday and then refused to bring Sister Mary Frances to the phone. It was suggested she call back on Monday. Pulling a face at the phone screen, Belle decided there was no point in arguing.

* * *

She was ready and waiting when Mary arrived. Another one she wouldn't have recognised. Belle remembered her as being average height. The woman who ran in out of the rain, shaking an umbrella over the lobby floor, to the obvious annoyance of the hotel receptionist, was large, in all senses. Tall, roundish with a face that immediately provoked a responsive smile, glancing eagerly around, spotting Belle, at first with a questioning expression and a pointing finger – is it you? – then exploding across to where Belle had stood up, and enveloping her in a hug.

'Sorry, I know we're not supposed to do that, are we?'

'No, Mary. But, all being well, we've both been careful,' Belle replied, indicating the armchair opposite hers as they both moved back.

'So, what's for lunch?' Mary asked as she threw herself into an armchair at one of the tables in the foyer area. Belle pushed a menu across the table to her and there was a minute's silence as Mary perused it, her head bobbing back and forth.

'I'll have the chilli. Make a nice change from sister-in-law's Sunday beef roast. She hasn't cooked anything else on a Sunday for twenty years.' She waved a hand in the air and the barista arrived immediately. Belle ordered, the same for both of them, plus drinks. Mary waited in silence until the drinks arrived. 'Don't want anyone overhearing what we're about to discuss, do we?' She stirred her coffee and took a mouthful, swallowed, then looked up at Belle, eyes narrowed. 'Now, what's this about?'

'You were at the reunion, you heard the story. Why are you scoffing?'

'Because I knew those girls, I mean, those of us who organised the party that no-one turned up to.'

'How do you know that's my focus, Mary?'

'Jane told me.' She shrugged. 'I think you're as crazy as Jane.'

'Then why are you here?' Belle drummed her fingers on the table.

'Now don't get annoyed with me. You sounded like there was something more to this, something you've found out.' She leaned forward. 'Look, the party was a horrible experience, degrading, embarrassing, despite everything Mags Jones and Jude Crawley did to help us out. Huh. No booze and no boys and no friends, present company excepted. But we've all moved on, in our different ways. Nowadays, I can look back and, well, not laugh, but shrug. I can tell you that I saw Kat Harris back in September and made a beeline for her, but she practically ran away from me.' She paused and laughed. 'How about that?'

Belle smiled.' You've changed.'

'Australia. I went with my family, not long after school, never looked back. I started again. I suppose not everyone can do that.'

'Angie Stephenson didn't die from an accidental overdose,' Belle said. 'Someone did it to her deliberately. Jane was in the nightclub where it happened.'

Mary's eyes widened. 'You think Jane was involved?'

'No, she has an alibi, and she doesn't fit the profile in other ways.'

Mary sat back as their food arrived. Again, they took a few minutes to arrange themselves. Mary poked a fork into the plate of food and stirred it around. 'Well, you don't say. And you think it was one of us.' Before Belle could respond she went on. 'You could be right, of course. I was in the UK. My first trip back. In fact, I've been coming back to the UK every five years, to meet up with my family since Mum and Dad died in Oz. Sometimes I've stayed for months and I've attended the reunions.' She put the fork down and stared hard at Belle. 'Now, here comes a shocker for you. The year Denise Goodright died, 2005, I didn't stay for Christmas. Mum was unwell, so I went home early. Denise was swimming off a Reef, at the southern end of Gold Coast City. Actually, she was snorkelling, alone. Immensely stupid thing to do. She got caught up, couldn't free herself. Drowned – at least that was the verdict. Thing is, Belle, that's where I live. And I was there at the time.'

Chapter 22
Hesitation

Belle put down her cutlery, sat back and stared at Mary. 'Did you know it was her? At the time?'

Mary nodded. 'Yes, I recognised the name.'

'But you didn't say anything?'

'Of course not,' Mary replied, shaking her head vehemently. 'I didn't want to get involved. It was 2005. I didn't know she was on holiday and I hadn't seen her at the reunion in September. If I'd said something I would have had to involve my family, probably give a statement to the police, and everyone was saying it was an accident. So, why should I have done?' Her tone had become belligerent.

'You just said something. You said, about the inquest "at least that was the verdict". What did you mean by that?'

'You don't miss much, do you?'

'No, I don't.'

'OK, I've been snorkelling there myself, many times, but always with at least one other person. You have to be a total novice to get yourself caught up on anything, but she managed it. Apparently, it was a line caught around her ankle and she was too far down to get it off. They didn't find a knife, although her husband said she had one with her. They assumed she dropped it. The line was caught under a rock. Another snorkeller had been there the day before and hadn't seen any line, so it was an issue how it got there overnight. Again, assumed to have been brought in by the tide, and wedged itself under the rock. But I asked myself, how did it get around her ankle in such a way it couldn't be easily released? And there was another diver in the vicinity, who was never identified. But that wasn't considered relevant.'

'Mary, when did you ask yourself that question? Because, I think you suspect there's more to this.'

Mary didn't answer. She applied herself to a couple of mouthfuls of chilli, before pausing to take a drink of water. 'Not at first, not when it happened. When I heard the story, though, I began to think back, and remember what didn't quite make sense at the time. Honestly, Belle, how could anyone have done that? I mean, deliberately? And why must it have been one of our party group? Kat Harris took her fury out on others in the class. Why not one of them? Have you even considered that?'

Belle shook her head. 'It's the timing, Mary. Every five years, three months after a reunion and on or around the date of that party. My belief is, it had to be someone affected by it.'

Mary nodded slowly. 'It wasn't me,' she murmured, staring at her plate. 'But I would say that, wouldn't I?' She grinned. 'Although, I wouldn't be too hard on whoever it was. Mind you, three of them disappeared, didn't they? There's no actual indication they're dead.'

'No, there isn't. But there's been no indication they're alive, either. Not a word to any members of their families since. No economic activity. Nothing; just – gone.' She shrugged. 'I know it happens, but it still seems odd to me. Eat up, please. Did you remember anything about Monica Smith, by the way, or find any reference to her?'

'No, name still doesn't ring a bell and there's nothing I've found so far. Have you asked anyone else?'

No, I …' she stopped as her phone rang. It was Bob Pugh. 'Excuse me, Mary, I have to take this.' She greeted Bob as she walked to the hotel exit and stood outside in the car park, trying to shelter from the driving rain under the short canopy.

'Any news?'

'Not really,' he replied.' We're struggling with Monica Smith. Are you quite sure you haven't heard of her?'

'Positive,' Belle replied. 'Bob, I'm having lunch with another of the old girls. I asked her to check any memorabilia she has about our school days. She says Monica Smith's name doesn't appear on anything she has, photos, whatnot. Have you checked with the woman who organises the reunions? She's likely to have comprehensive lists.'

'Yes, we have and she isn't on that list either. It's odd.' He paused, then said, 'Listen, we've taken a photo of her face. It doesn't look too bad. If I send it to you, could you tell me if there's anything familiar about her. See, she doesn't appear to have a past, as far as we can discover so far. But you can't show this to anyone else. I've had to get my gaffer to agree to send it to you.'

'Of course. Bob … listen, how about I just show it to the woman I'm lunching with, an old girl? She might see something I don't.'

He didn't respond and she went on, 'If you don't have anything at all, and she has even a vague recollection, surely that's better than nothing. I won't copy it, just show it to her.'

There was again silence on the phone for a few seconds as she guessed he was weighing it up. 'OK, show it to her. But you have to swear her to secrecy. I'll be in a shitload of trouble if she goes public.'

'Fair enough. I'll call you back after lunch. I'll have to go. I'm getting soaked here.'

Back inside Mary asked, 'Something interesting?' just as Belle's phone pinged. The photo had arrived.

'Maybe,' she said, sitting down and pushing away her half-eaten meal.

'If you're not going to eat that, can I finish it?' Mary asked. 'Saves me from having to eat the leftover roast.'

Belle pushed the plate across the table. Mary tucked in as Belle looked at the photograph. Whoever had taken the picture had done a reasonable job of not making it too gruesome. Monica Smith appeared to be asleep. Belle glanced at it for a few moments, shook her head and put the phone on the table. She could see nothing in the features of the dead woman that triggered any memory. The woman looked older than herself and Mary, at least in her sixties. The face was lined, the skin rough. The hair was grey, parted in the centre, long and straggling on each side of the face.

Mary finished the food and put the cutlery down with a smile of satisfaction. 'That was good.'

'Mary, I've been sent a photo of Monica Smith. Would you take a look at it, see if you see someone you might recognise?'

'Sure,' Mary replied, taking Belle's phone. She stared hard at it. 'This woman is dead,' she said. 'You didn't tell me that.'

'No, I didn't. I meant to, I'm sorry. What do you think?'

Mary looked again, stared hard. Then, for a fraction of a second, Belle thought her eyes widened. But she handed back the phone. 'No-one I know,' She replied. 'I have to get going.'

'You said you'd be out for hours,' Belle asked, puzzled, with a growing suspicion that Mary wasn't being truthful. 'Are you sure there's nothing familiar about her?'

Mary shook her head, unnecessarily vigorously. She stood up. 'Thanks for lunch. I don't like looking at pictures of the dead, that's all.' She put her coat on and picked up her bag and umbrella. 'I won't hug you this time. Let's meet up again soon. I'm probably here for a while yet.' She turned and marched out of the door into the rain without putting up the umbrella and disappeared around the side of the door to the car park.

Belle sat at the table, puzzlement and suspicion growing. Was it really about being upset at realising the woman in the picture was dead? Mary didn't seem the type. She remembered she was supposed to tell Mary not to speak to anyone about it, stood up and ran out of the hotel, just in time to stop her from driving away and signalled to her to lower her window.

'Mary, I'm sorry I upset you. I should have told you more before I showed you that photo. The thing is, please don't speak to anyone about this, don't tell anyone you've seen it. Please.'

Mary nodded. 'Who would I tell?' She said as she raised the window and drove away, leaving Belle standing in the car park. *I won't be seeing her again*, Belle thought, realising she was dripping. She walked back into the hotel, went straight to her room to shower and change her clothes. As she glanced at herself in the mirror she felt a rush of emotion and her stomach clenched. *What have I got myself into?* She brushed a hand through her hair. *Well, whatever it is, you're right up to your neck in it, Belle Harrington, so don't blub. Decide what to do next,* she lectured her reflection.

* * *

Next turned out to be switching off for the rest of the afternoon. The hotel bed was comfortable enough to prop herself up on pillows and turn on the TV, which served up an extensive menu of streaming services. She chose *Endeavour*, one of her favourites, and settled down to watch a couple of episodes. She liked the way he used elegant reasoning skills and thought outside the box. *Exactly what I should be doing.*

She awoke with a start at the end of episode two. Three hours asleep. She shook herself, sat up, switched off the TV and saw the light was fading outside. She checked her phone. No calls missed. Then she remembered Mary's momentary expression of surprise, and something that had come to her as her eyes closed. She called Bob Pugh.

'Sorry to disturb your Sunday afternoon, Bob. I've had an idea about Monica Smith. My lunch companion, by the way, said she didn't recognise the face, but something told me she might have.'

'OK. What's the idea?'

'Do you have the software that can age people from childhood to adult?'

'Not myself, but Maggie's son Jack's friend has it. We used it last year, on one of her cases. Why?'

'I have a photo of the bullies when they were in school. I can identify all of them. Could you get this person to take each face and update it to present time? I just have an inkling that it would be useful to see what they might look like now.'

'Hm. I've got an *inkling* you're thinking much more than that, Belle Harrington. But, OK, send me the photo. I'll see what I can do. I might have to use police software, though, and that will make it official. Can't ask the kid to do this.'

'That's OK, Bob. Thanks. Let's see what comes of it, shall we?'

'Fine. Send it to me. I'll get on to it first thing tomorrow.'

They ended the call and she sent the picture. Nothing more to do now, this evening. She thought about calling the convent but decided against. Best leave it all until tomorrow. Nothing more to do. She would order a sandwich later. For now, back to *Endeavour*.

Determined to put all thoughts of the dead and missing women out of her mind, Belle doggedly watched TV throughout the evening, ate a sandwich and slept.

The following morning, as she dressed and watched the local news, the leading item was the official announcement of the Covid firebreak, which would mean no travelling in and out of Wales from Friday. She had four days left before she had to return to Cornwall. Hopefully, enough time to make progress.

Chapter 23
Confrontation

Shortly after nine she called the convent again. This time, when she asked for Sister Mary Frances, a voice asked who was calling. She replied, 'an old friend', and was told to wait. The wait had been going on for almost ten minutes and Belle was thinking she would give it no more than another two minutes, when another voice said, 'Who is this? I have no old friends.'

The voice was flat, unemotional. 'Is that Sister Mary Frances? Helena Parry as was?'

'Who wants to know?'

'Helena, this is Belle Harrington, from Knyghton School. I was Belle Penning back then. Do you remember me?'

A pause. 'I remember you. Why are you calling me?'

'There's something I'd like to talk about with you, Helena. Do you think we could meet up?'

The response came immediately this time. 'No. I have no interest in the past. I have no old friends. There is nothing to discuss.'

Belle's instincts were ringing like a fire alarm. 'Oh, I think you know there is, Helena.'

'Don't call me that. My name is Sister Mary Frances.'

'OK, Sister Mary Frances. I want to talk to you about Kat Harris and the other girls – women – who bullied you. I'm guessing you know three of them are dead, the others are missing?'

'I know nothing and am uninterested in their fates. Whatever may have happened to them is God's will, nothing that requires discussion or opinion.'

'Well, at least one of them was murdered and, I've discovered, maybe two. Let me ask you a simple question, one which I'm sure you won't mind answering. How long have you been a nun?'

'That's not your business to know.'

'I can find out, but I thought you might like to be just a little co-operative. Jane Perry told me it was just after you left school, but I'm not sure that's right. Is it right?'

'I have nothing more to say, now please leave me alone,' Helena Parry replied and put the phone down.

'You are not a truthful nun, Sister Mary Helena Parry Frances,' Belle muttered, putting her mobile down on the bed.

* * *

Rose Teague absent-mindedly chewed the edge of her right-hand thumbnail, causing Harry to look up from the paper he was reading over breakfast. Harry liked a quiet, relaxed Monday, during which he and Rose could chat, do gardening, read books together, catch up on each other's news. Seeing her chewing, gazing into space and frowning, he sighed. Something was up. And when something was up with Rose, it was likely to be something Harry should know about.

'What's on your mind, my love?' he asked gently.

For a moment she didn't answer so he waved his hand in her direction, which distracted her. 'Sorry, Harry. Just thinking.'

'Not about anything good, I fear.'

She smiled. They each knew each other's expressions, body language so well that any instance of discomfort in one brought the same feeling to the other.

He reached across the table, gently removed the thumb from her mouth. 'Want to share?'

She nodded. 'Two things. Our new friend, Belle, asked me a strange question. About a boy who might have had an accident down at Cash Cove, and died, in 1976. Do you recall that, Harry?'

'No, I don't. 1976.' He closed his eyes for a moment. 'I was here then. Is it important?'

'I think so, for her. I don't know why. I offered to ask Bette, but she refused. It puzzles me.'

'I can check around, discreetly, if you'd like. I won't mention any names, of course.'

'I think so. I sensed that she needs to know. That's the first thing. Now, I told you we've organised a timetable to visit Tessa, for Mavis, so she's not so worried Tessa might have another accident.'

'Yes, and a very honourable gesture it is. So, what's wrong?'

'I don't think it was an accident. When she fell, I think she was meant to fall.'

Harry sat back. 'That's a serious suggestion, Rosey. If it was meant to happen, then someone must have been on the organising end of such a wicked event. Is that what you think?'

'Yes, Harry. I do think that. I don't have a clearness of sight yet. Just feeling.'

Some would have scoffed at Rose's *feeling*, but not Harry. He knew his esoteric wife well enough to respect this special and unusual part of her. He had never let it interfere with his own belief. He was a man of God, firmly and joyously. Nothing could or would ever change that. Yet, he knew that Rose, whilst never having explicitly said she believed in his God, viewed this aspect of her nature as a gift and who was he to deny that, or believe that it was anything but God-given. On the day they met he had recognised his soul mate. Few received such a benefaction. Therefore, he always took her seriously and never, ever disparaged anything she felt, strange or even preposterous as it might seem.

'Follow your heart and your instincts, my love, whatever they are telling you.' He squeezed her fingers. 'What time is your turn on the rota today?'

'Ten 'til twelve this morning. I'm sorry, I know we usually spend that time together, but ...'

'Don't apologise, please. Are you going to ask her about what happened?'

'Yes, I think so. I'll try to find a way to do it subtly, so Tessa doesn't become agitated. Mavis emphasised she must live quietly for the next couple of weeks, to allow her body to recover from the shock, as well as for her finger to heal. I thought I might read to her.'

'Good idea. Any thoughts about what she might like? A nice, simple romance, or a Cornish history?'

Rose giggled. 'She wants *A Game of Thrones*, according to Mavis. I'm not sure, from what I know, I'll be able to read it without blushing.'

Harry laughed. 'That's Tessa for you. Well, do your best.' His voice became serious. 'See what you can explore about the maybe-not accident.'

* * *

Towards the end of her rota time Rose had managed to get through five chapters of *A Game of Thrones* with her cheeks constantly hitting high degrees of beetroot embarrassment and taking only the odd peek at Tessa, who didn't seem in the least uncomfortable. They sat in the lounge with the log fire blazing, Tessa comfortable in her favourite armchair with a cup of tea and a pile of biscuits to one side. She looked thoroughly contented with the world.

'How's the hand?' Rose began, having put the book down with no little relief.

'Not too bad, my lover. Good job it was my right hand, not the left. I'm left-handed, you see. In my day they tried to make us write with the right hand, gave you a good smacking if you made a mess of it, which I did. Couldn't manage at all.' She tutted. 'Couldn't wait to get out of there. Went to work with my mother, cleaning houses, when I was twelve. I could read and write, just about. Never had too much need for it, but I made sure my children could, oh yes.'

Rose leaned over and took Tessa's good hand.' They're both gone now, I believe?'

Tessa nodded and jerked her head at photographs on the mantlepiece about the fire. 'Albert just a few years ago. I had him young. He was in his seventies when he had a heart attack. A fireman, he was,' she beamed with pride. 'A good man. He didn't have no children, though. And my Marla, she had the tuberculosis. Died when she was thirteen. Terrible, that was. Just me, now.'

'And Mavis,' Rose said gently. 'She cares a great deal about you. Remind me, what's the relationship between you?'

'She's my niece, my youngest brother's child. She's another good 'un, is Mavis. Not so sure about that husband of hers, though.'

This was Rose's opportunity. 'You don't like Andrew?'

Tessa shook her head. 'He's … I can't think of the word.' She paused and frowned. Rose waited. 'Calculating, that's it. Scheming. Oh, he's good enough, getting me moved, trying to sort out the business with this house. There's another layer, though. Another man, hiding under the one you see.' She stopped and nodded to herself, muttering.

'Spends too much time at the golf club, does Andrew. A nineteenth hole man,' Tessa said, tapping the side of her nose. Rose wasn't sure what she meant by the gesture, but didn't speak, in case there was more to come. But there wasn't. The arrival of the carer to organise Tessa's lunch and her afternoon nap interrupted them. Rose was disappointed she hadn't had chance to speak directly about the accident, but she would be back tomorrow. Twenty-four hours would also give her time to think more on the matter of the accident, and what Tessa was trying to convey to her. Calling goodbye, she walked out to the hall and stared up at the stairs. The hall itself contained only a small table with a cloth on top and a small glass vase, now empty. If there had been an object that caused the fall, it would have to be very small to have evaded the search by Mavis and Andrew, or have looked innocuous enough not to have been considered. What could it have been? Something was nudging at her, but she couldn't grasp it. Never mind. Bette would be next in, for the three to five shift, followed by the carer again for evening dinner, and finally Posy from seven to eight, before Tessa went to bed. The old lady was safe enough, Rose thought, then pulled herself up at the implication. *Safe from what, or who? Another so-called accident?*

* * *

After her unhelpful conversation with Helena Parry, Belle had decided she needed fresh air and distraction. The hotel was just across the road from the wall that formed the boundary of Knyghton House. It was a miserable, grey day, but dry. She decided to take a walk around the grounds, clear her head. The house itself was closing again, so this was the last chance she would have to walk around inside. Yet, she was reluctant to go in, feeling safer in the open air. On one side of the car park workshops had been set up in half a dozen old, converted garages. There was a leather worker, a candle maker, a saddler and crafts of various kinds. Despite having no visitors, the craftspeople were all present and working. Belle visited each, bought herself a new leather credit card holder and a few candles to take back to the cottage, then walked in the direction of the lake.

This was an artificial lake, built by one of the former peers to enhance his view from the house across the formal lawn with its central fountain and the sunken garden to one side. There was a small boathouse, now empty, originally for the ladies and gentlemen visiting to be rowed around at their leisure. On the near side the lake was bounded by a short wall. On the far side trees grew and a path had been made for present day visitors to stroll around the circumference. In their schooldays the girls had not been allowed on the lawn, never mind near to the lake. She began to walk slowly, hands in pockets, taking in the fresh air and the sounds of birds in the trees, trying to empty her mind of everything else.

The walk took half an hour, at the end of which she was ready to return to the hotel, sit with a coffee and resume her cogitations and, probably, make phone calls. As she headed back across the lawn in the direction of the car park, she saw another, single visitor, sitting on a bench at the side of the sunken garden. After a quick glance she went to walk past, but was stopped by a wave, indicating she should go over. She stopped, puzzled and alert. As she did so, the visitor stood up and turned to fully face her. With mounting horror, Belle recognised the face and form. It was Kat Harris, now heading in her direction. She must have been followed here. She marched over until they were face to face.

'Did you follow me here?'

'Of course I did. You haven't contacted me. We need to speak.'

'No, we don't,' Belle replied. 'Don't follow me again.' She began to walk away, but Kat Harris hurried forward to keep pace with her.

'Look, I know you despise me and I really don't care. I want to stay alive and I need your help. I have information that will speed up our discovery of whoever is planning to kill me.'

Belle kept walking until she reached her car. 'Kat, I have no intention of working with you. I hope to find out the truth behind whatever happened to your rotten gang of bullies. If that keeps you safe, so be it. I don't care about you, either, but I don't want to have it on my conscience that I had any responsibility for your death.' She wasn't going to say anything about the threats she'd received.

She put her hand on the door handle, but Kat Harris grabbed her arm. 'We both know none of their deaths were accidental, and they are all dead. I know more about two of the three who disappeared. Wouldn't you like to have that?'

'Let go of me!' Then she paused. Did she want that information? Yes, of course she did, but was she prepared to pay the price Kat would demand for having it? 'Give me a minute.'

Kat Harris grinned. 'Has to be a fair swap.'

'Don't push your luck, Kat. But tell me something. Do you actually care that they're probably all dead? Do you have any remorse at all for what you did to those girls who couldn't fight back?'

Kat Harris didn't hesitate. '*No*, to both questions.'

'You're a bloody psychopath, aren't you?'

'I don't like labels. And you know nothing about me.'

For the first time, Belle saw something in Kat Harris she had never seen before. Not fear, exactly, but hesitancy, wariness. A thought flashed through her head of a poem she had read not long before, about remembering that the monster was created after birth. Therefore, you shouldn't be afraid of the monster, but of whatever made it so. Reluctantly, she acknowledged that Kat Harris must have had something in her past that had turned her into the monster; she had seen so much of this, people turned into bullying monsters by their personal history. However, she reminded herself that such people still had choices. She had faced her own choice. Kat Harris had chosen to continue on the path that had been created for her, instead of stepping off to find an alternative, more humane way through life.

'I don't want to know anything about your personal demons, Kat.' Again, the flash of wariness. 'I only have a couple of days left here. So, I will – reluctantly – agree to trade information with you.'

'Good. Shall we go back to your hotel?'

Belle sighed. Of course the woman knew where she was staying. 'I told you I don't appreciate being stalked.'

'I'm not stalking you. I have superb hacking skills and I am an experienced investigator. There's far too much information out there, you know, to let you hide from people like me,' Kat said in an offhand way. 'If you know how, no-one is untraceable.' Her expression became serious. 'That's how I know Tina, Liz and Faith are dead. No footprint of any kind, ever.'

'Let's go,' Belle said.

* * *

Back at the hotel Belle decided the lobby was not a suitable place for this conversation. After a short discussion with the receptionist she paid for the hire of a small meeting room for an hour, then went to fetch her notes and laptop, leaving Kat waiting in the room.

On her way back to the lobby her phone rang. Bob Pugh. She decided to answer it before she was back in Kat's company. She might not want to share whatever it was he was calling about and when she heard his news, she was quite certain.

'Where are you, Belle?'

'In the hotel. I'm about to meet with Kat Harris.' She might as well be up front with him.

'Is that safe?'

'No idea, Bob. I'm about to find out. She says she has information about two of the three missing women.'

'Then she may have to tell me, officially. What I'm about to tell you is going to change everything.'

'We used the photo you sent me with the ageing software to take a look at how they might look now. It explains why Monica Smith has no history. She doesn't and never has existed. She's Faith Shepherd, the last one on your list, who supposedly disappeared in 2015.'

Chapter 24
Mutiny

'Belle, are you still there?'

She was leaning with her head on the door, eyes closed. 'Yes, Bob, I'm here. What does this mean?'

'Well, I'm afraid there's more to it. There's evidence of restraints, on her wrists. She was emaciated; fed, but poorly; quite dehydrated. We know she was an alcoholic and chain smoker. There's evidence of alcohol and nicotine in her body, but not the amount you'd expect. The pathology suggests she hasn't regularly drunk alcohol and has smoked few cigarettes for more than a year. She was also a drug addict, but the only sign of any drug is of a sedative, which is more recent.'

'Are you telling me … I'm not sure. I think you're telling me she's been, what, restrained against her will, for possibly a long period of time?'

'Could be, it's an odd one. We aren't sure, yet, but the initial indication of suicide is now an unexplained death. I'm heading up the investigating team. So, your unlikely story is now less unlikely and we'll have to talk in an official capacity, plus all of the people involved. I need all of the names.'

'I need to speak to Kat Harris. She's waiting for me. I might as well tell her about this, now. If that's OK?'

'Not yet, please, and I'll need to speak to both of you first. I'd like you to come to the station this afternoon. Speak to her, and call me back, then get down here.'

Kat Harris' reaction wasn't surprising. 'NO! Absolutely not. I am not going near any police station.'

'This is not a yes/no option. Visit them, or they'll be visiting you. I'm going now. Your choice.'

Looking mutinous, Kat Harris stood up and followed Belle out of the room and down to the car park, where she got into her car without speaking and drove away. Belle decided she had done what Bob had asked her to do and it was now up to Kat what came next. At the station Bob was waiting for her and took her through to an interview room. Another officer joined them.

'Thanks for coming promptly, Belle,' he began, giving her the impression that it had been a choice. 'Where's Ms Harris?'

'No idea, Bob. I told her she should come with me. I couldn't make her, though, could I? She drove off.'

He sighed and turned to his accompanying officer. 'Mike, go organise someone to find out where she's staying, please. Get her in here.'

The man nodded and left the room. 'We'll wait for him to come back; he's my sergeant and I want him to hear everything.'

'Are you convinced now that all of these deaths and disappearances have been part of a plan, not just random events?'

He rubbed his chin. 'Fifty-fifty,' he said. 'Which is why I want to hear more, from both of you. She does realise she could be next, if this is a plan of some kind?'

'Of course she does. She just wants to control everything.'

'That bird's flown, now, or at least until I make a decision.'

Sergeant Mike Goodman returned to the room. 'Got a couple of constables on it, put the word out.' He looked at Belle. 'Do you know what car she's driving?'

'Um, it was black, a Peugeot, I think. I'm not good on makes of car.'

He grimaced. 'Give me a minute. She's here from America, the boss says. Could it be a hire car?'

'Yes, possibly. I noticed it had this year's registration.'

'Well, that's better than nothing. I'll be back in a sec,' he said to Bob and left the room again.

'Is he going to be difficult with me?' Belle asked. 'Because if he is, you should remember you'd still be trying to find Monica Smith if I hadn't supplied that photo.'

Bob raised his hands, palms forward. 'Peace! No, he's not. I haven't given him the full picture yet. Let's wait until he returns and you can tell us both what you know, OK?'

Belle nodded.

The sergeant returned to the room. 'I've put them onto checking the main hire firms. Is Harris her maiden or married name?'

'It's her maiden name. I don't know if she's married or not … wait, yes, I do. It's Francois. Just a minute, she gave me a business card.' She fished in her bag and brought out the card, handing it over to him. Goodman rolled his eyes. 'A private investigator?'

'In the States,' Belle replied.

Bob decided it was time to intervene. 'Mike, we can go into this later, but for now, we need to hear everything Belle knows, so sit and listen. Belle, off you go. We're going to record this, if that's OK with you. This isn't a formal interview, so you can refuse.'

'Not a problem,' she said and began to speak, carefully, conscious of the machine and the two-way window taking up the upper half of one wall, starting with the story at the reunion. It took around ten minutes, with the sergeant scribbling notes. A few times he opened his mouth to interrupt, but Bob Pugh held up his hand. 'We can ask questions once Belle has finished.'

When she was done, Bob sat back in his chair and folded his arms, biting his bottom lip. 'You see, the thing that bothers me is this. It sounds like a plan, when you tell it the way you have. Now, I'm not a psychologist, but I can't see how one big incident, and it was a nasty one, but still, one big incident could turn someone into a serial killer. The thing with serial killers, and I've only ever in my career come across one before now, is that they don't wait five years between kills.'

'Well, I'm not a psychologist either, but I know someone who is. I've spoken to her. Sorry, I forgot about her. She works at the hospital. She agrees with you. She thinks a person who could execute this plan would have been feeling strong ongoing resentment. Then, another, further trigger occurred, something that tipped them over the edge.'

He nodded slowly. 'Maybe. So I can see two possibilities here. One: this person began with Angela, felt they had retribution, enjoyed it and decided to go through the group. Two: these were individual random events, but this person – let's give her a name – we might as well stick with Monica – Monica sees reports or finds out that Angela has died and it brings back the memories of bullying, and Monica wants more of these bullies punished. So, we may have one or more chance killings. But' – he held up a hand again to stop Belle intervening – 'the problem is with whatever happened to Faith Shepherd. That worries me.'

Belle nodded. 'That's what I was going to say. The first and the last. And restrained for a long period of time. That is unbelievably horrible. It's making me feel quite sick.'

Bob turned to his sergeant.' Mike, thoughts?'

Mike Goodman sat back and folded his arms. 'The three accidents are now doubtful as such. Of the three disappeared, one may have been restrained for a longish period and made to confess to the second death, then killed, but the death made to look like a suicide. I say there's enough there to make this a full-on enquiry into a potential serial killer. But, I am puzzled about one aspect,' he said, his head nodding.

'Go on,' Bob replied.

'I've never even been close to serial killing. I know more from what I've seen on the telly than in real life. I've made a study of psychopathy and there's evidence here, certainly. But also of incredible planning and patience, and the ability to keep a low profile.'

Bob stood up, hurriedly, surprising Belle and the sergeant. 'I need to brief the Super. She's going to have to commit resources to this and I think she'll be reluctant to do that until we have a more solid basis to convince her it's got legs. Belle, thanks, you can leave this to us for now. If anything else happens, though, any more notes in the middle of the night, whatever, you let me know at once. Mike will see you out.' He left the room.

'Is he always like that?' Belle asked.

'Yep. Action man. When he has something to get his teeth into, he'll not let it go. Drives us all mad sometimes, but he's a great boss. And he gets results.'

'So what do I do now?'

'You live in Cornwall, don't you?'

Belle nodded.

'Go back. You'll be safer there than here. We've got this. Come on, I'll show you out.'

A few minutes later she found herself standing on the pavement outside the police station, feeling thoroughly wrung-out and dissatisfied. She'd put all of the work in, and was now being dropped, more like a nuisance than a help. However, she was going to have to go home in a few days, as the formal announcement of the two-week firebreak was due to be made at today's five o'clock official government briefing. There was no chance of being included in whatever Bob and his team found in the next few days. Her pace quickened, along with her increasingly angry thoughts. The car park was a five-minute walk away. An idea was coming to her around something Mike Goodman had said, about the nature of the person involved. Quiet, able to remain silently in the background, patient, and, in his opinion, disciplined beyond normal human capacity. She reached her car and sat thinking over what to do next. Pack up and return to Cornwall? No, not immediately. She had a few days. The hotel was a safe place in the meantime. A second trigger, enough to make a bullied woman commit deliberate murder. Angela Stephenson. Had she been the one who had set 'Monica' off? She shook her head, unable to focus, thoughts darting from the party girls to the members of the bully group. She needed to stop, clear her head, get some aims. But she had been told to leave it alone, to go home. Well, no. She was about to start the engine when her phone pinged an incoming text.

Belle, where are you? It's Jane.

Damn! The last thing she needed now was Jane Perry trying to cling on yet again.

I'm in Newport, getting ready to go home.

Have you seen the local paper?

No. Why?

Get a copy!

Is it really important?

Yes!!!

Belle sighed, got out of the car and walked into the central square to the closest newsagent. She was horrified by the headline.

"LOCAL WOMAN COMMITS SUICIDE AFTER CONFESSING TO 25-YEAR OLD HIT-AND-RUN." They even had the name – Monica Smith – but confirmed that no further details were being released by the police. However, they did name the victim as 26-year-old Bernadette Dobson. A suicide note confirmed that it had been an accident and Smith had no longer been able to live with the guilt. She texted Jane back.

Oh no! Who is Monica Smith? Was she at school with us? She had no intention of sharing what she knew.

I don't know the name. But looks like I might have been wrong.

Well, there's an end to it, Jane

Yes. Can we speak before you leave?

Belle hesitated. She wanted to say no, but the pull was still there.

OK. But has to be today.

Can you come to my bedsit?

I can come now. Where do you live?

Jane texted the address and Belle set off. She could manage a half hour with Jane and at least this time it really would be their last interaction.

The bedsit was in the Bainswell area of the town, one of the early Victorian districts that had once been an area of substantial middle-class homes, but were now mainly flats, some in good order, others run-down and scruffy. Jane's bedsit flat was a converted basement, reached by steps leading down from the street. Jane was waiting, hovering at the door, dressed in a black skirt and a flowery blouse that gave off an odour of stale sweat.

'Come in, come in. It's not much, but I do my best.'

Belle glanced around as Jane led her along the hall. As she crossed the threshold Belle stood on an envelope lying on the floor. She stopped and picked it up, handing it to Jane. It was an official envelope, addressed to M. E. Cormorant.

'Oops, sorry Jane. I've left a shoe mark on the back of the envelope.'

Jane took the envelope, glanced at it, tutted and tossed it onto a small table next to the door. 'That's OK. It's for the landlady. Someone keeps sending letters to her here.'

'This isn't your own place?'

'No, I rent, from Mrs Cormorant. Can't afford to buy, not even this.' She looked away from Belle and led her into a small sitting room with a bedroom curtained off at the far end. A window faced the steps and wall, with a view of the pavement at the top. Jane would only be able to see legs and feet from this room. There was a settee and a small chair with a TV and a coffee table. There was also a fireplace.

'That's a nice feature, Jane,' she said. The furniture was threadbare and shabby and too big for the room. She had to turn sideways to get around the coffee table to the settee.

'I suppose. Doesn't work, though.' Jane sat down, then jumped up again. 'Oh, my manners. Can I get you something to drink, or eat? A tea or a coffee, or a soft drink. I have biscuits ...'

'A glass of water will be fine, thanks Jane. I've already had a lot of coffee today and I grabbed a plastic-pack sandwich on my way to the car park.' She smiled, but thought Jane looked offended. *Well, too bad.*

Jane left the room, returned with two glasses one of which she placed carefully in front of Belle and sat again, leaning forward, elbows on her knees. 'What do you think about this?' She nodded at the paper lying on the table, the headline showing the story of Monica Smith's confession and suicide.

'Do you know who Monica Smith is, or was?' Belle asked, her cheeks flushing slightly.

'Is it too warm in here? Shall I turn off the heating?' Jane asked.

'No, I'm just tired. Leave it,' she snapped as Jane had jumped up and was heading for the thermostat. She needed to get this visit over as quickly as possible.

Jane returned to her seat, hands fluttering. 'No, I don't remember anyone of that name.'

'Then it's unlikely she was at our school and the hit-and-run was a random accident. Sorry, Jane, I know this knocks your theory out of the park, but maybe it's for the best. It was always a stretch.'

Jane put up her hands to cover her face and muttered, 'I'm so embarrassed.' She began to sob. 'I started this, didn't I, got you involved. I'm sorry, Belle.'

'It's OK, Jane.' Jane didn't look up.' Look, I must go.' She took a few gulps of the water, and grimaced. Tap water, on top of a plastic sandwich. Not good. She stood up. Jane still didn't move. 'I'll see myself out. By the way, the police will be coming to speak to you.'

Jane's hands flew up to her mouth. Belle reached into her handbag and gave Jane a tissue. 'Why? What can they want from me?' She paused for a moment, then said, 'Did you tell them about me?'

'I've been talking to Bob Pugh, through Maggie Gilbert.'

'Yes, you mentioned that,' Jane said. 'What does he want from me? If I was wrong, I don't want to have to go through it with them, what I thought.'

Belle was torn. Should she admit that she knew who Monica Smith really was? No, it would only prolong her visit here. She was sweating and desperate to get away. 'I think he just wants to understand why you thought the accidents and disappearances were linked. Tell him about the co-incidence of the dates. You'll be fine.'

Jane stood up. Her hands were shaking. 'Thank you,' she whispered and went to hug Belle, who stepped back. 'Sorry, social distancing,' Belle said with a smile. This was one of the few occasions when she didn't regret the restriction.

At the door Belle glanced at the letter she had picked up, lying on the small round wooden table. 'Don't forget to send that on,' she said. Jane looked puzzled, then realised that Belle was referring to the letter. She nodded. 'I'll do it later. I don't suppose I'll see you again.' There was so much regret in the tone that Belle felt ashamed. 'No, unlikely, Jane. I'm heading back to Cornwall before the firebreak begins and I'm not going to be back for a while. Good luck.'

Jane nodded and closed the door. Belle ran up the steps and stopped on the pavement to breathe in the fresh air that had been absent in the stale basement bedsit. Poor Jane. Belle was a compassionate person, but still …

As she walked back to her car there was something itching in her brain. Cormorant. She knew that name but couldn't think why. It was something associated with the town. She shook her head. It might come back. It wasn't important. What was important was to get away as soon as possible, before Jane found out that Monica Smith was really Faith Shepherd.

Chapter 25

Contamination

It was dark and cold when she reached the hotel, battered by driving rain and winds as she ran in. A storm had been forecast with winds up to sixty miles an hour. Walking through the foyer she felt a wave of sickness added to the now profuse sweating. Racing up to her room, the nausea overcame her and she retched in the bathroom. Then, exhausted, she fell onto the bed and slept, but not for long.

Every half an hour for several hours into the night the nausea returned, followed by retching and heaving until she could barely walk. Eventually it slowed and ceased, allowing her a few hours' sleep before dawn. She was in a deep, dreamless sleep when what sounded like a loud clanging noise raised her to confused consciousness. *Phone.* She grabbed for it, groggy and finding it difficult to grasp the handset, for a few seconds unable to think where she was. She grunted into the speaker.

'What's the matter with you?'

'Who is this?'

'Kat Harris. Is something wrong?'

'Gastric problem. Been ill. Can't speak now. Call me in an hour.'

It took her almost half an hour of dozing to wake up, each time opening her eyes, trying and failing to raise herself from the bed. Eventually, she reached a sitting position and staggered over to the tea and coffee station to make herself a cup of tea. She drank half the contents of a bottle of water as she waited for the kettle to boil and wondered if she was going to be sick again. The nausea was still there but diminished. She drank the tea and took a few tentative steps around the room, then jumped at a loud knocking on the door.

She looked through the spyhole in the door but couldn't see a face. 'Who is it?'

'Kat Harris.'

Belle groaned. What did the woman think she was doing, turning up here? And how did she know which room was Belle's, never mind get past reception and up to the floor? Whatever, she couldn't leave her standing in the corridor. She opened the door and Kat Harris strode past her. Belle stood for a moment, gathering her temper and allowing her stomach to settle before she turned around.

'You look terrible. Who's tried to poison you?'

'No-one has tried to poison me. Unless it was you. I don't suppose you want to confess.'

Kat Harris shot her a dirty look. 'What good would that do me? We need each other, I told you that.'

'All I need right now is to go back to bed. Say what you have to say, then leave. Please.'

Kat looked at her, examining Belle as she swayed slightly. 'OK. I'll be back at lunchtime. I have interesting news.'

'I don't want to hear it. I'm going home as soon as I can.'

'We'll discuss it later.' She left the room as Belle fell back onto the bed and was asleep again within minutes.

* * *

She awoke with a start at loud knocking on the door, again. *What now*, she thought. *Why can't you leave me to sleep, whoever you are?* It was easier to get up this time, given she'd only been asleep for a few minutes.

Kat Harris swept into the room. 'Come on, time to get going.'

'I told you I need to sleep.'

'That was four hours ago.'

Belle grabbed her phone from the bedside table. It was almost one o'clock. 'Damn.'

'Go and shower, get dressed and come and have lunch. You'll need it after you lost whatever you ate yesterday.'

Belle didn't feel up to arguing, deciding that whatever Kat Harris wanted to say to her, it would get rid of her more quickly to listen, then walk away. She sent the woman out of the room and began to get ready.

Twenty minutes later they sat facing each other in the restaurant at a table in the far corner, well away from other diners. Belle was surprised to find that she was hungry, but wary of any food that might cause a re-occurrence of the pain and distress of the previous twelve hours. She ordered a simple sandwich. Kat Harris had no qualms about ordering a plateful of greasy food to eat in front of her.

'You said you had information,' Belle began once they had ordered. 'Have you spoken to the police yet?'

'I'm avoiding them for as long as possible. Why don't you tell me what you think and what you know, then I'll tell you what I've been doing.'

'No. If we're going to do this, it will be my way. I have a question for you, before we start.'

Kat Harris sighed. 'Go on, then. If it will speed things up.'

'Have you ever killed anyone?'

'Well, I didn't see that coming,' Kat said, sitting back and crossing her arms. 'Does it matter?'

'I never understood you, and I still don't. You go out of your way to insult and embarrass people who've done nothing to you, you appear indifferent to the deaths of women who were once your friends. You've been open about the fact your only concern is your own safety and survival. Outwardly you are a selfish, vicious, heartless woman whose interactions with others are based on trying to destroy any modicum of happiness or self-esteem they have. And I can see you really couldn't care less that I'm accusing you of behaving so horribly.'

'Did you enjoy saying that?'

'No, Kat. I'm just trying to understand who you are.'

'Don't bother, because you'll never succeed. To answer your question, yes, I have killed, more than once. I live in a country where guns aren't anything special. I live in Texas. Most women I know carry a small handgun in their purse; they're a fashion accessory. I've used mine to defend myself. Police usually accept the word of a white woman,' she replied with a complacent grin.

Belle felt her insides cramping in disgust. No, she thought, she would never understand this woman and she shouldn't waste time trying.

'Why do we need each other?'

'Because I think there's more going on, a great deal more, and potentially significant, that we haven't even scratched the surface of.'

'What do you mean?'

Their food arrived and they sat in silence whilst the waitress fussed around, offering condiments and asking helpful questions, until a look from Kat sent her scurrying away.

Kat leaned forward. 'Do you believe that one person is responsible for the deaths and disappearances of six women, getting away with it, successfully up until now, for thirty years?'

'That's one theory, yes, although a new piece of information might change that. Do you have a different idea?'

'No. And yes.' She picked up her fork and twirled it around. 'I mean, I could have done it, but I haven't. I don't care enough about people to want them dead. That's a lot of hatred living within one person, isn't it, to plan and execute six people so methodically. Beyond hatred. Emotions that don't even have a name.' She took a mouthful of burger.

She was right, Belle thought, looking at her sandwich and wincing. If her theory held, this was a sick mind at work, a very sick mind. What could such a mind be capable of? She was now the target of increasing threats. If the police were going to take this seriously, best leave it to them.

'So what did you eat yesterday, that caused you to be ill?' Kat asked, noting that Belle had picked up the sandwich and put it down three times without taking a bite.

Belle pushed the plate away. 'I ate very little. I had breakfast here, then I grabbed one of those plastic wrapped sandwiches from a small shop as I walked from the police station to the car park. I ate it as I walked then finished it in the car.'

'You should report it. Public health issue, you know.'

'I threw the wrapper away. No point.' She paused. 'Why do you care about my health, or public health?'

'I don't. I just wondered if you'd had anything else to eat and drink and if so, where did you get it and who gave it to you. You are at risk, you know. As am I.'

Belle snorted. 'Thinking about yourself again. Well, that was it, apart from several coffees and a glass of tap water at Jane's flat ..." She paused. 'It was a combination of stress and dehydration, plus a dodgy sandwich. Nothing sinister.'

Kat held a chunk of burger on the fork in front of her mouth. 'What were you doing at Jane Perry's flat? You know she could be the one?'

'Jane? Unlikely. She's too desperate to be helpful to hurt me. Like you. But I agree, The One could be any of the three remaining party-givers.'

Kat put more burger in her mouth and chewed slowly.

'Does the name Cormorant mean anything to you? There's something familiar there, but I can't think why,' Belle asked, watching the burger disappear.

'Garage,' Kat muttered through the food, then swallowed and took a mouthful of water.' There was a John Cormorant who had a garage, out on the Caerleon Road. Big, in its day. Sold high value cars, very posh. I think he died of a heart attack.' She stopped, frowned. 'There was a Teresa Cormorant at school. Odd sort. Loner. Kept away from everyone.'

'I don't remember her,' Belle replied after a moment. 'I do remember the garage. I used to pass it on the bus on my way to and from school. Probably why it came back to me when I saw the name. It was on an envelope at Jane's flat, addressed to M. E. Cormorant. She's Jane's landlady.'

'Little smelly Perry still renting?'

'Stop with the name-calling! In school it was cruel, now it's just childish.'

Kat shrugged. 'Picked up the habit in the States. Our President does it all the time.'

'And I expect you're a fan.'

'Of course,' Kat replied. 'Man after my own heart.' She pushed away the empty plate.' Can we have a serious discussion now?'

Belle nodded. 'Just use correct names. If you don't, I'm going back to my room.' She glanced at her watch. She had about five minutes at most. 'So, what's your suggestion and what's it based on?'

'You've been concentrating on the party girls. I've been talking to the families of the dead and disappeared. There's a lot more than Mal Jenkins ever picked up or if he did, never followed up on. And I've found something very interesting about …' She was about to carry on when, out of the corner of her eye she spotted a group of men enter the hotel and head towards them. 'You didn't!'

'Of course I did,' Belle replied, as Bob Pugh and two uniformed constables approached them. 'You were going to have to speak to them, so I thought, sooner rather than later. I don't care what you tell them, but I am interested in what you're saying now. Get back to me here, later. I'm going back to bed.'

Kat stood and faced the men, her hands raised in surrender, stopping Bob from having to arrest her. 'OK, OK, I'm coming.' She picked up her coat and bag. '*See you later*,' she mouthed to Belle as she began to walk away. Then she stopped, turned full around and mouthed, '*Teresa Cormorant*,' with a knowing look, and shook her arm free of one of constables as she walked out of the hotel between them.

Chapter 26

Players

Back in her room Belle drank a pint of water, then sank into bed for another six hours, before hammering on the door woke her again. She groaned. The nausea had passed but she still had stomach pains and a headache. Once she had let Kat Harris back in, she sat on the bed, shaking.

'I think that's food poisoning,' Kat said conversationally.

'Whatever, it's getting better, slowly, but I've lost a day. What time is it?'

Almost seven. Did you eat anything at lunchtime?'

Belle shook her head.

'Right, room service it is. Want to try the sandwich again?' Belle was about to refuse but decided it would be best to try to eat something. Kat ordered for both of them. Again, for herself, she had a large meal.

'Don't you put weight on, eating like that?'

'Nope. Good constitution. My diet is fat- and sugar-based heart attack-inducing food. Come on, let's sit and talk.'

There was a table with two chairs in one corner of the room, just enough for two of them to sit. Belle indicated her briefcase and Kat pulled out Belle's file of notes.

'Let's start with what you know about the party-givers. You've met all of them, haven't you? What was your impression?'

‘I’ve only spoken to Helena Parry by phone, but yes, including Jane, I’ve had a discussion with the four still alive. I’ve made notes in the file,’ she took it from Kat and opened a tab. ‘Read here.’

For the next few minutes there was silence while Kat read. When she finished, she looked up and said, ‘Very comprehensive. But there’s no indication in there which one. It could be any of them.’

‘First impressions,’ Belle replied. ‘I’ve not had time to follow up. Before we get into this, tell me about your police interview.’

‘Nothing too much, really. I must say, that policeman is quite attractive, in a rough sort of way. Mags Jones did well there. He just wanted to know what I knew. I told him the bare facts.’

‘How much did you keep back?’

‘We’ll get to that in a minute. Tell me about these notes.’

‘At some point you’re going to have to tell him more. Did he ask you about Monica Smith?’

‘He mentioned her name. I’ve never heard of her. Do you know who she is?’

‘Oh, yes.’

‘Then you’d better tell me, hadn’t you?’

‘I will. First, here’s what I’m thinking now about the party girls.’ She coughed for a moment, grimaced as the taste of vomit came back into her throat, took a long sip of water, then began.

‘Jane Perry: character still as it was, needy, irritating. She’s desperate to be liked. She put the story out back in September. I don’t think she took it seriously herself, it was more of a way to create a sensation. No-one took much notice, apart from me. They remembered what an attention-seeker Jane was. She still doesn’t see the implications of what she was suggesting. However, she may have been on to something, although not what it’s turning out to be. She'll be gratified if any of what she guessed at turns out to be correct. A good story to tell people, probably where she works, wherever that is. I haven't asked her.'

'Careless. I've checked. She's not working. She was employed at the hospital, in the pharmacy. Just a gopher, no training or skills. She took prescriptions around the wards for distribution by the nurses. She'd been there a long time but quit suddenly. Carry on.'

Belle bit her lip. 'Thank you, I will. Next, Gwen Williams. Not at all introverted, like she used to be. She's a teacher, at the school. She's married with kids. According to her it's a happy marriage. She's in touch with Mary Conroy, although Mary told me that, not Gwen. She doesn't believe the story. At the end of the conversation there was a flash of anger, actually of fury, aimed particularly at you. She still carries a lot of hatred for you.'

Kat shrugged. 'Big deal. Carry on.'

'Mary Conroy. Big change. Nothing religious about her now. Shyness all gone, according to her, knocked out of her by Australia. She's lived there for over thirty years, but comes home every five years; she's attended the reunions, and been around at the time of each death or disappearance, apart from 2005, when Denise Goodright drowned in Australia. Now, here's the interesting part. Mary didn't stay on in Wales that year. She was in Australia when Denise died.'

'Big country,' Kat interrupted.

'Not that big. Denise died scuba diving on the Gold Coast. Mary Conroy lives near the resort where Denise and her family were staying. She saw the reports of the death and knew it was Denise, but she didn't say anything to the authorities, didn't want to get involved. And, she suggested to me that it might not have been an accident.'

'So, she didn't come forward at the time, is that what you're saying?'

'Exactly. She thought there were strange aspects in the report of the accident, but kept her mouth shut.'

Kat put her fingers to her mouth, tapping her closed lips, contemplating. 'She didn't want anyone to know she knew Denise, which would have shone a light on past history. Interesting.'

'Finally, Helena Parry. Before I tell you about my conversation with her, you tell me why you asked if I knew how long she'd been a nun.'

'Do you remember she wasn't religious at school?'

'Yes; she was academically brilliant, way beyond any of us, but I don't remember religion coming into it. What does it matter? People change.'

'Mary Conroy was the religious one. You say she's not, now?'

Belle nodded. 'Didn't give me any hint in that direction. Quite the opposite.'

'Helena joined the convent less than a year ago. Before that, I haven't got to, yet. But I will. So, how did she react to you calling her?'

'She was cold, seemingly uninterested. Didn't react to me telling her that two of her former classmates might have been murdered and others were missing. She said it would be "God's will" and put the phone down. I did ask her how long she'd been in the convent and she refused to answer. That was it, with her.'

'Anyone else you've spoken with?'

'I met Lennie McGinnis. I wanted to speak to her about bullying, the long-term effect of bullying. She's a psychologist.'

'What did she have to say? Apart from it's all my fault.'

'She didn't talk about you, well, not much. She said the party itself, that you tried to ruin, wouldn't have been enough to trigger murderous psychopathy. There must have been something else, something that compounded it, after the original event.'

'Hm. So, it all began with Angela's death.'

Belle sat back. 'I suppose so, yes. The only person physically around Angela at the time was Jane Perry, although Jane thought others might have had a holiday job.'

'She's right, it wasn't just her. Angela worked at the government place down on Cardiff Road. So did Jane. So did the late Sue Jones' sister and I think we'll find Helena Parry did, too.'

Belle's brain was racing. 'Are you saying it could be any one of those three?'

'Any one of them, or something else. Gwen Williams was at university, in the final year of her Master's degree. She got her BA in Bristol, but then did her Master's in Cardiff. She might have been working there too, I'm checking that one. And Mary Conroy. She didn't go to Australia until 2003, seventeen years, not the thirty she told you. She gave you the impression it was straight after school.'

Belle nodded, and put her hands up behind her neck.

'I thought so. None of them is being entirely truthful,' Kat said, then paused for a moment. 'So who is Monica Smith?'

'There is no Monica Smith. She picked up her phone, found the photo Bob had sent and showed it to Kat. She was surprised at the emotions that passed over the woman's face. First, puzzlement. Then, anger.

'That's Faith Shepherd.'

'Yes, it is. You've seen the story in the local paper, that a woman called Monica Smith confessed to the hit-and-run that killed Bernie, and committed suicide?'

'I thought it was strange, to wait so long to confess. Is there something more I should know?'

'Yes. The woman was Faith Shepherd and there's a good possibility she was set up and killed, and the suicide note's a fake.'

'Oh wow.' Kat paused, stood and walked to the window, stared out for a few moments. 'So Faith is supposed to have killed Bernie Baloney, sorry Maloney, then waited twenty-five years to confess before killing herself. Five years after disappearing she suddenly emerges, dead.'

'Yes.'

'Do the police believe it?' She turned to face Belle. 'Do you believe it?'

'No to both. There's evidence that she was restrained before she died. That's why they're taking it more seriously, although he's still not sure of his boss. Budgets, et cetera. He's not sure there's enough yet to allow a full-scale enquiry.'

'Then we'd better find out more, to convince him and his boss.' Kat spat out the last word, and as she did, turned to pace around the room with her arms folded and her head down. Belle left her to it. She picked up her phone.

'Who are you calling?' Kat demanded.

'I'm calling Bob Pugh. I want to know if he's going to carry on investigating.'

Kat nodded, as Belle waited for the call to be answered.

'Hello, Belle, it's Bob. What do you want? I'm busy.'

'Sorry, Bob. I just wanted to know if there's any progress, about your investigating further.'

'No. My Super isn't convinced yet, but she hasn't said no. She's presented me with an alternative that *Monica Smith* was a name sometimes used by Faith Shepherd in her working life, and the restraints are something she might have used, in her work. She would expect an old prostitute to be emaciated and underfed and the fact she had lessened her smoking and drinking, well, lots of people doing that.'

'That sounds like a bunch of excuses to me.'

'That's how it is. Until we have more, she's not going to green light any more time. Your friend didn't help, either. I have to go,' he snapped.

'She's not my friend,' Belle began, but he had ended the call. She put the phone back in the table.

'Well?'

'No more investigating.' She outlined the response he had received. 'And she's given him grief, too, thanks to you and whatever you said.'

'Up to us then.' Kat sat down again. 'Faith was in her late forties. By what I've heard from my source she wasn't sophisticated. She was a heavy smoker and an alcoholic. She was a back street, back seat of a car quickie kind of working girl; she wouldn't have had a setup that included restraints and so on.'

'He probably knows that, but, well, he has to pick his battles, doesn't he, and if he says he can't win this one right now, I agree with you, we'll have to find more. We have two days, then I'm going back to Cornwall.'

'Why don't you just stay? No-one cares enough about you breaking the rules to make it a public case.'

'I care,' Belle snapped. 'This is too serious to be so bloody cavalier about other people's lives.' She wave her hand at Kat to shoo her away. 'Oh, I know you don't. But I'm not like you. Never have been and never will be. I'm going Thursday night. It's now Tuesday. We have today, tomorrow and a few hours on Thursday before I leave. Let's not waste time talking about morality, because you have none.'

'Fair enough. I'm not offended by your insults. Now I'll tell you about what I know. I've already said what I know about who worked at the government office. There's more to be learned there and I have an idea about how we get that.'

'Nothing illegal,' Belle warned. Kat grinned and tapped her forehead. 'Leave it to me. OK, first, Angie Stephenson.'

Belle sat back and folded her arms.

'Angela liked to taunt the shy girls publicly; she made sure there were enough classmates gathered around to hear what she was doing,' Kat said. 'She wasn't subtle. Did she have any idea what harm she was doing? Yes, but she didn't care. She loved seeing them squirm and blush. It could have been anything from a mark for an essay where they had scored low and she had scored higher, to the incident with Jane Perry.' Kat cleared her throat, then went on.

'She'd been taunting Jane for years. You may remember this one. Jane once turned up in the sixth form with a particularly dirty blouse, stained with food and with a filthy collar. Angie had a great time pointing it out.'

'I remember some of it. You egged Angie on, didn't you? Made sure Jane was thoroughly humiliated. And when she didn't come back for a few days? Angie kept on about it, I presume, after Jane did come back.'

'She tried, but Jude Winters shut her up. Everyone knew, though. Cartoons of "dirty Jane" were stuck on walls around the common room when we came back after the Christmas break. That was Angie, of course. She was a gifted artist. Jude and Mags Jones tore them down.' She paused and shot Belle an evil grin.

'Pity there weren't mobile phones back then. A picture for posterity would have been excellent. Angie was also the one who thought up "baldy bigfoot" for Susan Jones. Then, it all stopped.'

'That would be when you were expelled.'

'You know I didn't do that,' Kat snapped.

'Yes, and I don't care. They set you up beautifully and you deserved it.'

Kat pursed her lips. 'Whatever. Moving on. When Angie died, she was living with her parents. They were so proud of her, couldn't believe she had taken drugs, mummy's angel, and so on. Everyone outside her family, including her team – and God knows how she got promoted – knew about her habit. Mal Jenkins did investigate, a little. He knew she was disliked, because she played favourites and made life a misery for anyone who displeased her. I got the impression that, apart from her mother, no-one not only cared she was gone, they also were quietly pleased. And relieved.'

'How do you know this?'

'I was here at the time, so I went to her funeral, and I spoke to the colleagues who bothered to turn up. They were furtive at first, but afterwards we went to a pub, after attending the wake and telling her mother how wonderful she was and how much she would be missed. You should have heard them in the pub. That's when the truth came out.'

'Weren't you upset to hear your acolyte being spoken about like that?

'No, why should I have been? Nothing to do with me.'

Belle banged her hand on the table so hard the glass of water in front of her bounced. 'It's everything to do with you. You trained her. You told her it was OK to behave the way she did and let her loose to cause havoc. And misery.' She stopped and shook her head. Kat was looking at her with a puzzled expression.

'You really think that, don't you? Don't you realise, it would have happened without me.'

'No, Kat. With better influences around her, she might have gained insight into how her behaviour affected other people.'

Kat Harris shrugged. 'Whatever. You really don't get people, do you? You just don't get the baseness of the human soul, how easy it is to bring it to the fore, what people will do, and enjoy, given the freedom and the permission to do it.'

Belle shook her head. Nothing she could say would have any success in penetrating this woman's psyche. 'What next? And I don't want any more of your opinions, just facts and information.'

'Tina Lewis. She went out Christmas shopping and didn't go home again. She was thirty-one and in a loveless marriage. She'd married him – his name was Edgar – when they were both nineteen and she was pregnant. She lost the baby and never had another. The lovely Edgar had other women, used to taunt her about how useless she was at everything. Neighbours reported ear-splitting arguments and sounds of objects being thrown. She had bruises, so he was probably hitting her. Three days before Christmas she left the café in Cardiff and disappeared, but he waited until Christmas Eve to report her missing. Mal Jenkins did the basics but didn't follow up after he found that she was unhappy and probably being assaulted. He checked the refuges, discovered she hadn't tried any of them. Eventually, his pathetic excuse of a search was just dropped. Now, here's the interesting part. I've spoken to Edgar. He had her declared dead after seven years and he's married again. He told me he was glad to see the back of her, called her a miserable cow. Then he told me that she was probably encouraged to leave, by, and I quote, "that school friend of hers". Before you ask, he didn't know the name, but thought it was someone religious.'

Belle sat up. 'Could he describe her, this friend?'

'He never saw her, just heard Tina talking to her, complaining about him, saying how she hated him and would love to get away once and for all. The person said God would help her. She laughed and replied something like "there's no likelihood of that, is there".'

'Did he tell the police this?'

'Yes, he did.'

Belle put her hand up to her forehead, closed her eyes and rubbed her hairline. 'Then there wasn't much for them to follow up.' She stopped, then opened her eyes. 'Phone records. She died in, what, 2000? There were mobile phones around then, or he might have heard her on a landline. Did Mal Jenkins check the number to see who was making the calls?'

'No. He'd already made up his mind she'd decided to leave and that was her choice. Why would he make the effort? That's what he said when …' She paused and smiled.

'When you paid him for the information,' Belle said. 'When was that?'

'Two weeks ago. Can't get anything from him, now, since he's been suspended, thanks to you. That's one of my useful sources gone.'

'Serves him right. I hope he loses his pension, the corrupt bastard. That does mean another line of enquiry, doesn't it? Do you have the number?'

'I'm working on it. Next, Bernie Moloney. That was on the thirteenth of December 1995. She'd been getting poison pen letters. She believed there was a hate campaign against her.'

'Did the police know about that?'

'There's no evidence in the file she reported it, or that her family told them.'

'So that's the end of that one, and it might have been *Monica*.'

'Who's *Monica*?'

'It's a name for the potential murderer, provided by Bob Pugh. To make it seem more real, not just an unknown figure. It was the false name on the suicide note.

Well, I have more on that one. Bernie's husband still has one of the letters. I've spoken to the elder daughter and she thinks he may be willing to hand it over. I have an appointment to visit them tomorrow.'

'I'll be coming with you.'

'Fine. You can use your charming decency to persuade him to talk, once we're inside. Let's carry on. Denise Goodright, well, you know more about her than I'd got to. The final two, Liz and Faith. Faith we can leave for now as your tame Chief Inspector is investigating. Liz, though, I haven't found out much about, yet.'

'I have,' Belle said.' Or at least, part of it. She disappeared sometime in mid-December 2010. She'd gone to a pub after work, acting morosely and seemed angry. Drank a gutful then left saying she had to "sort someone out". Not seen again. I expect, given those words, we'll find she was still a nasty bully too.'

'That's interesting. She's unlikely to have been talking about someone at work. You sort them out in work, not at night in a pub after you've been drinking. How did you find out about this?'

'Newspaper reports. When she went missing there was an investigation. It was in the papers. The police arrested her ex-husband but had to let him go for lack of evidence. The landlord gave a statement to a reporter. He suggested she was pretty drunk when she left and it wasn't the first time.'

'Well, well. We'd better add him to the list of people we need to see in the next couple of days.'

'The landlord?' Belle said, momentarily flummoxed.

'The ex.'

'Right. Did she have children? I can't remember.'

'Whatever you ate has done a job on your brain. These are your notes. She had a daughter, aged seventeen, who reported her missing.'

Belle glanced at her watch. It was almost eight. She was feeling better but had had enough of Kat and of the investigation. Another good sleep and she would be ready to start again in the morning.

'Time for you to go.'

Kat scowled at her. 'We haven't made a plan yet.'

'Be back here at seven tomorrow morning. We'll plan it out over breakfast. We have forty-eight hours before I head home. And before you say anything, I'm not breaking the rules.'

Kat Harris stood up, shrugged her coat on. 'Have it your way.' She walked out of the bedroom, leaving Belle at the table. She hadn't agreed to be back in the morning, but she also hadn't refused. Belle collapsed onto the bed, switched out the lights, and without any further thought, slept.

Chapter 27

Regrets

At seven, as Kat Harris walked through the hotel lobby, Belle was ready and waiting, still pale, but with a clear head. She had sent Mavis a text and was just looking at the reply – which told her the rota was working well and Tessa was OK – when Kat sat down in front of her.

'Ready to go?'

'When I've finished my coffee. It's extra strong.'

'You'll need it. We have a full day.'

'I thought we were going to plan?'

'I did that last night. If you're clearing off tomorrow evening, there was no point wasting time. I don't sleep much. Right, this morning we're starting with Edgar Leonard. He's agreed to speak to us at half past seven.' She glanced at her watch.' Drink that up, we need to go. He's giving us twenty minutes before he leaves for work.'

'Where does he live now?' Belle asked.

'Not far, just up along the Risca Road, about ten minutes. I'm driving.' Belle didn't argue. She felt better, but not ready to face rush hour traffic. As they left the hotel Belle saw that the storm had passed and the day promised to be fine, from a meteorological point of view, at least.

* * *

'It's a complicated process, you must understand,' Edgar Leonard said as he showed them into the living room of his newly built detached home on a private gated estate on the outskirts of Risca. 'It took almost a year to receive the presumed declaration of death, which allowed me to finalise her affairs.'

'And marry again,' Kat said.

He nodded. 'So, please tell me why you are here and bringing all of this up? It was distressing at the time but I've moved on. I don't want to have to go over it again, unless it's absolutely necessary.'

Belle stared at the tall, grey-haired man, dressed in an elegant designer suit, who sat in a deep armchair, with one leg crossed over the other, trying to imply relaxation, but betrayed by a muscle quivering in his cheek that he poked at with his tongue.

They had agreed in the car that Kat would lead with the initial questions and Belle would follow up with anything she thought required a more forensic approach.

'Like I told you when I called, I'm organising a memorial for a group of women who went to school together, who have since died. Tina is one of them.' She glanced across at Belle next to her on the settee, with the slightest frown, to stop her commenting.

'You told the police, when you got around to reporting her missing, that she'd been talking to a friend. I was one of her best friends. I'd like to know who she was talking to,' Kat said.

'And I told the police I didn't know who it was,' he replied, curt now. They were distracted by the door opening and a woman's head tentatively appearing. 'The children need to leave for college, darling,' she said in a low voice.

'They can wait a few more minutes,' he replied, flicking his head at her. The woman jerked as if his words had physically slapped her and retreated, closing the door, without replying.

He hits her, too, Belle thought, just like he did Tina. She could see Kat balling her fists and decided it was time to intervene. 'Anything you can tell us, Edgar, anything at all?'

He put a hand up to his chin, rubbed it thoughtfully. 'Once it sounded like "Hattie", I may have heard that one time. Or Mary.' He jumped up. 'I have to go. There's nothing further I can do. Let me show you out.'

Belle didn't think there was much point in trying to press him further and she stood up and turned to the door. Kat, however, stood, but didn't move.

'One more thing, Edgar. How much did you have to pay Mal Jenkins to stop him investigating Tina's disappearance? Probably not as much I've had to pay him to give me information about her disappearance, and the others.'

The colour drained from Edgar Leonard's face. He stood rigid for a moment, staring at her, before his cheeks coloured to flaming red.

'Get out of my house,' he hissed.

'Going,' Kat said, leering at him and ushering Belle towards the door. As it slammed behind them, she said, with a triumphant grin, 'I knew I was right.'

'You're as bad as he is, and he's bad,' Belle muttered as they hurried to Kat's car.

'He paid off a corrupt policeman to stop looking for his wife. I paid off a corrupt policeman to tell me what he knew about said wife and I'm not apologising for that. Anyway, he's come on in the world, hasn't he? He runs his own plumbing company, doesn't get his hands dirty these days,' she said as she started the engine and drove away. 'He used to be a plumber. He set up the company with Tina's money. Once he had his declaration of presumed death, he took everything she had, sold the house she'd inherited from her parents, once he could claim probate, and set himself up very nicely.'

'Well, at least we know the friend might have been Mary or Hattie, which was probably a nickname, maybe Helena Parry, but were there any girls called anything like Hattie – which could be short for Harriet – in our year? Or a nickname? I don't remember anyone called Harriet or Hattie, and Helena Parry was unlikely to have become a friend of Tina Lewis Leonard, given the bullying she took from Tina.'

'I don't remember any "Hattie" but I can think of four girls called Mary in our year. I didn't know any of them well and I don't remember Tina being friends with any of them.'

A text arrived and Kat tossed her phone to Belle. 'Who's it from?'

Belle's eyebrows shot up. 'Edgar Leonard. It says: *Don't come near me ever again. Whoever the woman was Tina spoke to the one time I heard, in the end she was rude to her, shouted at her to clear off. That's it. I'm done with you.*'

'Why would Tina have been shouting? This couldn't have been someone trying to help her.'

'Maybe someone trying to be a "do-gooder", so it could point to Mary Conroy or Helena Parry or Hattie, whoever she might have been and it could have been nothing to do with school. I'll find out who the other three Marys were and check them out. Gets us nowhere. Still, had to be done.'

'Who else did Mal Jenkins take money from?'

'No-one I know of, at least not in relation to this case. Probably many, many others.' She grinned. 'Do you want to know? I can check out his bank details, if you want to give the information to …'

'No,' Belle said. 'What other horrors do you have in store today?'

'We're seeing Bernie Moloney's husband, Alan Dobson, and her daughter Karen, at ten. They've been visited by the police, to tell them someone has confessed. I've said that we're old school friends and have heard about the confession and the poison pen letters.'

'So I have to pretend I liked her,' Belle muttered. 'What are we hoping to gain from this one?'

'A name. Or anything about the letters Bernie'd been getting. They live near Cardiff.'

The rest of the journey was silent, Belle deciding that conversational small talk with Kat Harris was not an option.

Just before ten they arrived at a small semi-detached house on the outskirts of the city. It was well kept, with a neat lawn in the small garden area at the front of the house, and no rubbish bin at the front, unlike others along the street.

A woman who looked to be in her late twenties let them in and introduced herself as Karen. She was carrying a whining toddler, at which Kat pulled a face. The toddler began to cry. The woman led them into a small room with too much furniture and the floor covered in toys, into the middle of which she deposited the child.

'Sorry about him; he's teething. We're a bit up and down here; we had the police around yesterday. They told us someone had confessed to killing mum. It seems strange now,' she said, looking away from them at a photograph on the mantlepiece, in which Bernie Moloney Dobson was easily identifiable, with two toddlers, all smiling at the camera. 'I barely remember her. My sister Emily doesn't remember her at all, but she was a baby when mum died. Dad took the news with a shrug. I'm the only one who seems to care, much.' She turned back to them.' So, you were her friends at school. Did you know the girl who did it?'

'What name did they give you?' Belle asked.

'They said she called herself Monica Smith, but her real name was Faith Shepherd. Strange, I thought. Why didn't she own up to her real name when she wrote her note?' She was still looking at the photo and didn't appear to want an answer from them.

'We're puzzled, too,' Belle replied, which was at least truthful. 'They were friends at school, good friends. It must have been a terrible accident.'

The woman turned back to them. 'What was she like at school?'

Belle turned to Kat with an ironic look that said *I'm definitely not answering that one.*

'She had a good sense of humour, although occasionally people didn't get it,' Kat replied. 'She could wind people up, but she had a good heart,' shooting the look back to Belle.

'Dad thinks he remembers your name,' she said to Kat.

'You said she had been sent nasty letters,' Belle hurried on. 'Can you remember any more about that? Do the police think they were associated with the accident?'

'Dad never told them, at the time. He didn't think so. There was something a bit odd about it all, but I was just a small kid. I remember a big argument and him saying "serves you right".' She glanced around, suddenly nervous. 'Don't tell him I told you that, please.'

'Of course not,' Kat replied with a sweet smile.' Do you know what the letters were about?'

Karen shook her head. 'I just know he kept the last one, but he's never shown it to me and I don't want to see it.' She snapped round to face the door. 'He's here. You can ask him yourself, but he's still in shock. He may not want to talk about it.'

A man entered the room, elderly, stooped, with sparse hair and a scowl. He sat down on the available armchair and stared at them. 'The police told you? Why?'

'A friend told me. She has a connection to the police. I was so shocked, given I knew both of them. Thank you for agreeing to talk to us. It must have brought back so many bad memories after all this time.' Kat Harris could sound charming and compassionate when she chose.

The man grunted. 'So what do you want?'

'I was upset to hear she was being sent nasty letters. I'm worried it might have been someone else at school. Never mind about how long ago it was, that person needs taking to task for doing something so horrible, especially as Bernie died shortly after.'

He stared at Kat for a few seconds that dragged on until it was becoming uncomfortable. Kat was about to speak again, when he held up his hand. 'Are you the Kat she hung out with at school?'

Kat nodded, wary.

'Then cut the crap. I know who you are, and what you did. Bernie changed, after she left school. She was ashamed of what she was like, especially after that girl killed herself.'

Kat said nothing, but Belle looked at her then back at Bernie's husband. 'What girl was that?' she said, with an air of surprise.

'Which one are you,' the man spat out.

'I wasn't one of them,' Belle said.

'A girl called Sue. I can't remember the surname. Very tall, lots of problems. Lost her hair,' he muttered, then turned back to face Kat. 'You drove her to it, Bernie said, and she was part of it. Now, you, get out of my house. Karen, see her out.' He turned to Belle. 'You can stay, if you really weren't part of it.'

Kat tutted, but stood up and left, before Karen could follow her.

'I wasn't, truly,' Belle replied. 'I expect you're wondering why I'm here with her … sorry, I didn't catch your name.'

'Alan,' he said. 'Why are you with her?' He spoke Kat's name with contempt.

'I don't know if you know this, Alan, but the bully gang – sorry to call it that – but it was, are all dead or missing. Kat Harris is the only one left. And the way in which they've died suggested to me it hasn't been co-incidence. I began to investigate after I received a threat, telling me to leave it alone. All I had done was heard a story and put a photograph online. That was enough to tell me there was something more than random chance and I want to know more.' She paused, not sure how far to go, but with a gut feeling this man might have something valuable to tell her, so she might as well exchange as much information as possible with him, if he was willing to give up what he knew.

He nodded. 'Good enough.'

'Before we go any further, what can you tell me about Sue Jones, the girl who killed herself? She was another of the girls who organised the eighteenth birthday party. I was one of the three girls who actually turned up.'

'What's that all about?' Karen interrupted. She'd returned to the room after locking the front door and was sitting on the floor next to her son.

'I'll tell you later, love,' Alan said. 'I don't know much. Bernie was distraught when she heard. I couldn't understand why, after all, it was just someone who'd been in the same class as her at school. They would have been out of school for a year when it happened and they hadn't spoken since they left. So I asked her why and she said "It's my fault. I've killed her." Then she broke down and told me the whole story.' He put his head in his hands. 'We were courting at seventeen, married when we were just twenty-one. Bernie was lively, bit bossy, but she calmed down when Karen was born. She changed then, she was a nicer person. She was always guarded about her past, she told me she hated school and wouldn't ever speak about it. She opened up to me eventually and it all made sense.'

He had tears in his eyes. Karen jumped up from the floor and put an arm around his shoulders. 'I think you'd better go,' she said to Belle.

'No,' he said. 'She needs to hear about the letters.'

'Thank you, Alan. I would like to hear more, if you're up to it.'

He brushed his eyes with his sleeve. 'There were three, at the beginning of 1995. The girl, Sue, had died around the anniversary of her birthday, apparently, a few years before. Bernie had gone to the funeral. It had upset her. I asked her if she had seen any school friends and her reply was odd. She said: "Not the ones I had hoped to see. They were just cowards, in the end". She wouldn't say any more than that. I didn't see the first letter. She burned it, wouldn't tell me what it said, just it was nasty and best ignored. A week later, the second one arrived. This time, whatever it said – and she still wouldn't show me – she was upset for days. She burned it again. The third one was at Easter. This time, she showed me. It was vile, accused her of killing the girl, Sue. Said she would pay for what she'd done. I told her she had to take it to the police, but she wouldn't do it and that made me angry. I yelled at her that she was being threatened and what about Karen and Emily, but she wouldn't go. Then—' He stopped. 'Karen, love, would you fetch me a cup of tea?' The girl left him, scowling at Belle.

'I'll tell her later. I didn't want her to hear this part. Finding out her mother was a disgusting bully is going to devastate her. She was her mum's girl, when she was little. Anyway, that was when Bernie finally told me about everything they had done, and how it had culminated in ruining that birthday party. I couldn't believe it. This wasn't the Bernie I knew. And loved. She could see my disgust and she begged me to forgive her. She said that woman, out there' – he waved at the car outside the window where Kat Harris was sitting – 'that woman had them in a kind of, I don't know, a hold of some sort. The ideas were all hers but they did the doing, if you know what I mean.'

Belle nodded. 'I was there; a few of us tried to intervene, but they managed to avoid us. Sue Jones suffered horribly.' She felt her own eyes watering and shook her head. 'We should have done more.'

'You were schoolgirls,' he said. 'The school should have done it. Did you report what was going on?'

Belle nodded, unable to speak.

'It wasn't your fault, then. You did what you could. That, that … thing … out there, she's responsible. She's a monster.'

'I know.'

'So why are you with her?' he snapped.

'I want to find out what happened, Alan. You see, apart from Kat Harris they're all dead or missing, one every five years. You said Bernie had changed. If she was deliberately run over by someone who wanted revenge, that's even worse than what Kat Harris did. Kat, well, she knows she's the last one standing and the December five-year anniversary is approaching. She wants to save herself from another "accident". Alan, if I just let that happen, then I'm as bad as her, aren't I?'

He said nothing for a moment, then nodded. 'So you think this Faith Shepherd could be responsible for the other deaths?'

'No,' Belle said, instinctively. 'There are aspects of her death that I know about but can't say. I'm sorry, but I can't. There's still more to come.'

Karen returned with the tea and glowered at Belle again.

Belle stood up. 'I'll leave you to it. Thanks, Alan. Just one last question. Was there anything in any of the letters, especially the one you saw, that gave Bernie any clue as to who was sending them?'

'I don't think so,' he replied, 'but see for yourself.' He reached into his pocket and produced an old, dog-eared piece of paper. 'Take it. I've held onto it for too long. I don't want it back.'

Taking the paper, Belle thanked him again and said she'd be back in touch if there was new information.

Karen walked with her to the front door. As she opened it, she gripped Belle's arm. 'Don't come back. He's ill – cancer. You wouldn't believe he's still in his fifties, would you. He doesn't have long.'

'I'm so sorry and I understand. But Karen, what if there's something that would finally give him closure? Wouldn't you want him to have that?'

The woman shook her head. 'He's been upset enough by the police visit. Leave us alone.' She pushed Belle over the threshold and slammed the door shut.

As she walked slowly to the car, the paper burned a hole in her hand. Should she even show it to Kat Harris? She was blazing with anger again, re-living the worst instances of Kat's manipulation, which had brought about the suicide of a depressed young woman. But, she wouldn't have been here, met Alan, have the letter if not for Kat Harris' efforts.

However, this visit had raised many more questions. She thought back to what Alan had said about Sue Jones' funeral and the school friends who had been there. '*Not the ones I had hoped to see*.' She wanted to know more, but without Kat's involvement. She would pursue this particular new knowledge alone, no matter what the consequences.

Chapter 28

Deception

Kat drummed her fingers on the dashboard as she waited for Belle to leave the house. Irritated at having been dismissed in such a humiliating way, she had wanted to shout at Alan Dobson, *Don't you realise I'm next? I'm the one in danger, not your stupid wife. It's about me now, you pathetic little man.*

She saw the door being slammed in Belle's face and felt better, prepared to be conciliatory. The feeling dissolved as soon as Belle sat in the passenger seat and the atmosphere dropped to freezing.

'Did he give us anything new?'

Belle shook her head. 'Is there anyone else for us to see today?' she asked, staring out of the front windscreen.

'Yes, Liz Maynard's daughter who reported her missing. She might be able to tell us who it was Liz was angry with. What's the matter now? You look like you've had your face slapped.'

'In a manner of speaking, I suppose I have. You did know Sue Jones killed herself.'

'Yes. What's it got to do with anything?'

Belle slowly turned her head, took a deep breath in, then blew it out. She thought of many things she could say but decided there was no point. 'Then we'd better get going. What time is the daughter expecting us?'

'Not until three this afternoon. Do you want to get lunch? It's almost midday.'

'Don't treat me as if I'm a friend, Kat. Please drop me at the hotel, then give me the address. I'll meet you there.'

'Whatever.' She started the car and drove off. Neither spoke until they reached the hotel. Kat scribbled down the address and Belle went into the hotel, saying nothing and not looking back.

Kat sat for a few minutes, wondering what had been said at the Dobson house. Well, whatever it was, Belle wasn't going to share, which was irritating, but not irretrievable. Hopefully, she'd get over it by the time they met Liz's daughter. Could it have been something to do with Sue Jones' suicide? She couldn't think why. If old 'Baldy Bigfoot' had had enough of life, so be it. Her choice. Everyone had choices and she had made hers. Kat couldn't see how she had anything to reproach herself for. She shrugged and drove off.

* * *

Back in her room, Belle had two phone calls to make. The first was to Lennie Maginnis who she caught on a lunch break.

'Belle, what can I do for you today?'

'Are you being sarcastic, Lennie?'

'Not at all. Let me start again. How can I help?'

'Did you go to Sue Jones' funeral?'

'Yes, I did.'

'Who was there from her school group, can you remember?'

'Um, let me think. Gwen definitely. Not sure about Mary. Was Helena there? Yes, of course she was. She was with Sue's sister, who was, as I recall, inconsolable.'

'Were any of Kat's group there?'

'Actually, I thought I saw Bernie Moloney, at the back. I don't remember anyone else. Is this important?'

'I'm not sure, Lennie. I told you Sue's suicide note contained accusations against the school bullies.'

'Yes, you said her sister was specific about that.'

'Could Sue's death have sent someone over the edge, enough to make them decide on revenge, for Sue?'

'This is related to our last conversation, isn't it? You asked me about triggers. Yes, someone else who might have suffered in the same way Sue did, it's possible. But that's theoretical.'

'That's all I need, for now. Thanks, Lennie. I'll let you get back to your lunch.'

'Belle,' there was a pause, 'if something comes of this, you'll let me know, won't you?'

'Of course. By the way, do you remember Teresa Cormorant?'

'I have a vague memory of the name.'

'Do you remember the girl?'

'No, can't picture her. Just the name.'

'OK, thanks, Lennie. I'll be in touch if there's more.'

The next call was to Bob Pugh. He had nothing more to tell her.

'I wasn't expecting anything, Bob, but I have to ask for another favour.'

He sighed. 'Go on, then.'

'When a person commits suicide, if they leave a note, I'm guessing it would be kept as part of the evidence to present to the coroner?'

'Yes.'

'Would such a note be kept in the file? And how long would the file be kept?'

'I sense you're going to ask me to find a file, if it's still available. When was this suicide?'

'Er, it was in …' she realised she didn't have the actual date. 'Sorry Bob, I think it was 1987, at the end of the year.'

'Unlikely. Is this part of what you've been looking for?'

'I thought "we" are looking?'

'Not at the moment, Belle. For now, it's just the death of Faith Shepherd. We don't have the coroner's report yet and until I see it, I can't say where we go next. Anyway, back to your request. Everything's supposed to have been digitised, but I don't know how far back it goes. I'll get someone to check for you. What's the name I'm looking for? And a date of birth would be useful.'

'Susan Jones. It was the thirteenth of December, the day of the party. I'll ask Maggie to verify, though.'

'Let me take a look, or I'll get someone to take a look. Text me when Maggie's confirmed the DoB. I'll call you back.'

An exchange of texts brought a quick response from Maggie Gilbert. Sue's eighteenth birthday was the thirteenth of December. Belle sent the information on to Bob.

She was about to leave the hotel again when a call came from Bob Pugh.

'She was on the database, but only the high-level information which means the paper file is somewhere in the archives. I've sent a lad down to find it, but it may take time, if it's there at all. Belle,' his voice softened, 'it was a gruesome death and it happened on the anniversary of the party, the thirteenth of December 1988, the day of her nineteenth birthday. I'm not going to tell you any more at the moment. Let's see what the file turns up, OK? Are you on your way home yet?'

* * *

She would have liked to know, despite his warning, but she really had to set off now, if she wasn't going to be late at Liz Maynard's daughter's house. Frustratingly, the direction in which her satnav guided her was held up by roadworks. It was a few minutes after three when she turned into the road. As she looked for somewhere to park, she caught a glimpse of a car leaving a space up ahead. As she approached, the driver waved to her. It was Kat Harris. Gobsmacked, she stamped on her brakes, expecting Kat to stop, but she didn't. The last Belle saw of her was the car turning at the end of the road, out of sight.

Kat Harris must have changed the time of the meeting to be earlier, Belle realised, fuming with anger. She must have spoken to the daughter to make sure she could leave before Belle arrived. That was it, she was done. She wouldn't call her, text her, or in any way try to get in touch. She didn't care where Kat Harris had gone. She never wanted to see her again. She was sure this was reprisal for not being told what Belle had learned from Alan Dobson. Ridiculous behaviour. The problem was – did she get anything from the daughter? Belle couldn't go to the house and ask the woman to repeat what she'd already said.

She slammed her car around and headed back to the hotel.

Chapter 29

Demise

Kat Harris reached her Airbnb at breath-taking speed. She had never had much time for speed limits, but today she had driven knowingly through several speed cameras without concern. By the time any attempts at prosecution caught up with her she'd be long gone.

At last – she had a name. *The* name. Liz's daughter had given it up without any thought of consequences, unaware of what she was letting loose. All Kat had to do was pay her a visit. If she had expected to remove Kat in December, she was going to find herself removed in October. No time for finessing or discussing, or even bothering to find out more detail. She already had the basics, from investigations she hadn't shared with Belle Harrington, beyond the immediate and obvious. It would be quick, then she would leave. Her bags were always packed in preparation for a rapid departure. All she had to do was book a flight to one of the Central American countries still open for business, then buy a cheap car and make her way up to the US border and into Texas. No border wall security for her, not that she expected to face interrogation. Her work in Texas had revealed many ways of entering the US on quiet back roads, if you knew where they were. She had her US passport, having become a US citizen years before. And it was in her full married name. No-one would know that Kat Harris was leaving the UK, until it was too late.

There was a flight leaving tomorrow to Mexico City, which was still open for business, but only just, as reports told of a huge increase in Covid infections and there was talk of shutting down airports. Just as well she was ready to strike, then leave. She booked herself a first-class seat and decided to reserve a room at an airport hotel, stay overnight, ready to be at the check-in well ahead of time. She loaded her luggage into the car, which she'd abandon in the hotel car park. She was ready to go.

She considered how she would get the woman alone. She might have to lure her out to a quiet spot. She drove out to the venue, and had been watching for half an hour, trying to decide on her approach when the door opened and the target came out, got into a car and drove off. Kat followed, discreetly, until they reached a house on the outskirts of Newport.

The house had a large enough frontage to accommodate several cars. There were now two parked up. As soon as the woman was inside Kat left her car on the road . She didn't lock the door and left the keys in the ignition for rapid departure if necessary, then marched up to the front door. She didn't need to knock. The door opened as she reached it. Must have CCTV. She hadn't spotted the cameras. Didn't matter.

The person at the open door was not who she expected, and a shock of concern bubbled in her gut. She was invited in politely enough, though. Where was '*Monica*'?

'We've been expecting you, Kat.'

We? Could she handle two people? Of course she could but it would be inconvenient. She was tempted to turn back, but, too late. The door shut behind her and she heard the click of bolts being drawn. Still, she had the weapon in her pocket and would use it, if she had to. She put her hand on the gun, made it ready.

She was ushered along a corridor and through a door. She managed a quick glance at the person sitting in an oversized armchair in the middle of a large but scruffy, rundown room before a sharp pain hit her neck. She stared in amazement at the calm smile of the woman in the chair as her own head spun and her mouth opened. Then, arms flailing, she reached out as a blanket of panic and blackness hit together.

The woman in the armchair watched, one elegant leg crossed over the other. She put her hand out to the side and picked up a cigarette from a pack on the small table, lit it, drew in a long drag, then blew it out with a whole breath, watching the smoke fill the space between herself and the body on the floor. The last one. All gone, at last.

* * *

Belle Harrington, in her hotel room and with her bags packed, ready to leave an hour ago, was still sitting on the bed, not sure why she couldn't bring herself to move. Driving back to the hotel the adrenalin that had kept her angry had dissipated, leaving her tired, upset and disillusioned, and she had decided in that moment to return to Cornwall, immediately, give it all up, decisively this time. She'd had enough of Kat Harris and the ripples in the pond that were still affecting people's lives over thirty years after their school days. She had friends to go back to, the comfortable cottage, the gorgeous garden. So why was she still sitting here, unable to pick up her bags and go, despite being threatened, used and lied to by Kat Harris and caught up in what was more than one case of murder?

The only word that came to mind was – justice. For Sue Jones. What about Gwen, Jane, Helena and Mary. Didn't they deserve justice too? The problem was – could one of them be '*Monica*', as unlikely as that now seemed. Or was it something to do with the Cormorant family? Why had Kat Harris mouthed '*Teresa Cormorant*' at her? But what could she achieve if she stayed? Did she actually care if Kat Harris died? Her inner demon said no, the woman was a psychopath. Would the world be a better place without her? Probably. Then, inevitably, another, deeper but nicer demon said yes. If she didn't do everything she could, she was no better than whoever was behind this. And, this same annoyingly fair and decent demon told her, the women who died had been bullies, but they hadn't deserved to die. Bernie Moloney had felt remorse for what she had done. The letter! She had put it in her pocket when she got back into the car after visiting Alan Dobson and had forgotten about it. Reaching into her pocket she pulled it out and read.

You are an evil bitch. She died because of what you did. You killed her. You will receive your just deserts. You are scum. You should be the dead one. Keep looking over your shoulder.

It was handwritten, ink once black now faded. She noted that 'desserts' was incorrectly spelled. It wasn't exactly a death threat, but she could imagine how Bernie Moloney must have felt when she read it. Did she know that Angie Stephenson was already dead? Maybe, though it was reported as a drug overdose. She wondered if Bernie had tried to contact any of the others. There was another question to ask their families, but not by her. She was going to hand the note over to the police. Then a thought occurred to her. Had Bernie tried to contact Kat Harris to tell her about the letters? She no longer trusted anything Kat Harris said. Only one way to find out. Despite her best intention she picked up her phone and dialled Kat's number. No reply, and the phone went to voicemail for the next ten minutes. Give up, then, hand it all over to Bob Pugh and go home.

As she stood up her phone rang. For a moment she was tempted to ignore it but couldn't help herself. It was Bob Pugh. She answered.

'Belle, my clever lad found the file on Sue Jones' death and her note was still in there. You sure you want to know?'

'Yes, Bob. I think it's important.'

He read it out to her. Sue had written of her despair, how she had become unable to leave her home because of the way people looked at her, lost all of her confidence and her friends, believed what had been said about her in school, that she was 'an ugly freak show'. She saw nothing but hopeless, pointless darkness ahead. Now the pain had become so great there was only one way to stop it.

'Stop,' Belle said. 'What did she do?'

Bob swallowed. 'She hanged herself.'

Belle let out a small moan. 'Would it have been quick?'

'Probably less than a minute.'

'Could she have changed her mind, tried to stop?'

'Yes, probably.'

'But she didn't.'

Bob didn't reply.

Belle wiped her eyes with the sleeve of her coat. 'I'm going back to Cornwall, Bob. I've had enough of this. First, though, I'll tell you about the people we met today.' She was about to start speaking but he interrupted.

'Could you come to the station? It would help if you spoke to Mike Goodman and me together. If I'm going to have another go at making a case to take back to my Super, it would be good to hear it all in one go. Are you OK to do that?'

‘I’ll do that, but then I’m leaving, OK?’

‘Thanks. See you in, say, half an hour?’

For the next ten minutes Belle sat on the bed, unable to move, trying to deal with the images in her head. How someone could be driven to take such a terrible way out by the actions of another person, or people, was almost beyond belief, yet it had happened. She tried to calm the rage that was now boiling in her blood. Kat Harris. She picked up her phone and dialled again. No answer. And again. No answer.

She picked up her bags, checked out of the hotel and headed to the station for what she hoped would be her last act of involvement in this mess.

Chapter 30
Firebreak

It took almost two hours to take Bob and Mike through everything she had learned. They wanted to know about each discussion, meeting and conversation as closely and exactly as she could remember, and to go over, yet again, every thought she had from the time she had learned there was something off, to missing the meeting with Liz Maynard's daughter. By the time they finished it was dark and Belle was exhausted, and too tired and emotional to think about driving home.

Bob offered her a bed at his and Maggie's house, but she refused, deciding she would prefer to spend one final night in her flat. She could ensure the door was locked and bolted, so if anyone had a key to her door as well as a pass to the lobby, they would not be able to get in. Her plan was to leave as early as possible the following morning. And she was going to sell the flat.

Before going to bed she called Bette, to let her know she would be home by early afternoon.

'Then we must have a get-together, so you can tell us everything that's happened. Can you face that tomorrow or shall we make a date for Friday?'

'Friday please, Bette. I'm still shaky from the stomach upset. I'd just like one night of quiet and calm at home, if you don't mind.'

'Well 'course not, fine with me, as it will be with the others. Let's say eleven, Friday morning, in the café. Posy says it's really quiet now. The Welsh visitors are heading home. We'll probably have the place to ourselves. You drive careful, now.'

Her last act before sleeping was to try Kat Harris again. This time the number was unavailable. So Kat had decided to not speak to her. So be it.

* * *

After an undisturbed night Belle set off at nine, found the roads to be reasonably clear and was back in St Foy at two in the afternoon. She couldn't be bothered to put her car in the garage along the back lane, as this would have meant lugging her bags along the lane and through the garden, so she parked outside her front door. The road was narrow here and careless motorists venturing to drive down through the narrow streets into the town square had been known to knock off a wing mirror, or scrape a bumper, and drive on, in the hope that no-one had seen them and they would soon be gone, but she was tired enough to take the risk. In the living room she threw her bags on the floor, decided unpacking could wait, lit a fire and flopped down on the settee, where she immediately fell asleep.

A soft knock on the door woke her, bringing her struggling to her feet and it took a moment to remember she was home. A voice called out 'Belle? Are you there?' It was Rose, who took one look at Belle's dishevelled appearance, put her hand up and started to walk away. 'I disturbed you, I'm sorry. I'll come back later.'

'No, wait, Rose. I'm pleased to see you. Come in, give me a minute, I'll be fine. I shouldn't sleep any more, anyway. I need a good night's rest tonight. I haven't been well.' Her stomach churned again. 'Sit down. I'll make us a cuppa.'

Rose took a place on the settee closest to the fire and leaned in to warm her hands, but sprang to her feet at a scream from the kitchen. She raced in to find Belle staring out of the back door window, pointing at the garden. Rose looked out and covered her mouth with her hands. Every plant, bush and tree had been hacked to bits, the dead branches, flower heads, stalks and leaves lying on the ground where they had been chopped down. Belle was shaking so badly Rose thought she might faint. She took Belle by the arm and guided her back into the living room where she dropped onto the settee and put her head in her hands.

Rose took out her phone. Her first call was to Harry, then she called Bette, explained what had happened and asked her to let Posy and Mavis know. Then she sat down next to Belle and put an arm around her shoulders as she sobbed.

Harry arrived at a run. Rose mouthed, '*Garden*,' and nodded in the direction of the kitchen. He returned a few moments later, his face thunderous. Before he had chance to say anything, Posy appeared.

'What's happened? Bette said I was the closest and to get around here pronto.'

Again, Rose nodded at the garden. Posy returned, waving her arms and was about to shout when Rose put a finger to her lips. Posy nodded and sat down. Belle was now hiccupping, the sobbing done with. She wiped away the tears from her blotched face.

'Who on earth could have done such a horrible thing? Who could hate me so much?'

'I can think of a candidate,' Posy growled.

Rose looked up at her husband. 'Harry, put the kettle on, will you? Make us all a cuppa.'

When Harry had disappeared into the kitchen Belle pushed herself up from Rose's shoulder. 'Has there been any change with Tessa and Pearl Hawkesworth Fox? Anything that could have set her off to do this to me?'

'She's still pushing for a social services review,' Rose said. 'She's got that tame social worker under her thumb still. She's not getting anywhere, though. With us going round there two or three times a day, plus the carer, she can't make a strong enough case to have Tessa moved out. Trouble is, she's angry and when Pearl is angry, watch out. If you're asking if she's capable of this, though, I'm not sure she would resort to something so … crude? It's too obvious, even for her.'

'I sort of agree,' Posy added. 'But who else is there?'

After a few moments' contemplation, Rose said, 'Is there anyone from Wales who might have come down here and done this?'

Belle shook her head. 'I'm certain none of them would do this. There's a lot going on, but for a spiteful act like this? I can't think so.'

'Then it's puzzling,' Rose replied.

Again, no-one spoke until Harry returned with the tea tray.

'Where's Mavis, by the way?' Belle asked.

'She's with Tessa, it's her turn. I'll give her a call later on, after she's handed over to the carer,' Rose replied. 'Do you want to tell us about what's happened in Wales, then? If it's gone too far for spite, that sounds like it's become beyond serious.'

Belle nodded, her cup to her lips. 'It's … what can I say? It's become dark and threatening. I had to leave because of the firebreak starting midnight tonight, but I wouldn't have stayed anyway. The policeman I told you about, Chief Inspector Pugh, he has everything now. He'll have another try tomorrow to persuade his Superintendent to allow him time and resources, given all of the information I handed over to him. That reminds me.' She fished down in her bag for her phone and gave Kat Harris' number another try. Still unavailable. She threw the phone onto the settee. 'That's it, I'm done with her. She can do whatever she wants now. Bob Pugh will track her down, she can't hide from him.' She yawned and Rose gave the others a brief nod.

'We'll leave you alone, I think, Belle. No need to talk about it now. Tomorrow, we'll see what we can all do to help with your garden. Don't worry too much, between us we'll restore it. Plants are resilient.'

Belle returned a weak smile. It was comforting they had descended on her so rapidly but energy had deserted her and all she wanted was to go to bed, although it was barely five o'clock. Still, if she could sleep well, she would be more in the mood to think of solutions tomorrow.

The group took the hint and departed. At the door, Harry Teague squeezed her arm. 'Be as strong as you can,' he whispered, his voice quivering with concern. 'We're all here for you and I think you will need us in the coming weeks. I believe there's more to come.'

Belle thanked him. Nothing to think about tonight. Thinking was for tomorrow.

'Thank you, all of you, for coming round. I'll see you at eleven tomorrow.'

She turned out the lights and fell onto the settee, closing her eyes and falling into an uneasy sleep.

* * *

The following morning Belle awoke at six. It was still dark, and she was cold. The fire had gone out. She shivered and thought about going upstairs to bed, but it was too late. She had slept for almost eleven hours. Best thing, get a shower and a change of clothes and take a walk by the sea. She hesitated. Would that be safe? Was there someone close by determined to do her harm? She gave herself a shake, went into the kitchen and made a flask of coffee, keeping the blinds closed so as not to look at the ruins of the garden. After showering and dressing she glimpsed early dawn light, enough to venture out, she decided. There would be tradespeople about, making deliveries, to prevent anyone surprising her.

By seven she was down on the seafront. It was light now, but dull, a fresh breeze whipping up wavelets that slapped against the wall. She sat on a bench overlooking the harbour, breathing in fresh, tangy sea air. After quiet meditation, breathing exercises and coffee, it was time to return to the cottage, open the back door and step out into the garden.

The shock was still great, and her knees buckled with an immense wave of sadness. Slowly she began to walk around the beds, taking in the damage to each plant. Smaller ones had been torn out by their roots. There was no chance of saving these. Medium height shrubs had been reduced almost to ground level, taller ones hacked and mangled. It was an act of both destructiveness and cruelty. As she stood there surveying, there was a knock on the gate. She glanced at her watch. Just after eight. She had seen a text from Bette, sent last night, to say they would all be arriving at nine, as they couldn't wait for the café meeting at eleven. Who could this be? She tentatively drew back the bolt and lifted the latch. There, belligerent and angry, was Pearl Hawkesworth Fox. Without waiting for an invitation she strode past Belle onto the top step.

'I have heard a rumour that you believe damage has been done to your property, by me, Mrs Harrington. I am here to demand an immediate apology, as I …' She stopped as her eyes left Belle and glanced around the garden. For a moment she seemed quite dumfounded. Her angry gaze returned to pierce Belle.

'I did not do this.'

'I haven't said it was you, Mrs Hawkesworth Fox. Now, if you will excuse me, I have a great deal to occupy myself with, as you can see.'

Pearl didn't move. She adjusted the paisley silk scarf around her neck and swallowed, her eyes flickering over the garden. 'I can assure you, this was nothing to do with me, nor with anyone connected with me.' She had spoken in a lower voice, with a touch of sadness. 'I am a gardener. I would never do such a dreadful thing.'

'Maybe not you, but someone close to you?'

Pearl looked as if she was about to snap a reply, but a questioning look appeared on her face, as a thought came to her, one that she was not going to share. 'I am quite certain not. I'll go now.' She backed up the step and stood in front of the open gate. 'I am sorry this has happened to you,' she said as she turned away.

Belle closed and bolted the gate. A thought crossed her mind – had she actually locked the gate when she left for Wales? She couldn't remember. She was always mindful to lock the front and kitchen doors, although she knew that many of the older inhabitants in the town didn't bother, but she hadn't considered access to the garden. She had fitted an electronic video device to the front door when she moved in, but she had given no special thought to the old wooden garden gate.

The garden was better protected from the breeze that blew in the harbour, so she decided to drink the rest of her coffee whilst she sat on the patio, with pen and paper to make a list of what she needed to do and what plants would have to be replaced. At least it would stop her mind focusing entirely on events in Wales. How ironic. Yet, she couldn't help thinking about Pearl Hawkesworth Fox's visit. The woman did seem genuine in her sadness about the state of the garden, but there had been something that gave her pause when Belle spoke about someone close to her. Maybe her husband? Or someone else? Throughout Pearl's interference in the fate of Tessa Glaston the only other person Belle had seen had been the social worker: a tall, thin woman with a pinched face that held a permanent look of resignation. Many social workers probably had that look, these days. She hadn't seemed the type to destroy a garden out of anger or frustration, but who knew?

Her thoughts were interrupted by her phone telling her there was someone at the front door. It wasn't quite eight thirty. The face on the screen was Bette and Belle could see someone standing behind her.

'Come around to the back. I'm in the garden.'

Bette arrived, followed by a man Belle hadn't met before, tall with wide shoulders and the tanned face of an outdoor worker. He was dressed in an old parka over a set of black combat trousers, the pockets bulging with string, twine and metal, and wearing heavy, steel-toe capped boots. He held out a rough and calloused hand.

'My nephew, George,' Bette said. 'He's a gardener. He's going to take a look and advise us on what to do and where to start.'

'Oh, that's lovely of you,' Belle said to the man, whose face flushed red.

'He don't talk much,' Bette said. She patted him on the back. 'Off you go, Georgie.'

He turned away from them and began to walk around the garden, his face concentrated and often frowning.

'He's a bit slow,' Bette said, watching him. 'He don't get people, on the whole, but he's a genius with plants.'

'Everyone has a talent,' Belle replied. 'Is he a local man?'

'Oh yes, he lives in Par with Mandy and his boy.'

'He's married?'

'Just because he's a bit slow don't mean no-one loves him,' Bette said. 'He and Mandy been together since they were in little school.'

'Sorry, Bette, I didn't mean to imply …'

George turned around before Bette could reply.

He had taken a pen and paper from two of the pockets. Belle and Bette watched his progress around the garden, staring then making a note each time he stopped, before he ambled over and gave the paper to Bette.

'Some can be saved, others not. You 'ave'nt lost many, though. Plants are resilient. They'll come back 'fore you know it. I've drawn you a picture of what you need to do.' He stopped and glanced around. 'Terrible, this. Someone has a bad mind.'

'Yes, they do. Thanks, George.' Belle had taken the paper and was looking at a carefully drawn diagram of the beds of her garden, with, in small writing, a few words about what to do to each plant. 'This looks excellent.'

He looked at Bette. ''Ave to go now, Aunty Bette. Couple of gardens to see to today.'

'Thanks for taking the time to come down, George. Love to Mandy and Will.'

He nodded and let himself out by the garden gate.

'He's the last person who's going to have unimpeded access to the garden through that gate,' Bette said. 'Bert's coming down later this morning when he's finished on the farm. We're going to fit an electronic opening device with a code.'

For a moment, Belle couldn't speak. She squeezed Bette's arm. Bette shook her off. 'Don't you be thanking me, Belle Harrington. It's what friends do.'

As she finished there was another notification through the phone in the robot-like voice, of more activity at the front door.

'Not sure I'd like that too often,' Bette muttered, as Belle went to let them in.

Posy, Mavis and Rose were waiting, all dressed ready for the outdoors and carrying a selection of garden tools.

'We weren't sure what you'd have, so we brought our own,' Posy said, holding up a rake in one hand and a spade in the other, as Belle ushered them in. 'We'll go straight through to the back, shall we?'

* * *

By midday most of the clearance had been done and the clipping and trimming of bushes and shrubs completed. George had also sent a list of suggested replacement plants for those that couldn't be saved. The least she could do for the owners was to return the cottage as she had found it, when she finally left.

Posy was planning to open the café for a few hours after lunch, Rose had a committee meeting to attend and Mavis, who had been quiet during the morning, had an appointment, so they left Bette and Belle with the final half hour of clearing up. Bert hadn't arrived, having called Bette to explain there had been an issue with a tractor he had to sort out and would be there after midday to sort out the back gate and take her home.

Once they had finished, Belle offered Bette lunch. They sat on the patio, surveying their morning's work.

'Doesn't look so bad now, and it'll be better when you get the new ones in.' Bette said, sipping coffee and cautiously eyeing a hefty slice of frittata full of veg.

'Yuk test,' Belle said.

'What?'

'Something I always insisted on with my son. You have to try it and say 'yuk' before you refuse to eat it.'

Bette laughed. 'I never allowed my kids such luxury. You ate it or you went hungry. At least they've grown up with no food fads.' She paused, cut off a mouthful and chewed. 'Quite nice. Actually, very nice, although I don't think I could persuade Bert.'

'I'm looking forward to meeting him,' Belle said. 'He's the only husband, partner, whatever I haven't met yet.'

'He's not much of a one for socialising,' Bette replied, tucking into the food and breaking off a large slice of garlic bread. 'He's a good man, though.'

'How did you meet him?'

'Young Farmers dance. We were both eighteen. Got married a year later, never looked back. I was brought up on a farm, so the life came naturally. Wouldn't have it any other way.'

'And you had four children. Can't have had much leisure time.'

Bette laughed. 'You can say that again. But it does seem quiet sometimes, with just the youngest still at home. Even he'll be leaving soon.'

'Do you think any of them will return to Cornwall, Bette?'

Bette sat back. 'I don't know. What I do know is – we'll be the last of the family on the farm. The kids all mucked in when they were growing up, but it didn't give the feeling to any of them. Not a love of farming enough to make them want to take it on. They've seen how hard we work and how difficult it's been at times to keep going. No, if we have to sell in the end, it will be OK with me. Don't tell Bert I said that,' she said, leaning forward.

Belle smiled and put a finger to her lips to mimic a zip.

'What about your family, Belle. You don't say much.'

'I don't have much to say,' Belle replied. 'I'm not one of these people with dark and dirty secrets. My life had been straightforward, the usual story. Most of this isn't news to you. Married, had a son. He's in Africa now, volunteering, a doctor. Had a good career, husband died of cancer. Mother had a stroke and I moved in to take care of her. I'm an only child, so I inherited the family home in Kensington when she died. Retired, moved here. That's me. Simples.' She smiled. She had maintained this story for so long that it came naturally now.

Bette Jones also knew a lie when she was hearing one but had no intention of probing. Whatever it was, she was sure Belle would talk about it when the time came. Nothing to be achieved from pushing.

The back gate opened and a man stood on the top step, waving tentatively at Bette.

Whatever Belle had expected, it wasn't this. She had imagined the archetype of a farmer: small, ruddy cheeked, cheeky grin, or perhaps bald, taciturn and frowning. Bert Jones fitted none of those stereotypes. The man on the step was around six feet tall, dressed in blue overalls that didn't disguise a powerful, muscular build. He had a shock of thick, white hair. And he was one of the handsomest men Belle had ever seen. His complexion was dark, but smooth, his eyes a deep penetrating colour that she saw was a liquid brown as he moved towards them.

Bette saw the look on Belle's face and grinned. 'Hooked a good one, didn't I?'

Belle laughed out loud, which she turned into a greeting as she held her hand out to Bert. 'Thank you so much for coming to do this for me, Bert.'

He grinned. 'I'll just get on, then we have to get back for the milking,' he said to Bette. 'No problem. Happy to help.' He looked around. 'You've done OK here. Bette said it was a right mess.'

'It was,' Belle replied, 'but thanks to Bette and the girls, the worst is over.'

'Any idea who done it?'

'I thought it might have been Pearl Hawkesworth Fox, but she came here this morning to deny having anything to do with it.'

'I still think she's involved, somehow,' Bette muttered. She turned to Bert. 'I suppose you'd better get on. We'll clear up here.' He smiled at her and ambled back to the gate, picked up a bag of tools and began to work.

'I bet he turns heads when he's cleaned up,' Belle said to Bette as they took trays back to the kitchen and began to load the dishwasher.

'Might do, except he's hardly ever dressed up,' Bette said. 'He's the most contented person I've ever known. He's never wanted any more than his farm and his family. Mind you, at first I used to think he loved them cows better than any of us.'

'Used to?'

Bette paused, bending over the dishwasher.' We had five children. When Marcy died – she was just two – I thought I'd never get over it. She was our third and a little beauty, angelic, kind of. I had a breakdown. I wouldn't have recovered without him. He took on everything, the two older kids who were just six and four, as well as the farm. Wrapped me up in cotton wool and let me grieve as long as I needed. Never asked anything of me, until I was ready to come back and try again. He's been my rock and my strength.'

'I'm so sorry to hear that, Bette. It's terrible to lose a child.' She almost said more but caught herself in time. 'The bond between you two is strong, I can see already. Your children must have had a great time growing up in such a loving family.'

'I believe they did; they're a happy bunch,' Bette said, standing up. 'We don't talk much about Marcy outside the family. I was a right mess, did things I'm not proud of. The girls know, and now you, but that's all.'

'Thank you for telling me,' Belle replied. 'Of course I'll respect your privacy.'

'Right, then.' Bette was back in bustling mode. 'What else can we do?'

'Make more coffee and watch the workman work?'

'Excellent idea.'

* * *

They made small talk for the hour it took Bert to complete the work on the lock and make sure Belle understood how to programme it.

'You should think about having that CCTV to cover the garden, also,' he said. 'Whoever did it, might come back.'

'Worth thinking about, thanks, Bert,' she replied. 'I'll probably do that, if the owners agree. It doesn't feel like my safe haven, not now.'

He opened his mouth to speak again, but Bette got in ahead of him. 'Time to go,' she said, taking him by the arm. A look passed between them, and he nodded.

'Thank you, both, for everything you've done today.'

'Nonsense,' Bette said gruffly. She put on her coat and marched Bert to the gate. 'We'll see ourselves out. Will we see you tomorrow?' she shouted back over her shoulder.

'Probably,' Belle replied and waved them gone.

She was relieved to be alone again, despite her pleasure in their friendship, but she still felt raw and unusually agitated. There was so much rattling around in her head and whilst she and Bette had been talking, another part of her brain was rumbling, snatching at ethereal shadows and motes of dust in the light, to almost catch one, only to have it dissolve before it formed anything useful.

The agitation came from a feeling that she was close to something, but just couldn't see it. After another hour of sitting she decided there was no point in trying. Whatever it was would not be forced. The only way to get to it was to ignore it. Deliberately, until it wouldn't be ignored and, hopefully, present itself in a more graspable form.

* * *

By Monday morning, nothing further had occurred to her, and she had heard nothing from Bob Pugh. The group had met up on Saturday in the café, where Belle had updated them on everything she knew.

'Can you leave it to the police, now, do you think?' Posy had asked as she served their usual drinks, then joined them at the table.

'I still don't know if Bob Pugh has the go-ahead to investigate properly,' Belle replied. 'I know he'll call me when he has anything. He must have spoken to Liz's daughter by now.' She shook her head. 'There's something I've heard, that I know has an important meaning, but I just can't put my finger on it.'

'Stop trying,' Bette said. 'Works for me. I just forget about it, then it suddenly comes at me when I'm not expecting it.'

Belle smiled. 'That's what I'm trying to do.'

As she was about to leave, Mavis had jumped up and said, 'I'll go with you. I should get back home. Andrew will be expecting me.'

'Sure,' Belle replied turning her head so Mavis couldn't see. Her raised eyebrow received a return shrug from Bette.

They had begun to walk along the High Street.

'This is the wrong way for you, Mavis.'

'I need your help with something.'

'Of course. What I can I help with?'

'I need to get into my husband's study. I need you as a look-out to intercept him and spin him a story if he comes home suddenly.'

'Oh. Before I ask what you're going to do—'

'I'd prefer you didn't ask, not yet.'

'Well, OK. But, Mavis, why me?'

'If he finds you waiting in the garden he won't brush past you, as he would the others. He knows them too well. I was thinking, if you see him coming, you can ring the doorbell three times. That'll tell me he's approaching, then you can hold him up in conversation to give me a few minutes to get out of the room and open the door to you, as if you'd just arrived. You see?'

'I see. Well, if it's important.'

'It's important.'

'When would you like to carry out this piece of subterfuge?'

Mavis blushed. 'Soon, when I know a time he's more likely to be out. Once I've found what I'm thinking I'll find, I can tell you all about it. Will you do it?'

'Of course I'll do it. But first you'll have to give me an idea of how I can engage Andrew in conversation on his own doorstep, enough to keep him away from his front door for more than a few minutes.'

'I'll give you a few ideas.'

They'd linked arms and walked to the end of the street, parting at the steps leading up to Tessa's cottage. Mavis had given Belle a weak smile. 'Thank you,' she'd whispered and ran up the steps, leaving Belle wondering what had happened, but suspecting that whatever it was, Andrew being mainly in conveyancing, it might involve Tessa and her property.

* * *

At lunchtime on Monday her phone rang. It was Bob Pugh.

'Can you get back up here, Belle. I'm going to need your help.'

'If that's allowed,' she replied.

'I'll make sure you're OK travelling.' He paused. 'We arrested Helena Parry yesterday. On a charge of unlawful abduction.'

Chapter 31

Confession

By nine on Tuesday morning Belle was in the station and Bob took her through to the back area and his office, where Mike Goodman was waiting.

'Can I get you anything?' he asked. 'Tea, coffee, whatever?'

'No thanks, Bob. Just tell me about Helena, please, and why you need me here.'

He sat forward in his chair, grasped his fingers together, then rubbed both palms as if trying to remove something stuck on them. 'OK. The not-so-good news, then the really bad news. We arrested Helena Parry. She's refusing to answer to that name, by the way. Says she'll only answer to Sister Mary Frances. Anyway, we made the arrest following the information from Liz Maynard's daughter. Her mother had said she was going to deal with' – he paused and checked his notes –'"that silly little wannabe nun freak I was in school with. I'm going to sort her out once and for all". According to her daughter, that was between the end of work and going to the pub, which she left after saying something similar and wasn't seen again. We went to the convent and tried to speak to Sister Mary Frances, but she just laughed at us. Told us we had no idea what we were dealing with. I asked her to elaborate. She refused so I arrested her, on suspicion of the unlawful abduction of Liz Maynard.' He sat back.

'Do you have any evidence she's been responsible for any of the deaths or disappearances, Bob? Liz or any of them?'

He shook his head. 'I'm going to have to let her go.'

'Has she denied being responsible for any of it?'

'That's the odd thing. She says she is culpable, but not why. I can't continue to keep her, based just on that. Now, the very bad news. My Super won't let us carry on. She can't commit the time and the money to a wider investigation. We're still looking into whatever happened to Faith Shepherd, but that's all we can do.'

'That's disappointing. But it doesn't tell me why you've brought me back.'

He sat back and folded his arms. 'Helena Parry says she'll talk to you. If you're willing to speak to her, of course.'

Belle sat for a moment before she replied. Then she leaned forward, putting her arms on the table, hands resting under her chin. 'Do you want me to just talk, or do you want me to ask your questions for you?'

'Just talk, we think. But, if you could throw in a couple of our questions, I would be grateful.'

* * *

Helena Parry irritated Belle from the moment she walked into the room. It could have been her air of condescension, or her smug smile, or her assumption of superiority, or all of those signs leeching off her like a malevolent miasma. Or maybe Belle was just annoyed anyway. The headdress and what appeared to be an extra-large cross hanging around her neck were Helena's badges of office and authority. Belle took a deep breath. Her strategy would be to act uninterested. Let Helena make the running. She sat back, crossed her ankles and folded her arms.

'Good morning, Helena. So, we meet at last. I understand you want to talk to me.'

'They have to let me go.'

'Yes. So, talk to me.'

'Don't you have questions for me?'

'Me?' She shook her head. 'No.'

Helena shifted in her chair and fingered the cross. 'I have been accused of unlawful abduction. I have not abducted anyone, as I have repeated, throughout the past twenty-four hours, although I am culpable.'

'Annoying. I suppose you could sue them. Or, then again, perhaps your Christian charity will prompt you to forgive them. After all, they're trying to identify a potential murderer. You know something. You could help. But you won't, you've made that clear. What do you want to say to me?'

Helena Parry's mouth formed an annoyed moue. 'You know as much as I.'

'No, Helena. I have clues. You have evidence.'

'No, not evidence. But, I can tell you that you're looking in the wrong place; missing the obvious.'

Belle sat up. 'I have no idea what you're talking about. You'll have to tell me more than that, if you want to help solve a murder. What will your Superior say when she finds out you know something, but are refusing to help the police? Not a good look.' Belle was longing to ask what she meant, but held it in.

Helena sat back in her chair, folded her arms, mimicking Belle. 'I would suggest you think in a different direction. Go back to the beginning.'

'This is getting us nowhere.' But it was; she could see small signs. Helena sat forward now, put her hand to the top of her head, making sure the head covering was straight, then both hands to the cross. Now was the time.

'Helena, I believe there have been six murders and one more to come. The problem for the police is they can't make the link between them. If that's something you can provide, then do it. Give it up.'

'That's what they need, a link?'

'Yes. I don't have enough for them.'

'Why did they arrest me?'

Belle wasn't sure she had permission to say what she knew, but, what the hell. If she was going to force this woman to speak, she had to give her something. 'Because Liz Maynard's daughter said that her mother was going to deal once and for all with, and I quote, "that silly little wannabe nun freak I was in school with". That would be you.'

Whatever reaction she had expected, this wasn't it, as Helena threw her head back and laughed. 'You've completely missed the obvious, Arabella Penning. I didn't always see myself in the religious life, but others did. As I said, you have to go back to the beginning. Look at it again, but from their point of view. Think about what they said about themselves, back then.'

'You mean, Kat's lot?'

Helena nodded. 'Yes them, but also, look more widely. That's where you'll get your link.' She stood up. 'I'd like to go, now.'

'Helena, did you have anything to do with the deaths and disappearances? Anything at all? Why did you say you're culpable?'

'I have had nothing to do with any of it, but I am culpable, in the same way you are,' the nun replied. 'I know some of the history. My memory is good, better than yours, as it turns out. Look in the side-lines, in the shadows, too.' She frowned, suddenly. 'Someone once told me something, in confidence. About who they really were. I will never, ever repeat what I heard that day. Not even under oath.' She looked up at the two-way mirror. 'I wish to leave now, Chief Inspector.'

Mike Goodman entered the room, indicating to both women to stand. At the door, he nodded Belle to Bob's office and took Helena's arm to lead her to the exit.

At the last minute Helena turned around. 'I hope we never meet again, Arabella.'

'Mutual,' Belle muttered as she watched the tall, straight-backed figure walk slowly down the corridor and through the exit.

Bob was already back in his office, waiting for her. 'What was that about?' he snapped. 'You didn't ask her anything we discussed.'

'Sorry. It just seemed to me as soon as I was in front of her that she wasn't going to give anything up. But, I do think what she told me has great significance for both of us, if I can figure it out.'

'Well, get thinking. I've nothing left, now. She had an alibi for most of the times I could question her on. We're checking them out, but so far they stand up.'

'Look, help me here, Bob, please. Something has been in my head for days. I don't know if it's related to what Helena just said, but it's part of the story, particularly what she just told me, about someone being not what they seemed. She said go back to the beginning, think about it from their point of view. If I can work out what she meant—' Whatever she was about to say was interrupted by the door opening.

‘I got a message you wanted to see me, Sir?’ The last word was spoken with such contempt Belle expected it to solidify as it came out of Mal Jenkins’ mouth.

‘No, I don’t want to see or hear from you, Jenkins. Someone was winding you up. Go back into your hole.’

Jenkins grinned and slammed the door.

‘I thought he was suspended?’ Belle asked.

‘Super decided to bring him back in. He’s only got a week to go. Then he gets his pension and a full hypocritical send-off, without scandals or adverse publicity.’ Bob’s contempt was equal to that of his departed colleague.

Belle shook her head, then stood up. ‘I’ll go, I think. I’m going to head back to my flat. Do you need any more from me?’

He laughed, bitterly. ‘Nothing, unless you can come up with a miracle to give me the opening I need to get properly into this.’

‘I’m going to drive back to Cornwall later on in that case. I can think better, away from here.’

‘I’ll show you out. I’ve got enough on my plate anyway. Thanks for coming back.’

‘Sorry it didn’t work out.’

‘Sometimes, you just have to let go, despite what your instincts are screaming at you.’

* * *

Back at the flat Belle wrote notes on as much as she could remember verbatim of what Helena had said. This would be the end of the road, unless she could work it out. Damn the woman! Four women were dead and two still unaccounted for. Over the weekend, having made the decision to put the apartment on the market, she had emailed an estate agent. A reply was waiting for her. Would two this afternoon suit? She replied that it would and began to tidy and clean up, her mind all the time on Helena's advice to go back to the beginning. Nothing came.

By three she was on the road. The agent had suggested a fair price. There being no chain, she was confident the apartment would be an attractive offer to a young, up-and-coming business person. Belle didn't care who bought it. She just wanted rid of it. She had bought it out of nostalgia. That past had turned out to be horrific. Where she would go after the lease expired on the cottage in St Foy she didn't want to think about.

She arrived just after six. Because of the travel restrictions the roads were clear. If only it could stay that way.

Before leaving she had called Mavis to put her off, explaining that the police needed her in Wales. Mavis was disappointed, but Belle promised to let her know as soon as the plan was on again. A quick phone call established that Andrew Tregoss would be at his golf club the following morning, leaving at around eleven. They set the kick-off for eleven thirty.

Chapter 32

Discovery

Still not sure what she was doing, or why, Belle walked up to the front door of Mavis' house at eleven thirty the following morning and stood, hovering from foot to foot, watching the road at the end of the front garden. Mavis' plan was to enter the study at eleven thirty and begin searching. For what exactly, Belle had no idea, but Mavis had promised to tell her, if she found what she was expecting to find. Too vague for Belle but, she had to trust Mavis. Ready to ring the bell if there was any sign of Andrew returning, her mind began to wander back to the conversation with Helena Parry. No! She had to give this her full attention. Concentrate on watching out for Andrew Tregoss.

Mavis had said that she expected the search to take about fifteen to twenty minutes, after which she would come out to join Belle in front of the house. After twenty-five minutes there was still no sign of her. Then, the worst possible – Andrew Tregoss' car pulled up in front of the house and he got out. Belle began to ring the bell, three times for three seconds each, as they had agreed.

He paused, frowning. 'Good morning, Mrs Harrington. Can I help you?'

'I've come to meet Mavis, but she doesn't seem to be answering. But, actually, this is an opportunity I've been hoping for, Andrew. I have a question about the possibility of buying my cottage, and I thought you were exactly the person to help me.' She smiled at him. It wasn't true, but he wasn't to know.

'You can make an appointment at my office. Call my secretary.' He went to walk past her. There was still no sign of Mavis.

'Oh, I could, but I thought perhaps we could chat informally, save setting up a formal meeting. After all, we are friends, aren't we?' Her smile widened.

'I'm sorry, Mrs Harrington. I don't do favours for my wife's friends. I am a professional solicitor. Now, could you please move out of my way.'

Belle pouted. 'I'm sorry you feel like that. Mavis is such a good friend.' She was desperate now. 'Surely you could make an exception …'

'Please move, Mrs Harrington.' He had a key in his hand. She had no choice and was praying that Mavis hadn't been so caught up in her search for whatever it was that she hadn't heard the bell. She took a step to the side, as the door opened and a flustered Mavis appeared.

'Belle, so sorry, I was in the bathroom. Andrew, you're home early.'

'I forgot certain papers,' he snapped, scowling at Belle. Mavis stood aside. 'Oh, sorry. Well, Belle and I are going to lunch. I'll see you later.'

Andrew Tregoss didn't reply. He marched into the hall, opened a door opposite the stairs and slammed it behind him. Belle opened her mouth to speak but Mavis put a finger to her lips. She darted back inside, opened the door to a cupboard underneath the staircase, brought out a large suitcase and wheeled it quickly to the front door.

'Let's go, before he finds out. I've got what I need, in here.' She patted the top of the case. 'Your car's close by?'

'Right next to Andrew's.'

They ran down the path to Belle's car, threw the case into the back seat, threw themselves into the front seats. Mavis was still putting on her seatbelt as Belle drove off.

'Where are we going, Mavis?'

There was no reply. Glancing across she could see Mavis' hands fumbling on the seatbelt catch and her body shaking. She pulled over, but Mavis shouted, 'No! Don't stop. We're going to Bette's farm.'

As they travelled Mavis stared out of the front window. In the farmyard Bette was waiting and ushered them in, shutting and bolting the door behind them. She sat Mavis down in front of a blazing fire, as Bert arrived with a tray of tea.

'Special sweet one for you, Mavis,' he said, putting a cup between her hands. 'If he turns up here, he'll get the business end of my pitchfork.'

Mavis giggled, which turned into a hiccup, then a sob.

'She's left the bastard, at last,' said a stone-faced Bette. 'Told me everything last night. Did you find it, Mave?'

Mavis nodded.

'Can someone please tell me what's going on and if I've just been party to something illegal?' Belle demanded.

'He's the illegal one,' Bette said. 'Are you ready to tell her, my love?'

Mavis nodded. 'Andrew has been advising Pearl Hawkesworth Fox behind our backs, about Tessa's cottage and who owns it. He's discovered the row of cottages all belong to a trust, except for Tessa's, and Pearl's nephew has been wanting to buy them up as they become vacant. He's negotiating with the trust, with Andrew helping him. He wants to convert them all into luxury holiday lettings. He's had plans drawn up. I've found them. And the correspondence. The thing is, the numbering is all wrong.'

'What do you mean?' Belle asked.

'Give her a minute. You drink down that tea, my dear,' Bert intervened. He turned to Belle. 'She's had a big shock. Give her a few minutes.'

Belle nodded and sat back, eyes closed.

'I'm fine, thank you Bert. I owe Belle an explanation, 'specially after what she did this morning to help me. Right, so you know Tessa has always claimed the cottage was given to her family a long time ago.' Belle sat up. 'Yes, but she hasn't been able to find any proof, I thought.'

'That's right. Because Andrew stole it and probably destroyed it. I had an idea, though. Tessa once said that His Lordship was the original owner. So, I went to see him. Walked right in there, I did.'

'His Lordship's a good man,' Bert explained to a wide-eyed Belle. 'You know the place, up on the headland, beyond the castle.'

'You mean, *that* house? The one that ...'

Bert grinned. 'Yep. The Trevellowses keep the public away, but His Lordship agreed to speak to Mavis, her being a local woman with a problem.'

'Lovely, he was,' Mavis said, sighing. 'So helpful. He got his people to check into all the old papers and they found the deed that made over the cottage to Tessa's ancestors, or rather, her husband's. It was number seven, Fish Row.'

'Hang on,' Belle interrupted. 'Tessa's cottage is number six.'

Mavis beamed. 'That's what people think now. But it's really number seven. You see, about a hundred and fifty years ago, the same person had number one and number two. Whoever it was, I can't remember the name, got agreement to convert them into one and called them number one. Over the years the others, what didn't have any numbers on the front, assumed the next number up from the new number one. So, Tessa's cottage was assumed to be number six.'

'But it's really number seven,' Bette said, grinning. 'And it never had a number anyway. It was called the Captain's Cottage. It being the biggest one, on the end of the row.'

'They all lost their numbers over the years,' Mavis said. 'Next door to Tessa is Cream Cottage, then Red Cottage, then The Lodge, then Blue House, then St Foy Place at the other end, which is the old numbers one and two.'

'But what about the land registry?' Belle asked. 'Surely, it must be registered in Tessa's family's name?'

'It doesn't seem to be registered in anyone's individual name, which is why the deed of transfer is so important. The nephew's been plotting to get number six, which is now number five on the changed numbering. He thinks he's getting Tessa's Captain's Cottage because it's the sixth cottage, but it's number five he's in the process of negotiating with the trust, who still own it. The tenant died, you see, and the trust want the money. They just re-let in the past, but times have changed. Anyway, he'll find out his mistake soon enough, when Andrew has to unpick the whole thing and tell Pearl and her nephew they're looking at the wrong house.'

'Surely they looked at the plans, and documents. What on earth has Andrew been telling them? This is very confusing,' Belle said. 'I think I get it, but it's going to need a good solicitor to work it all out.'

'Indeed,' Bette said. 'Andrew Tregoss knows, though. Although I don't know if Mave will be able to prove that, since there's no proof he ever had the original documents.'

'He kept a copy,' Mavis said, digging into her suitcase and extracting a sheaf of papers. 'And I found the correspondence between him and Pearl, explaining what needs to be done. Fortunately, they haven't made the final offer, so there's enough time to have the rest of the cottages in Fish Row sorted out proper, as well as Tessa's.'

'Is that why Pearl has been trying to get Tessa out of the cottage?'

'Yes. It would have been so much easier without her in residence,' Mavis replied.

'Golf ball!'

'What?' Bette said to Belle, who had shouted out.

'That's what she tripped over on the stairs. Something small and hard. A golf ball. I'll bet as soon as Mavis and Andrew reached the cottage he found it and popped it into his pocket. You said he spends a lot of time playing golf.'

'I do remember he bent down, to tie a lace,' Mavis pondered.' That's what he was really doing? Picking up a golf ball?'

'Again, you'll never be able to prove it,' Belle said. 'But, it does sound like both he and Pearl are thwarted, for the time being. Probably permanently, given you have those papers. I must say, Mavis, you gave me a fright. I thought Andrew was going to push me out of the way, in the end.'

'Sorry,' Mavis muttered. 'I had to put the papers into my case then shut the case away, make sure he didn't see it.'

Belle rubbed Mavis' arm. 'Not to worry. It's done. What's next?'

'She's going to stay with us for now,' Bette said. 'Bert and the lads here will make sure Andrew can't get at her. Then, we'll figure out next steps.'

'And Tessa is safe, too. For the time being, that is.'

'What do you mean, Belle?'

'She's getting weaker, Mavis. She won't be able to stay there much longer. Not on her own.'

Mavis' face lit up. 'Yes, you see, that's the answer. Once Andrew knows how much we know, I can move in with her. Look after her. See, I know she's not got much longer. Now, she can have what's she's always wanted, to die in her own bed.'

Bette moved in and gave Mavis a hug. 'I think it will all work out nicely. And wouldn't we all like to be there when Andrew has to tell Pearl that her rotten nephew will never get his hands on the property! What people will do for money, eh? Pure greed, nothing more, nothing less. No concern about Tessa or her health or wellbeing. Just ugly human greed.'

Chapter 33

Realisation

It came out of sleep at five in the morning two days later.

Belle sat up, her head spinning slightly as she adjusted to the room. She had to blink a few times to fight to rising panic that came with the dizziness. But this time, it wasn't about the past, or at least not about *her* past. She had remembered, somehow her brain had moved it from subconscious to conscious level.

What they said about themselves? Not quite. It was what they had called themselves. Because there had been no boys in the school, the girls had been discussing social hierarchy and Kat Harris had decided to designate her group the Alpha Girls, or the Alpha Kat Crowd. Belle remembered Kat laughing. They were the top dogs, the ones with power over others. The memory was fragmentary. Just the laughing and the way they all strutted round afterwards, in what they thought was the way an Alpha Girl should behave.

But what had that to do with a lead on the deaths and disappearances? The full answer hadn't come, but still, it was a start. Nor was there anything about side-lines or shadows. Unable to return to sleep she got up and dressed and made notes.

The picture was almost whole, yet still with whisps of fog that stopped her from seeing the something, which faded in and out, with glimpses of strutting teenage girls.

She banged her fist on the table.

There was to be a get-together at Bette's farm at ten and Belle was there ahead of time. Mavis' story had already been shared. Belle told hers.

'So there it is. It's so close, but I can't grasp the full picture. Anyone got any ideas to propose? Doesn't matter how daft they seem, because I'm going to rip open my head if I can't find a better way.'

'Maybe,' Rose muttered. She had been looking at the original set of notes Belle had given them, about the two groups of girls. All eyes turned to her.

'Helena Parry said to look at it from their point of view. I think the key might be Tina Lewis and Liz Maynard.'

'Why them?' Belle asked.

'And Kat Harris,' Rose went on. 'Can you call your friend Maggie with a couple of questions that might help confirm what I'm thinking?'

'Of course. What are the questions?'

Rose told her and they all stared as Belle dialled and asked. 'Maggie says give her ten minutes.'

The wait was only ten minutes, but seemed much longer. Belle's phone rang. She answered, listened, thanked Maggie and ended the call.

'OK. Tina was registered at birth as Christina Ellen Lewis and Kat Harris as Georgina Kathryn Harris. Tina and Kat. And, of course, Liz, who was actually Elizabeth. Does that help?'

'Oh, yes,' Rose whispered. 'Can you see it now? Look at the notes with those names instead of what you've written, and think about it.'

Belle stared. And stared. Then, she saw it. She slapped her hand to her mouth. 'Rose, you brilliant woman! This should be exactly what Bob Pugh needs to convince his Super there's been nothing random about it and give him the resources to carry out a full investigation.' She leaned across the table and enveloped Rose in a breath-stopping crush.

'What am I missing here?' Bette demanded.

'It's the names, the order in which the killings – because I'm quite sure now that's what they were – were carried out.' She pointed to the list of the bullies. 'Change the three on my list to what we now have, then look at them again, just the first names.' She paused. Posy saw it, then Bette, then Mavis.

Belle confirmed it, as they stared, wide-eyed. 'Not Alpha as in top dog. Alpha as in alphabet: Angela, Bernadette, Christina, Denise, Elizabeth, Faith and Georgina.'

'Well I'll be damned,' Bette said.' You'd better call that policeman and tell him. We'll wait.'

They sat in silence around the large farmhouse kitchen table, as Belle dialled the number for Bob Pugh. He answered. Belle asked him for five minutes of his time. He agreed. She went through the names, without interruption on his part.

'I'm going to put you on speaker now, Bob. I'm with my friends in Cornwall. It was one of them who spotted this.'

'Well, whoever it was, that's excellent work,' he said. 'And yes, I think this is enough to confirm these deaths and disappearances weren't random nor accidental. Give me half an hour and I'll call you back.'

'Before you go, Bob. Is Maggie at home? There's something else I want to know about.'

'Yes, last time I spoke to her she was planning to spend the day in the office with Zelah and Nick. Is it something that could be useful to me?'

'I think so, let me talk to her. By the time you call me back I hope she'll be on the case.' He ended the call.

'Belle,' Rose began. 'You do realise what this means, about Kat Harris?'

'Oh, yes. She's known all along. She named the gang. It must have been a huge joke, the alphabet of names.'

'Why didn't she tell you, do you think, when she asked you to work with her?'

Belle took a few minutes to answer; no-one spoke. 'Kat Harris is a psychopath; no empathy, no compassion, no conscience. Yes, she knew, she told me she'd been watching, "with interest" she said. So, she knew there was planning and deliberation behind the deaths and disappearances. I think she kept it to herself because she thought she could discover who was behind it all and deal with them herself, in her own way, with me as her patsy.'

'That's horrible,' Rose muttered. 'But why did she wait so long?'

'That's Kat Harris,' Belle replied. 'She could have voiced suspicions years ago, yet she let her friends – if that's what they ever really were to her – fall in the path of whoever is doing this and never told them.'

'But why?' Bette demanded.

Belle shrugged. 'Because she doesn't care about anyone other than herself. Her arrogance may yet be her downfall. I haven't been able to contact her. We'll see.'

'Are you going to point this out to your policeman?' Mavis asked.

'He'll have realised; be hopping mad, I expect. He had her in for questioning and she didn't say anything. Stupid, stupid woman. Anyway, no point speculating on anything to do with Kat Harris. I'm going to call Maggie.'

Belle dialled again, and Maggie Gilbert picked up. 'Hello, Belle. How's it going?'

'Interesting,' Belle replied. She gave Maggie a quick summary of the name discovery.

'Of course! I remember now, the Alpha Kat Crowd. God, they were so arrogant, weren't they. So, what can I do to help?'

'Do you remember Teresa Cormorant, from school?'

'Vaguely remember the name. Why?'

'She would have been born in the same academic year as us. Could you do a search for me, just a basic one to start: birth, marriage, et cetera? My gut is telling me that I shouldn't ignore the Cormorant connection, but I have no idea why. Kat Harris did say her name before she left and Helena Parry told me to look at the side-lines.'

'No problem, leave it with me. An hour?'

'Great. Bob's calling me back soon, hopefully to tell me he's got the go-ahead to start a proper investigation. If there's anything significant about Teresa Cormorant, I can tell him it's in the pipeline at least.'

No-one wanted to leave before they heard the outcome of Belle's phone calls. Bert provided more tea, with biscuits and cake that Bette proudly announced he'd made himself. 'I'm the cook, he's the baker,' she said, tucking into a slice of ginger cake.

'This is just like the one you serve, Posy,' Belle remarked.

'It is the one I serve. Bert's my best supplier.'

Bert blushed and faded into the background.

'Well, farming isn't enough these days. We had to diversify,' Bette said, straight-faced.

They went back to the subject of Tessa's cottage, talking over how easy or difficult it might be to find a solicitor who would be willing to take Andrew on.

‘He’s still well-known and respected in the legal community,’ Mavis said. ‘It won’t be easy.’

‘What about your new friend, Lord what’s-his-name? Could he help you find someone?’ Belle asked.

‘It’s Trevellows,’ Mavis said. ‘Maybe, I don’t know. I did promise I’d update him, so I’ll do that later. He seemed genuinely concerned about Tessa’s safety, so perhaps he’ll be upset enough to offer me assistance.’

The chatting was interrupted by the phone. ‘It’s Bob,’ Belle whispered. She answered the call, putting it on speaker again.

‘We’re all here, Bob.’

‘Good news. The Super has agreed we have to look into this. The alphabet of names with the Alpha Kat Crowd was enough to convince her this isn’t a series of co-incidences. I’m putting a team together. We’ll begin with all of the available documentation. I’m expecting to be able to hold a briefing by five this evening. Belle, I may need you back again in the next couple of days.’

‘Of course. I’ve asked Maggie to start basic information on a woman called Teresa Cormorant, by the way. I’m not sure why, but the Cormorant name has come up a few times and I just feel it’s worth checking her out. I’ll let you know if there’s anything to add to the case.’ She paused. ‘Bob, thanks for sticking with this.’

‘No prob. Right, I have to go. Let me know if Maggie comes up with anything we need to know.’

As soon as the call ended the phone rang again.

‘Maggie, hi, that was quick. I’m with friends and you’re on speaker.’

‘Hello, Belle’s friends,’ Maggie said. ‘Right, I haven’t found much as yet, but as a bit of background, John Cormorant was born in 1935, the son of Peter Cormorant and Helen Brass. He inherited a small garage from his father and built it into a major car franchise. He married Annette Wilson and their daughter, Helen Annette Teresa Cormorant was born in March 1969. She was the only child of the marriage. I can also confirm that Teresa Cormorant is dead. She died ten years ago, following a car accident. Seems she was drunk and ran into a tree. Died instantly.'

'Do you know who identified her?' Belle asked.

'It was her step-mother, Mary Elizabeth Cormorant. Is any of this helpful?'

'I'm not sure, yet. What was the actual date of her death?'

'Uh, let me check. There, it was the thirtieth of December 2010. The car caught fire and she died from internal injuries and burns.'

'Her step-mother was able to identify her?'

'So it says. Also, I can't find a marriage under her name. But her father was definitely John Cormorant, the car guy.'

'Thanks, Maggie. I'll let you know how it's going. I might need more, if that's OK with you?'

'Of course, especially if it helps Bob. He'll be buzzing right now,' she laughed.

***

At the Newport police station Bob already had the first half-dozen detective constables assigned to his team. In addition to Mike Goodman, who he put in charge of the first three teams, he was also expecting another sergeant. And, to his satisfaction, Mal Jenkins had been placed on gardening leave, at last, pending his retirement, and an imminent disciplinary investigation.

He had assigned each of the first three cases – Angela Stephenson, Bernie Moloney and Tina Lewis, to a pair of constables, leaving Sergeant Goodman to brief them on the case and set them to work on finding and assessing any remaining papers and other evidence.

'There's going to be a lot of work, Guv,' Mike Goodman said. 'Once they've got to grips with the evidence they'll have to start interviewing any remaining witnesses they can find.'

'You're getting help. I've just heard Donna Lewis from Ponty is joining us later today, with two of her team. We can round up another four, from uniform.'

That's good news, Guv. I've worked with her before. She's a stickler for detail, which is just what we're going to need. What should I tell her, apart from the history?'

'What we're looking for is a name, I don't know what name, but one that keeps appearing, in each case, when it shouldn't.'

Mike shrugged. 'OK, Guv. I'll let them all know. They're enthusiastic right now, but that'll wane after a few days of reading papers and reports.'

Bob grinned. 'If they want to be detectives, they're about to find out it's ninety per cent boring slog that gets us to the answer. It's just the TV cops who get to run around in fast cars chasing villains. Us poor sods usually have to walk, or take the bus.'

They walked off along the corridor to the incident room that was being set up.

Within days, Bob Pugh was to be proved wrong.

Chapter 34
Information

For the next couple of days Belle heard nothing from Wales. She took a trip with Rose into Truro to look for curtain material for the living room. Rose showed her around the older parts of the city and took her to a tearoom she would never have found on the tourist trail, a small, seventeenth century crooked house.

On the third day she decided to wander down to the café. There was no definite arrangement to meet up. She knew that Mavis was still at Bette's farm. Posy had no customers and was leaning on the counter, reading a magazine.

'Interesting?' Belle asked as she sat in the usual corner.

'Very. Travel brochure. I'm hoping by next year this pandemic will be over and I'll be able to take my Christmas break. I usually go off somewhere hot and exotic. It passes the time, at least, looking at the pictures.' She glanced at her watch. 'Something for lunch?'

'Oh, yes please. I'll have a toasted sandwich. Holidays, eh? I haven't been abroad for a long time. I renewed my passport last year, too.'

Something was clicking inside her head. Passport. Something knocked, like a woodpecker using her brain as a tree trunk, about passports. She had seen one recently, but where?

'Belle, I said, "did you want the Emmental or the Brie?"'

'What? Sorry, Posy. There's something about passports. It's important.'

'What exactly?'

'No idea, that's the problem,' Belle said, exasperated.

'Try this. Put your head back, close your eyes and take deep breathes in and out, each time count down from five. It's relaxing and helps access deep memory.'

'Nothing to lose,' Belle said and started. She'd reached the fourth breath when she stopped, put her hand up and slapped her head.

'Got it! I know what I saw, and when.'

Posy waited a few minutes as Belle frowned. 'Well, are you going to share?'

'Sorry, yes. When I was in Jane Perry's flat I stood on an envelope and picked it up for her. It was addressed to M. E. Cormorant. She said it was nothing, just a bill, I think, something for her landlady. She put it down on a table. But it wasn't any such thing. It was a passport. I recognised the envelope, not at the time, but that's what it was. Now, why would a passport for M. E. Cormorant, the landlady, be going to Jane's flat and not her own home?'

'Interesting question,' Posy replied. She opened her mouth, paused, opened her mouth again, and stopped again. 'I can't think of a reasonable answer, although there probably is one. Where does this Cormorant woman actually live? And who is she and how does she fit in?'

'I don't know the answer to either of those questions, but I need to find out.'

'Can your friend Maggie help again?'

'Probably.'

'Well, eat your sandwich then go home and ask.'

* * *

As she walked, Belle thought through and discarded most of her ideas. This was an official document. It should have gone to the registered address of its applicant. By the time she reached home there was just one idea left. Jane Perry was doing an illicit favour for M. E. Cormorant, probably the Mary Elizabeth Cormorant who had identified the body of Teresa Cormorant, in having the passport delivered to Jane's flat. Why? It still didn't join up any dots in the puzzle, in fact it just added more. But somehow, it had to be significant. Jane had never been the type to do anything illegal. Maybe she was in debt to this woman, couldn't pay her rent, or something similar. Damn! She hadn't wanted to speak to Jane again, but it was unavoidable. First, though, she could ask Maggie to research the Cormorant family, digging deeper.

She made the call, explaining that somehow this was crucial, but she couldn't say why, just a gut feeling. She offered to pay Maggie and Maze for the time she was spending on Belle's research, but Maggie refused.

'If it's going to help Bob in the end, I'm happy to do it for you. You'll probably have to wait until tomorrow or the day after, though. I have a looming deadline on one of my trickier brick wall cases and I've managed to make progress. Rather like yours, indirect, but adds just that bit more to the picture. As soon as I've drafted the interim report and sent it to the client, I'll have a few hours free. What in particular would you like me to look for?'

'Nothing too complicated, Mags. Just who they are, or were. I have what you told me about John Cormorant, the patriarch and we know that his daughter Teresa is dead. It's the second wife, Mary Elizabeth, I want the information on. Whatever you can find.'

'No prob. I'll call you tomorrow.'

Belle's enthusiasm moved from trot to canter, but she had to be patient. Maggie was prioritising her highly enough and she was grateful for that.

Back at the cottage she tried to read, but couldn't concentrate as she thought over what was still outstanding, people to whom she could speak. She had given up trying to call Kat Harris. Waste of time. She could go back to Gwen. She might remember a girl called "Hattie", the name Edgar Leonard had said was who Tina might have been talking to before she disappeared.

'Hello, Belle. How's it going?'

'It's moving on, Gwen.' She still couldn't say too much, just in case. 'A few more names have come up and I was wondering if you remembered any of them. One is a girl called "Hattie". Does that ring any bells?'

'Um, let me think. Yes, I do remember someone, but I think it was … no, I'm not certain. Can you give me more time? It may come back to me.'

'Of course. And what about someone whose family name was Cormorant?'

'I do remember a Cormorant. Now, what was her first name?'

'Might it have been Teresa?'

'Maybe. Sorry, Belle. They are familiar, though.'

'That's fine, thanks, Gwen. If you do remember any more, could you give me a call?

'No problem.'

'How's Mary Conroy, by the way? I'd hoped to meet up with her again but I had to get home, with the firebreak looming.'

'I haven't seen her. We keep planning to meet in person, but something always comes up. Mary's changed since we were in school, hasn't she.'

'She's a lot more confident than I remember. She puts it down to Australia,' Belle replied.

'Well, that's true of many of us. Roger, in my case.'

'Thanks, Gwen.'

Another conversation with Mary Conroy wouldn't do any harm. Gwen was right, Mary had changed since their school days. Belle remembered a quiet, small, round-shouldered girl. Mary certainly wasn't small, not now. Maybe the round shoulders had been deliberate, to make herself look smaller than she actually was. Given the way in which Sue Jones had been goaded because of her height, that was understandable. Mary had been the religious one in school, very intensely so. Well, she'd grown out of that, too. She'd like to get more of Mary's insight into her treatment by Kat Harris, and the others. She didn't remember Mary being particularly close to anyone. Gwen, but not especially so. But it was Jane who had given her Mary's contact details. Yes, definitely another chat with the ebullient Australian.

Eventually her brain couldn't hold another thought or idea. She closed the book and went to run a bath.

* * *

A buzzing noise close to her ear woke Belle with a start. She sat bolt upright. Wasp! Phobia reaction kicked in and she jumped out of bed, clutching for a weapon, picked up the towel she had left on the bed and headed for the source. It was the phone on the bedside table.

She huffed, dropped the towel and grabbed it.

'Were you asleep?' Maggie Gilbert said.

'Yes. What time is it?'

'Almost ten.'

'What! I've slept for almost twelve hours, yet again. Sorry, Mags. Give me a minute. I'll call you back.' She fell back onto the bed. Having been in a deep sleep she had awoken unsure for a few seconds of where she was. Of course, she was home. And there weren't any wasps this late in Autumn, or there shouldn't be. She sat up again and reached out for the phone.

'Sorry. Bit disorientated there. I thought the phone was a buzzing insect.'

Maggie laughed. 'I have initial news for you about the Cormorants. I've found the first marriage. John Cormorant married Annette Wilson when they were both in their early thirties. As you know, Teresa was their only child. Annette Cormorant died when Teresa was five. He stayed single until Teresa was twenty, when he married again, this time to Mary Elizabeth deSouza. He was fifty-five and she was twenty-one. Less than two years later he died of a heart attack. The probate was claimed by Mary Elizabeth as his widow. There doesn't seem to have been a will.'

'Interesting. And who was Mary Elizabeth deSouza? Have you been able to find out anything about her?

'No, that's it so far. I can't find any record of a birth in the UK for Mary Elizabeth deSouza. I'm going to get the Cormorant/deSouza marriage certificate today, see if it tells me anything new. We'll get their marital status and where they were living at the time, plus the names of the witnesses and where the marriage took place.'

'I'm guessing the status will be that he was a widower and she was single. Big age difference, wasn't it?'

'Yes. Thirty-four years. One wonders.'

'I won't speculate until you have the certificate. Can you give me a call back when you have it, Mags?'

'Of course. I must finish my client's report and call them this morning. I'll head down to the registry office this afternoon and give you a call this evening.'

'Thanks, Mags. I know you're busy.'

'It's no problem. By the way, I was right, Bob is buzzing. When I first met him he told me about his "copper's nose". It twitches when something's up and he said last night it's in full twitch mode now. Belle, you will be careful, won't you? You have been threatened, after all and the damage to your garden was nasty.'

'I promise. I'm heading down to Posy's café in an hour or so. They're a good bunch. They have my back.'

'That's good to know. Call you later.'

At midday the group assembled in the café. Belle brought them up to date on the news about the Cormorants.

'So Teresa Cormorant and Mary Elizabeth deSouza were almost the same age,' Rose said, 'and you think Teresa was in school with you?'

'Yes, that's right. What are you thinking?'

'Was there a Mary Elizabeth deSouza at school, too? Maybe that's how she met Teresa's father. If they did know each other, it must have been odd for them, when Mary Elizabeth became Teresa's step-mother.'

'I don't recall anyone of that name,' Belle mused. 'She could have been either a year below or a year above, depending on when her birthday fell within the academic year, but it's a good point. They must have got on well enough, because it was Mary Elizabeth who identified Teresa's body after the accident.'

'But they could have hated each other,' Bette said.

'I don't think so, Bette. According to the death certificate – I haven't seen it but Maggie has given me the details – they lived in the same house at the time of Teresa's death, which was also the address of John Cormorant at the time of his marriage to Mary Elizabeth.'

'Do you know anything about the house? Would it help to know?' Mavis asked.

'I don't and you're right, Mavis. Every little bit of information helps. I wonder if it means Mary Elizabeth Cormorant is still at the house?'

'That's a reasonable supposition, Posy. I'll text Maggie to see if she can add it to her list of research. I don't want to overburden her, though, until I know if it matters.'

'I'd ask her anyway,' Bette interjected. 'Like you said, every bit of information helps and even if she can't get to it today, it's worth the ask.'

'Agreed. I'll text her later. Now, what news, Mavis?'

It was Bette who answered. 'We've been having fun, haven't we, Mave?' she said with a grim smile. 'Didn't take him long to figure out where she'd gone. He came hammering on the door, demanding she come out. What he got was Bert with a pitchfork and a couple of our workers. They can look pretty fierce when they have to. They're lambs, actually, but they'd been practising scowling all morning. I thought they looked like pantomime villains, but Andrew Tregoss didn't. They saw him off in a trice. All right, Mave?' She put her hand on Mavis' shaking arm. 'He won't come back. Bert saw to that, told him that he couldn't answer for what would happen. Called him a thief and a wife beater and told him if he tried to call the police, the whole town would know soon enough who was the real Andrew Tregoss. I think it did the trick. Andrew knows Bert's family has lived in St Foy for eight generations. Bert has respect in these parts.'

Belle covered Mavis' hand with her own. 'Don't worry, Mave. Bette's right. I know his type. He's a coward and a bully. He won't be back. How's it going with the new solicitor?'

Mavis smiled. 'Very well, actually. I mean, it's early days, but His Lordship recommended him and he's keen to please His Lordship and the costs are very reasonable, much less than I expected.'

Bette raised an eyebrow at Belle over Mavis head. '*Very keen to please His Lordship*,' she mouthed.

'That's good news. Does he say how long it's going to take?'

'Quite a while, apparently, because of the confusion over the house numbers and the trust will have to be involved. He's says I have to be patient, but he also thinks it's a good idea if I move in with Tessa, so I'm doing that this coming weekend.'

'Is Tessa pleased?'

'Delighted,' Rose said. 'I was with her earlier. She's looking forward to the company. I told her all about the problem and about Andrew's part in it, as Mavis said it was OK for me to tell her.'

'Bert's going to help with the rest of Mavis' belongings, and she's having a few pieces of furniture too. There's no room in Tessa's, but we're going to store it in one of our barns. The bastard's not getting everything. I don't think he'll object when Bert and the boys turn up.'

'Probably won't be there, if Bert lets him know he's coming. He's not a man for confrontation, at least, not with other men.'

'I can help, too,' Belle said, 'if you want someone else with you, to pack up your personal stuff.'

'Bless you, Belle, and thanks, but Bette is coming with me.'

'He usually crosses the street when he sees me coming,' Bette said.

Belle was torn about whether to speak up about something that was bothering her. She knew Andrew's type of mind. If Bert warned her they were coming it was likely he wouldn't be there. But it was also likely he would destroy whatever he knew was most precious to Mavis. Anything he could do to hurt her would give him pleasure. Personal mementos, photographs, precious inherited china and so on. She feared they would find it smashed or gone. She decided she had to say it, and did so. The result was silence, with Mavis looking at her in horror.

'You're right,' Mavis said, after a few moments as the implications of Belle's speech sunk in. 'He's nasty and spiteful. But what can I do? There's so much in that house that I can't lose.'

They all sat, staring at the table, before Rose spoke.

'Before Saturday, we have to lure him out of the house. I think he's changed the locks, Mavis, so your keys won't work. I happened to walk past and saw someone at work at the front door. So, we'll have to figure out another way to break in and gather up your stuff.'

'Breaking and entering! And you a vicar's wife,' Bette said, with a wicked grin.

'I'll tell Harry, of course. He'll be cross, but he'll understand why we have to.'

'Is there an alarm system, Mavis?' Posy asked.

'Yes, but it's an old-fashioned one. You have to put in a key and turn it. The key is usually on top of the box in the hallway next to the door. The only door alarms are the front and kitchen, and the French windows at the back.' She gave Bette a knowing look.

'What he doesn't know, and I don't know why I never told him, but now I'm glad I didn't, is that I have a spare alarm key.'

Bette clapped her hands together. 'Excellent, Mave. All we have to do now is figure out how we get into the house.'

Posy stood up. 'You can leave that to me.'

'Were you a burglar in your past life, Posy?' Bette said.

'There are many things you don't know about my past life,' Posy said, as she began gathering up plates and cups.

As there is for all of us, that we don't want anyone else to know about, Belle thought. 'Right, let's meet up again in the morning. Posy, I'm thinking you'll have a plan by then?'

'Oh yes. Leave it to me. I have preparations to make.'

Chapter 35

Revenge

Bob Pugh and his team had been hard at work for two days; they were weary, with sore eyes and their initial enthusiasm had begun to wane. There was also an air of unease about the discovery that one of their own had been more involved in the cases than anyone had previously realised. In the early evening of the second day he called them all together, as the local pizza and Italian restaurants delivered a mountain of food. Thanks to the descendants who remained from the war-time immigrant Italian community in the area of Pill, not far from the police station, there were stunningly good takeaway outlets.

'Tuck in and enjoy, ladies and gents. Tomorrow, we hit the streets to interview, and re-interview as many of the family members, friends and witnesses as we've been able to identify. Right, I'm going to hand over to Donna, to summarise what we know so far.'

Donna Lewis stepped up to the whiteboard and began to take them through the history of each case. She opened with the story of the party and how the group of women whose deaths and disappearances they were investigating had ruined it, and how one of those they'd bullied had committed suicide a year later.

'So we believe they are actually all dead, and these are revenge killings?' a constable asked.

'Yes,' Bob replied. 'And before any of you ask a sceptical question, I'm not going to ask how many of you sitting here bullied others at school and how many of you were victims, but the latter will know what it's like and may understand how this group of victims felt.'

A hand went up at the back of the room, a female constable. 'I know what it was like, Guv. I hated every minute I had to spend in school. I used to truant and it was me who ended up getting into trouble, not them.'

'Thank you,' he said, smiling in acknowledgement. 'That's so often the story. As adults we can look back and shrug, or at least some of us can.' He spotted uncomfortable shifting in seats and heads looking away. 'Now, here's what we also know. The leader of the group, a woman called Georgina Kathryn Harris, AKA Kat Harris, married name Francois, was in Newport until a week ago. She's now missing. She'd been investigating, in the hope she could save herself, but went off the radar last Wednesday. She'd booked herself a flight to Mexico and I believe from there she was going to drive up into Texas where she now lives. Update: she's disappeared. She didn't get on the flight and there's no sign of her elsewhere. She'd hired a car, but that's been found at the Airbnb, where she'd been staying under the name of Francois, and she hasn't used her bank account since last Wednesday. Normally, I wouldn't be concerned yet, but under the circumstances, we need to find her. The final thing, I've reason to believe that members of the Cormorant family may somehow be involved. Some of you will remember Cormorant Motors. The owner, John Cormorant, died about thirty years ago. His daughter, Teresa Cormorant, is also dead, ten years ago, in a car crash. There's just the widow, Mary

Elizabeth Cormorant, remaining. She's off the radar, too. We'll be starting on her tomorrow, so another long day coming up. Donna will have the assignments first thing. Enjoy your food, go home, sleep and be back bright and early tomorrow.'

They chatted amongst themselves as they left the office over the next half hour, leaving Bob, Mike and Donna.

'Are you really concerned about Kat Harris?' Donna asked, munching pizza.

'Yes,' Bob replied. 'We had her in last week. She's arrogant enough to think she could sort this out herself.' He picked up papers from a file he had brought in with him. 'I did background research, in the US, today. Here's the result. She is a registered PI, but she's a nasty piece of work. Killed a few people in the course of her enquiries. Unscrupulous type who'll take on any case for money.'

He handed a copy of the report to Mike and Donna. 'I'm going to ask Belle Harrington to come back again tomorrow. She knew all of them personally, and she's met with the victims of the bullying in the last few weeks. Kat Harris was trying to have them work together, on her own terms of course. I'll be asking Belle to speak to us. She might have useful insights we'll never pick up from paperwork and computers. Anyway, that's me done. You two should head off, too.'

He headed out of the station, leaving the two sergeants discussing the assignment pairings for the following day. His gut was troubling him; nothing to do with the pizza. Something was telling him that they were about to break open something huge. The next few days would tell.

Chapter 36

Disclosure

Bob's phone call to Belle came the following morning. Reluctantly, she agreed to go, but only after a demand for assurance from him that her presence was necessary as well as useful. After all, she could have given the team her insights by phone.

'It will be better coming from you in person, Belle. You're an expert witness. They can ask questions; they're paired up, with each pair concentrating on a case, so twelve in all, plus my two sergeants. Please believe me, it will make a difference. It's tough for them, especially the pairs looking at the first two cases, it being so long ago. Some of them weren't born when those events took place.'

'So it's true, policemen are getting younger.'

'Tell me about it. I know they call me 'grandad', behind my back.'

She laughed. 'OK, Bob. I'll drive up tonight and be with you tomorrow. What time would you like me there?'

'How does eight o'clock sound? I have an early briefing, seven thirty, then you can talk to them and then we're sending them out again to interview the family members and friends and colleagues we've been able to trace. If you're willing to stay on, we can get back together around sixish for a progress report. I'm hopeful by then they'll have picked up insights they can share.'

'OK. One question. Has the name Cormorant come up at all, and is there any news about Kat Harris?'

'That's two questions, and the answer is the same to both. No, and before you ask, I am now officially concerned about Kat Harris. She's gone silent. Of course, she'll be good at that, but there's no evidence that she made any preparations to do so. She had a plan to return to the US, but never made it.'

'She's a devious woman, Bob.'

'I know; I have a report from the US about her activities in her PI role. They don't make pleasant reading. But, these days, it's not easy to go silent. Too many ways to track people.'

'Not one of the better aspects of our modern society. Anyway, let's not get started on that. I'll see you tomorrow, then.'

'Thanks.'

This meant she couldn't be part of Posy's plan to enter Mavis' house and extract her belongings, and she had to let Posy know. Posy took it well enough.

'There are enough of us and we couldn't all go in with her. You head off to Wales. That's your priority right now. We can manage, but let's keep in touch. You'll let us know how yours is going and I'll tell you about the big raid.'

'When are you planning for?'

'Day after tomorrow.'

'Well, let's wish each other good luck. Would you let the others know for me? Tell Mavis I'm sorry.'

'Of course. Now, get yourself ready and drive carefully.'

* * *

At the apartment block Belle checked around before letting herself into the building, making sure there was no-one waiting to tailgate in behind her. When she reached the fifth floor, after the lift had whooshed to a stop she poked her head out, checked the foyer and waited a few seconds with her hand on the 'close door' button. Again, it was silent. She only had to cross to the right, to her front door and let herself in. Could there be someone waiting behind the door that led to the stairwell? For a moment she almost pushed the button to go back down again, but steeled herself. Apart from Bob and the girls no-one knew she was travelling tonight. 'Get a grip, Belle Harrington,' she murmured. Taking a deep breath, head up, she marched out of the lift and to her flat, put the key in the door and let herself in.

A few minutes of checking confirmed no-one was in the flat and she flopped down onto the settee, aware of how quickly her heart had been beating. This was ridiculous. She got up again, put the deadbolt on the door and settled herself down for the evening.

* * *

The following morning, just after six thirty, she opened the curtains to a dawning grey sky with clouds bearing down and obliterating the view of the hills and the channel. Below, the river looked muddy and sluggish, as the tide turned and made its way back down to the sea. It felt depressing. She would call the estate agent as soon as they opened their doors. There had been a couple of immediate viewings, but nothing since. Still, it was only just over a week, and she wasn't in a rush to sell.

After half an hour of coffee and reading the news on her tablet, she showered and was ready. For what? There was nothing much to do before the walk down to the police station. She thought about calling Maggie, but decided against it. Maggie would let her know if there was any update.

Her phone pinged an incoming text. Thinking it might be from Cornwall, she checked. It was from Jane Perry.

Hi Belle. Just wondering how you are?

Should she reply? There was probably no reason why not. She didn't need to mention that she was in Newport, nor that Jane would be receiving a visit from the police during the day, as a witness at the time of Angela Stephenson's death.

I'm fine, thanks Jane. You?

Yes. Do you know if anything more is happening, about the dead and missing girls?

Not really.

So where are you at the moment?

Now what did she say? Lie or admit to being local? No more lies.

I'm back in Newport. Meeting with estate agents. I'm selling my apartment.

Oh no, that's so sad. Would you like to meet up one more time?

Sorry, Jane, appointments all morning, then driving home. Next time.

I understand. Hope it all goes well for you. Goodbye.

Jane, just one question. Does the name 'deSouza' mean anything to you? Or a girl called Hattie?

Why? Is it important?

Probably not. Kat Harris said something about Teresa Cormorant so I followed up. Turns out your landlady, Mary Elizabeth Cormorant, was a deSouza when she married. And Teresa Cormorant is dead.

I don't know anything about that. But, name is not unfamiliar. Not sure why. May have been someone at school. I'll think it over.

Thanks. I'll be driving home later.

Bye.

It was time to leave for the police station. As soon as she arrived she told Bob Pugh that she'd mentioned the Cormorant and deSouza names to Jane Perry, but it hadn't led to anything.

'One of the teams will be calling on her later. Did she say where she was?'

'No, but I didn't ask. I don't want to get too involved with her. I told her I'm selling the apartment and that I'm going home later. I'm assuming that's OK with you?'

'Yep, can't see why it should be a problem. Anyhow, the boys and girls are almost ready for you. They have questions.'

He walked Belle into the incident room and took her to stand in front of the whiteboard. It was now divided into six sections. Each one had a picture of a schoolgirl and, where it had been available, the matching adult. The only one missing detail was Faith Shepherd.

'That's because it's an ongoing criminal investigation,' he replied to her question. 'We're liaising with the team handling it while we concentrate on these. We have the other five. Is there anything there that doesn't seem right to you?'

She walked along the length of the board, looking at the photographs, reading the notes, becoming lost in the memories of this innocuous looking group of schoolgirls and thinking of the devastation they had caused to other, innocent lives.

'It was my photograph on the reunion website that started all this,' she murmured to Bob, who was following her along. 'If I hadn't put it out there, none of this would be happening. I'm not sure if that's a good thing, or not.'

'Why would it not be a good thing?'

'Because I'm now constantly looking over my shoulder. Last night, and again this morning, my heart was in my mouth at the apartment. Someone out there is watching me, threatening me.' She paused and shook her head. 'There's nothing out of place here, at least, no factual errors.'

As she studied the board the room had filled up and she turned to face a dozen or so eager and interested young faces. Bob introduced her. Belle was used to standing in front of groups, giving presentations on difficult subjects. Over the years she had trained hundreds of people in senior management positions on the legal aspects of employee relations, as well as ways of dealing with difficult employees, hopefully to avoid formal disciplinary action, but also on how to manage the internal processes, if it became unavoidable. Most of the people she had trained had hated the subject, she had known that, so she had developed a way of presenting that allowed them to be as comfortable as possible with this most unpleasant of managerial responsibilities, along the way gaining herself a highly favourable reputation in a major international company. She gazed out now at the eager faces all turned to her. Her usual dress these days was cargo pants, jeans or sweats, with sloppy jumpers and t-shirts. Today, she had wanted to make sure her audience would respect her presence and her knowledge, so she had un-mothballed one of her expensive, now redundant, business suits and a pair of shoes with heels so high she had to take each step carefully, having forgotten how to walk in what she now considered the most ridiculous and uncomfortable item of women's wear. Still, she could see them forming their opinions. The world hadn't changed a bit, she thought sadly.

'Good morning. I'm going to give you what I hope will be insights into the ugly, nasty atmosphere this group behind me created, albeit a long time ago. The effects of bullying never, ever go away from the soul of any human being who has suffered it.

Ever. I will also talk to you about the effect it had at the time on a particular set of victims. You won't be hearing anything you haven't heard before, but I hope that, hearing it from someone who was there – and I'm not going to hold back – will help you understand the environment this group created until they were finally stopped. Someone eventually decided to put an end to it, to fight fire with fire.' She paused and took a quick glance at Bob, not certain how much he knew. The slightest of returning nods and raised eyebrows with a tight smile, told her that he knew everything. 'I'm not going to say who it was, but I will tell you what they did and the extent of the relief it brought. But, for the worst sufferers, the scars were still there.'

For the next twenty minutes she held them in thrall. She was an electrifying speaker. There wasn't a movement in the room. Apart from Belle, no-one even noticed the two people, a man and a woman, both in uniform, who had entered the room as she began to speak.

At the end she said to the group, 'OK, questions?' Every hand shot up. She picked them out, one by one, told them as much as she could. Eventually, she asked the couple at the back if they had anything to ask, thinking she might as well acknowledge their presence. As she did so, Bob, who had taken a seat at the front of the room, turned round and jumped out of his chair.

The man shook his head. 'No, thank you, Mrs Harrington. I was visiting and interested in the subject and I have to say, that was very impressive.'

The sound of his voice caused every head to turn.

'As you were,' the man said smiling and ushered the accompanying woman out of the room.

Bob grinned and nodded to the woman as they left.

'Well, not every day we get a visit from the Deputy Chief Constable.' He turned back to Belle. 'From all of us, I think, thanks. That was informative and, honestly, fascinating. As you've probably realised, it will help the team when they go out to continue their interviews.' He turned to them. 'Right, off you go, you lot.'

They jumped up, chatting in pairs as they left the room. As soon as the room was empty apart from Bob and the two sergeants, Belle took off her shoes, leaned down into her briefcase and took out a pair of pumps, which she put on with a sigh of relief.

'Couldn't stand those damn things a minute longer. They're going to a charity store as soon as I get home. So, was that OK?'

'That was beyond OK,' Donna Lewis said. 'It takes something to hold a group like this, amongst whom were, I have to say, sceptics who honestly believed bullying was no more than a bit of banter, like. They don't think that now, I could see.'

'And a few biting their lips, I saw,' Mike added. 'Guilty as charged, at some time.'

'It's the psychology and the human experience that gets to them,' Belle said. 'Emotions they've all known. The soul of the victim. And in this case, someone has been so badly affected they've turned into the avenger. By the way, I guessed those other two were senior. The Deputy Chief Constable, eh? And the other was your Chief Superintendent?'

'Yep,' Bob replied with a grin. 'She must have had quite a job to convince him to let me run with this. He doesn't just happen to be in a building. He wanted to see for himself and you did a great job impressing him. Not easy. Thank you. He won't hold us back, now.'

'The team was impressed, too,' Mike said. 'It will give them sensibilities they didn't have when they carry out their interviews. Your two case studies were … moving.'

‘I thought they would be,’ Belle said. ‘Personal experience goes a long way.’

Bob nodded.’ Horrible stories, Belle. Were you involved in both of them?’

‘Yes. I was the last person to speak to the first one, before she hanged herself. The memories and images stay in your head.’

A few moments’ silence followed.

‘Right, time to get on with it. I’m going to speak to the Super. The Man will have gone by now.’

‘Elvis has left the building,’ Belle said and they all laughed. ‘I’m going home later, Bob. I just need a quick meet-up with the estate agent, then I’ll head off.’

‘You’ve made a difference,’ he said.

* * *

Belle decided she needed a walk to shake off the agitation of speaking about the two case studies. It hadn’t been part of her original plan, but came to her as she was speaking, that to widen out the stories she could tell them, from her personal experience, would give them a better feeling of the devastation that bullying could cause. But it had been hard for her. Although the cases were now a decade old, she still felt the impact. She took a longer route back, down through the town to the famous Transporter Bridge and followed the footpath alongside the river back to the apartment. The early morning mist had not lifted, instead thickened into a dense fog that swirled around her and over the river, lying low on the water. It was disorientating and she was relieved when the footbridge came into view. As she started to walk across, her phone rang. It was Jane Perry, again. She dismissed the call. It rang again. Gritting her teeth, she answered.

'Yes, Jane. What is it?' She hoped her tone was sufficiently off putting.

'Sorry, Belle, sorry to call. But it's important,' Jane whispered breathlessly. 'After our texts I thought I remembered about someone called deSouza. I went back through my school mementos, and there was someone. But not who I thought it might be. So, I've been checking out Mary Elizabeth Cormorant and I've found out where she actually lives, can you believe!'

As the woman was Jane's landlord, Belle was surprised that Jane didn't already know, and said so.

'Oh, no. I pay my rent by bank transfer, to a company address.'

'OK, so what's the deal?'

'Look, it's a bit shocking.'

Belle sensed what was coming.

'I think we should go to see her. She's involved. Please, Belle, come with me. I'm too nervous to do this alone.' There was a pause, then, 'I think she may be the person who's been threatening you.'

Chapter 37

Deceit

'Belle, are you still there?'

Belle had said nothing for several seconds. 'Yes, I'm here. Why do you think that, and if she is, why would I want to meet with her? After all, if she really is the person who threatened me, that would mean she's involved in multiple crimes. I really don't want to meet someone that dangerous.'

'I've tracked her down to a house on the outskirts of Newport, towards Risca. I've been to watch it this morning and she's on her own. Now, please don't be cross with me, but I've been talking to Mary Conroy. She says she'll come along if I need her. I was thinking of her as a backup, if you said no, but maybe the three of us together would be more than a match for Mrs Cormorant. What do you say?'

'You haven't told me why you think she's the person who's been threatening me, Jane. And frankly, I think we should leave this to the police.'

'No,' Jane shouted. 'If I'm wrong I'll make a complete fool of myself, and I'll also lose my home. She's my landlady; she can have me thrown out. Belle, I can't lose my little flat. I know it probably doesn't seem much to you, but it's everything to me.'

'I understand that. But you still haven't told me why you think Mary Elizabeth Cormorant is the person who's been threatening me.'

'No, well, it was the email address. I had to contact her yesterday over a leak in my kitchen. Usually the company answers, but this time she responded personally. The email name was *lizzibird.* You told me that was the address of the emails you had.'

Belle stopped walking and leaned on the handrail of the bridge. 'Did I? I see. Give me five minutes, Jane, please.'

'Well, OK, but please, please don't speak to the police. Not yet. If I'm correct, then you can call them right away, after we've seen her. I promise I'll be very careful in how I speak to her. I won't give her any notion that we suspect her.'

'Just doorstepping her doesn't sit right with me, Jane. It's too dangerous.'

Jane sighed. 'Well, it's up to you, but Mary will come with me. I'll let you know what happens.' She ended the call.

Belle walked slowly across the footbridge to the apartment block entrance, thinking furiously. Jane had said she couldn't do it without her, then told her Mary Conroy was also involved. Nevertheless, could she really let Jane and Mary go alone? Did she really want to go? The answer to that question was easy. Of course she did. But she also didn't want to be reckless. She decided to speak to Bob Pugh, who would probably advise her to stay well clear, but when she dialled the call went to voicemail. Three times. On the third attempt she left a message, telling him where she was going and why, knowing she had just committed herself. So be it. She called Jane back.

'Jane, OK, I'll come with you and Mary, if she's in. But I'm not going past the doorstep. I just want to get a look at Mrs Cormorant, maybe ask a few questions.'

'Oh, thank you so much, Belle. Um, actually, Mary's already there, in her own car. I'll come and pick you up in five minutes.'

Belle waited in the car park, thinking about what they would say to this woman. Despite many potential ideas, none of them felt better than asking a direct question: *Did you warn me to stay away from the deaths and disappearances of former school pupils? And if so, why?*

Jane hadn't told her yet who she thought Mary Elizabeth deSouza was. And Maggie hadn't called with the marriage certificate information. This must have been someone from their schooldays, but Maggie hadn't recognised the name, either, nor any other Mary Elizabeth, nor a Hattie.

She decided to give Maggie a call. It had been over twenty-four hours since they had last spoken, so she felt sure Maggie wouldn't mind. But as she began to dial the number Jane arrived and she got into the small, aged Fiat Punto.

'Sorry, the heating doesn't work,' Jane breathed as they set off out of town on the road towards Risca. The fog hadn't lifted at all so Jane drove at a snail's pace. 'Horrible morning, isn't it? It should only take us ten minutes. It's just across the motorway junction, about five minutes on from there. It's a huge house and ...'

'Jane, please tell me about Mary Elizabeth deSouza. You said you think you remember her from school.'

'Yes, that's right. I think she was a year above us.'

'You think? You aren't sure?'

'No, but Mary's remembered the name, too, although she thinks it was two years above.'

They had reached the motorway overpass and Jane began to drive even more slowly, looking out for the road on which the house was situated.

'I don't remember anyone of that name, but I don't suppose that matters. Anyway ...'

'There it is!' Jane turned slowly off the road into a driveway. Belle couldn't see a property but assumed that was because of the fog. However, she did spot the name carved into one of the two stone pillars at the entrance to the drive. Hill House.

Jane's car crawled up the drive, rolling to a halt as the first glimpse of a house came into view. She pulled towards a rhododendron bush at the side of the drive. The house was a honey-coloured stone building, in the Georgian style with a portico and three floors of windows. Belle's immediate impression was that it was deserted. Many of the sash windows were boarded up and weeds grew out of the guttering along the length of the roof. There were holes in the façade where the brickwork had deteriorated.

'I can't believe anyone lives here, Jane, in this rotten state. And where's Mary?'

'I don't know. She was supposed to wait in her car, but as we passed it on the road it was empty. Mary can be impetuous; I hope she didn't decide to go ahead without us. Oh, look.'

The fog swirled and lifted slightly for a moment and a car came into view, a sleek, black Porsche Cayenne with a personalised numberplate.

'MET 1,' Belle said. 'I'd take a guess that the ME is for Mary Elizabeth.'

'So that's where my rent money goes,' Jane muttered. 'Nice for her. Come on, let's get closer.' She crept out of the car and tiptoed towards the house, beckoning Belle to follow her. As she reached the front window she ducked down and crept along underneath it. Belle almost laughed. *She's actually loving this*, she thought. As Jane reached the front door, she paused, gave it a push and it swung open. She beckoned to Belle again. Belle didn't move. Why would anyone leave their front door open, unless they had just gone in temporarily and were about to come back out again? She shook her head and beckoned to Jane to come back to the car, but this was met with a frown and another call to move forward. The silly woman was going to go in alone, damn it.

Reluctantly she left the car and walked towards the front door, without the dramatic creeping. The door was wide open and Jane had pinned herself against the door jamb underneath the portico.

'Do you think we should go in?'

'No, Jane, I do not. Ring the bell.'

'There isn't one.'

'Then knock. This must be an inhabited house, or at least it's not abandoned. We should give the owner a chance to come out. Jane gave a tentative single knock. No-one answered. There was only silence from within the house. Then, the sound of a door slamming, which made them both jump. But still no-one appeared. Belle stepped forward and knocked hard, three times. They waited. Nothing.

'Come on, let's go in, at least into the hallway,' Jane whispered and stepped forward before Belle could stop her. Belle put a foot over the threshold and looked around, then took another step inside. The carpet covering a scuffed parquet floor was threadbare and worn through in places. The décor was 1950s, but some of the original features, including a chandelier and ornate coving, remained. To their left a double width staircase led up a short flight of stairs, then turned ninety degrees and ended in a balcony above. An unpleasant smell permeated the corridor. Belle was so busy looking around she didn't notice that Jane had silently closed the door behind them.

As she was peering around, a low vibrating buzz started. Belle had put her phone in her pocket. She took it out.

'Don't answer that now,' Jane muttered.

Belle took no notice. 'Hi Maggie,' she whispered. 'Everything OK?'

'Why are you whispering?'

'Because I'm in a property called Hill House, somewhere off the Risca Road, with Jane Perry. We're supposed to find this Mary Elizabeth Cormorant here, but the place seems to be deserted. And Mary Conroy is also supposed to be here, but she's missing, too.'

'Oh my God! Get out of there now. And it can't be Mary Conroy, she ...'

Jane had grabbed the phone out of her hand.

'What are you doing! Give that back to me.'

Jane grabbed her arm. 'You're coming with me.' She pulled Belle a few steps forward, opened a door to their right and dragged her in, then pushed her down into an armchair.

Belle was shaking. Something was terribly wrong here. 'What is this Jane? It's not what you told me, is it?'

Jane grinned at her. It wasn't a pleasant grin, but spiteful and triumphant. She turned her head to the side. 'You can come out, now, my love.'

Another door opened. Mary Conroy walked into the room. In her right hand she held a long, gleaming kitchen knife.

Belle's heart was thumping, her stomach churning.

'You aren't Mary Conroy really, are you. Maggie Gilbert was about to tell me something about Mary.'

'Of course she isn't,' Jane replied, still smiling. Meet Teresa Cormorant. My wife. And, if you hadn't guessed yet, and I don't believe you've managed to put it together, I'll tell you. I'm Mary Elizabeth Cormorant. Mary Elizabeth Jane Perry, then deSouza and now Cormorant. Gotcha, Belle Harrington.'

Chapter 38

Transformation

She couldn't, mustn't, look afraid. Her shock at Jane's revelation and the change of demeanour that accompanied it had stunned her. Yet, no matter what they'd done, there was no excuse for them to kill her, or to hurt her in any way. Maggie knew where she was, too. And she'd guessed that something was wrong. Jane had brought her there. The question was why. She might as well ask it.

'Why am I here, Jane?'

Teresa answered. 'You wouldn't leave it alone, would you? I told you to, but you just kept ignoring me.'

'Oh, it was you, Teresa.' She paused for a moment. 'Teresa, was it you who destroyed my garden?'

The woman nodded. 'Yes, I thought it might put you off. Didn't work, did it. You keep coming back. You're like a pesky bluebottle. No matter how much you're shooed away, you keep coming back. You even got over Jane's attempt to poison you.' She tutted and rolled her eyes at Jane. 'She didn't put enough of the drug in the water. Well, this time, we'll make it permanent.' She said it matter-of-factly as she held up the knife.

Belle bit her lip. 'Do you want this, Jane? I can understand why you hated them, all of them. I have sympathy. But hurting me isn't going to help you, is it?'

Teresa began to walk towards her, but Jane put a restraining hand on her arm. 'Not yet, my darling. We need to think this through. Maggie Gilbert may well tell the policeman. She,' she nodded at Belle, 'managed to tell her where we are.'

Belle watched as Jane began to pace around the room. She couldn't help marvelling at how Jane had changed from the needy, small, hopeless persona into an upright, confident woman. Rather like a butterfly emerging from its cocoon. But this was one of those dangerous butterflies, the ones that retained toxins as they transformed. But you had to eat them, didn't you, to suffer. Stop! She knew her mind was wandering off into the absurd, staving off the rising panic, tasting bile in her throat. She could only hope that Maggie had done something. Anything. She needed to keep them talking, for at least ten or fifteen minutes, before she knew she was on her own, with no help coming.

Jane had pulled her ratty hair out of her face and put it up into a bun on the top of her head.

'You look, smart, Jane. Quite a transformation.'

Jane Perry stopped pacing and folded her arms, but couldn't prevent a self-satisfied smile and a nod.

'How long have you two been a couple?'

'Since we were in school,' Jane replied as she paced around the room. Teresa had moved to stand next to Belle's armchair, between her and the door, so there was no chance of distracting her and running out.

'None of you realised,' Teresa added, 'did you? You didn't even remember who "Hattie" might have been. That was me, Helen Annette Teresa Cormorant. H.A.T. You were all so stupid. Everything was going well, until Jane came up against Angela Stephenson at work. She saw us together, and she was going to tell everyone.'

'So what?' Belle replied. 'No-one cares if you're gay.'

'That's now. Back then, it wasn't the same. Jane would probably have lost her job, or would have been hounded out. Lovely Angela would have made sure of that. She had a go at blackmailing us, first. When we refused to pay, she announced she was going to tell the world about Jane. Said Jane was a pervert.' She spat on the floor.

'It wasn't that bad, surely, back in 1990?' *Keep her talking.*

'You don't have any idea, do you? We were just trying to live quietly. The awful deSouza had died. He was the pervert, he abused her. He married her when she was nineteen, sold to him by her mother.' Teresa's eyes flashed.

Belle guessed the 'awful deSouza' didn't die without assistance, but she wasn't going to question that now. And she wondered about John Cormorant, too. 'So what happened to the real Mary Conroy?'

'Brain tumour,' Teresa replied. 'She was thirty when she died. Tragic, but useful for us. We were in Australia at the time. Now that was a co-incidence, but beneficial for us. She had no family, she'd gone there alone. She was a nurse, but not working and she had no friends out there. Mary never had the knack of making friends. We presented ourselves as old schoolfriends, told the authorities she had no family.' She paused and laughed. 'We were the only people at her funeral. We got our hands on her birth certificate and her passport. Fortunately it needed renewing, so with her original birth certificate I made myself look as much like her as possible, hair, eye colour, you know, and renewed it. It worked. I've been Mary Conroy whenever I needed to be, ever since. I also had my own passport, of course, but that ran out when I "died",' she made the quotation marks in the air. 'Jane and I have been travelling for years, until this Covid thing.'

'And you've been stuck here since?'

'Yes, bloody annoying. We're leaving soon, for good. We'd planned to go in a couple of days. We anticipated the police might want to speak to us, as old school friends and witnesses, in Jane's case. As soon as that was done we were going to leave. But you've ruined that plan. God, I hate you.'

Belle glanced up. Teresa's expression was so intense she had to look away again, but what she'd seen convinced her the woman was as mad as a box of frogs. Jane knew it, too, she could see from the frequent worried glances at her wife. She began pacing, again.

'We have to go. The bags are ready upstairs, aren't they?'

Jane nodded. 'We'll take her with us. We'll keep off the motorway, use the 'B' roads in Kent and leave her somewhere in the middle of the countryside without her phone. By the time she gets to a phone we'll be long gone.'

'Kind of you,' Belle said, forcing a note of sarcasm.

'We'll put her in the boot,' Teresa said, ignoring her.

'No!' Belle shouted. 'I'm horribly claustrophobic. I'll have a panic attack and throw up. Look, you can lock me in the back of your car. You're right, by the time I get away from you it'll take me hours to contact someone. I take it you're going to Dover?'

'As if we'd tell you,' Teresa said.

Belle glanced at her watch. Ten minutes since Maggie's call. If no-one came in the next five minutes, she'd have to travel with them.

'I'll go for the bags,' Jane said. 'Keep her here. Don't give her a chance to run.'

'If she does …' Teresa replied, waving the knife.

'What happened to Kat Harris?' Belle asked. 'I haven't been able to get hold of her. Do you have her?'

Teresa smiled and waved the knife in the direction of the ceiling. Through the windows Belle spotted a newly dug pile of earth in front of the back fence. She felt sick.

'We couldn't wait until December, although that was the original idea, but she showed her hand, silly bitch. Asked to meet me. We knew she'd sussed me. I know what she intended; she probably expected to kill me, but between us we overpowered her.'

'And killed her?'

'Well of course we did.' She pushed herself down into Belle's face and shouted, 'It wasn't like she came here for a nice cup of tea and a cucumber sandwich, was it?' She stood again. 'Same way Sue Jones killed herself. Thought we'd let her feel what it was like to suffocate to death on the end of a rope. I thought it was too quick, given the misery she'd inflicted on Sue, but Jane said it was only right and proper.'

This time Belle thought she was actually going to throw up. She took deep breaths, blowing each one out slowly. However much she had hated Kat Harris, what they had done was barbaric.

The sound of thumping down the stairs told Belle that it was too late, Jane had brought their cases down to the hall. She came back into the room.

Belle tried to think of another delaying tactic. 'Teresa tells me you've killed Kat Harris, Jane.'

Jane nodded. 'She overplayed her hand. She wasn't expecting me, Just Teresa. Evil bitch that she was.'

'Yet, you always wanted to be one of the Alpha Kat Crowd, didn't you? I remember how you used to —'

'She found me,' Teresa interrupted, waving the knife. 'She didn't need them, after she found me.'

'Well, you kept up a good pretence of being "poor little Janey No-Mates", didn't you?' Belle said. 'Right through school and since. Good acting, Jane.'

Jane stared at her. 'You have no idea, Miss Goody Two Shoes Harrington. No idea what it was like to be me, to have to pretend to like that bunch of—'

'You weren't pretending,' Belle interjected. 'You were desperate to be one of them.' She knew provoking Jane might be the most dangerous, and last, thing she did, but she had to take the risk.

'Until I found Teresa, as she says.' She shook her head, pushing away the inconvenient memories, Belle thought.

'Right, enough. I'm just going to close all of the shutters and turn off the gas and electricity and water.'

'What for?' Teresa said. 'We're not coming back.'

'Habit,' Jane replied.

As she left the room, panic rose in Belle's chest. That was her last card. She couldn't think of anything else to delay them; then, so quickly she wasn't sure she'd seen it, there was a movement at the window. She blinked and looked again. A man ran past. The cavalry had arrived. Her hands began to shake. She wanted to laugh out loud with relief, but she had to keep Teresa's attention for a few more seconds. It wasn't over yet.

Her voice was faltering, but she turned to Teresa and called her attention. 'Teresa, is anyone else buried out there?'

'Tina Lewis. The veg are doing nicely,' Teresa giggled. 'She was a useless moaner in life, but she's made good compost.'

Jane came back into the room. 'Ready to go. Let's put the bags in first, then we can—'

She got no further as the French windows burst open and half a dozen men stormed in, screaming at them to get down on the floor. Each man carried a weapon, including Bob Pugh. Jane looked at them in disbelief, then horror, but sank to her knees, her mouth wide open.

Teresa did not. She howled in fury and grabbed at Belle, brandishing the knife. In the few seconds it had taken the men to enter the room, Belle had prepared herself, guessing at what Teresa might try to do. She grabbed the cushion that had been at her back and threw it up in front to shield herself, as Teresa's knife descended. It deflected the blow, giving her a few seconds to jump up and push out at Teresa. As she hoped, the woman was caught off balance and fell backwards, throwing out her hands to save herself as she fell, turning over and crashing face down.

The men were still yelling. 'Hands behind your head! Get down on the ground! Put your hands behind your head!'

Belle complied. They could sort out who was who once they secured the room. Teresa was not complying. She lay still, with two of the men now standing over her and shouting. She kept perfectly still, and Belle watched as blood began to ooze out either side of her chest. One man looked at the other, then leaned down and turned her over. Teresa had fallen on the knife, which had penetrated her chest up to the hilt. She was wide-eyed and staring. The man put a hand to her neck, then shook his head. Teresa Cormorant was dead, for the second and permanent time.

Bob Pugh pulled Jane up from the floor and had started to caution her, when she looked over and saw Teresa. The howl she let out was more animal than human, high and keening. Bob indicated to his sergeants, both of whom had entered the room, to take Jane away. He walked over to Belle and helped her up.

Belle's legs were no longer working. She collapsed against him.

'It's OK, it's over,' he said quietly. 'We'll get you seen by a doctor, then we can talk it over.'

She shook her head. 'It's not over,' she said as tears ran down her face. 'You have to get people in, forensic people. Tina Lewis is out there.' She looked up at the garden and Bob's jaw dropped. She nodded and added, 'and Kat Harris is upstairs. The bad smell in the hall.' She turned away from him and threw up over the threadbare carpet.

Chapter 39

Aftermath

It had been a cold, wet winter in St Foy. The Curiosity Club continued to meet regularly, occasionally to discuss local issues, more often to chat and support. Mavis' Aunt Tessa had died a few days into the New Year, at home, quietly. Mavis had been upset but resigned. Tessa had reached her ninety fifth birthday a few days earlier and the group held a quiet gathering. They could already see her deterioration. Pearl Hawkesworth Fox was not invited.

The support was mainly for Belle.

Jane Perry had, in the end, given up everything, pleaded guilty to six counts of murder and her part in three further deaths. Her barrister had tried to persuade her to enter a plea of insanity, but she hadn't agreed. He had spoken at length about her upbringing, resulting in her mother selling her to Johannes deSouza. But it hadn't made any difference. She stuck doggedly to her plea of guilty and received a life sentence.

Tina Lewis' remains had been removed from the garden. Jane revealed that it had been Teresa who had organised and carried out Denise Goodright's drowning, being an expert scuba diver. The alcoholic, drug-addled Faith Shepherd had gone to Bristol in December 2015, to hide from the police after the death of a client. Jane and Teresa had found her there, a year later and taken her to the Cormorant house, having convinced her she was wanted for the client's murder, from which they could shelter her. The woman had been so confused by her addictions that she hadn't objected. They had even taken her out on shopping trips and visits to the seaside, made her 'one of them', Jane had explained. But she had become restless and was demanding to be let go, so they had drugged and restrained her, until she had come in useful when they needed to have the police discover the person who had run down Bernie Moloney and confess to it, then kill herself.

Kat Harris had been the last one, found in one of the upstairs bedrooms. No matter how vile the woman had been, her death must have been terrible.

Belle also hated that she had believed the killings were all down to the bullying. Jane and Teresa had had terrible lives, and she felt compassion for that, but they had killed out of self-preservation, then greed, then madness.

Belle hadn't attended the trial, such as it was, which wasn't much. Because of the confession there was no gory detail and the press quickly lost interest.

Then, a month after being jailed, Jane asked for a visit from Belle, who's initial reaction was 'no way', but after much discussion, reluctantly agreed that she would go. The visiting order was sent and she set off, driven by Posy to the Category A prison.

It wasn't Belle's first visit to such an establishment. At one point in her career she had worked with prison teachers and lecturers and had met them 'on the job'. So, the procedure of entering, being searched then taken through the series of locked doors didn't faze her.

In the car en route she and Posy talked about how she would handle the visit.

'It depends on what Jane has to say,' Belle said. 'If she's difficult, I'll just leave.'

'If she's difficult, you won't have a choice. There'll be a guard present, who'll stop the visit as soon as there's the slightest hint it might get out of hand.'

'I don't know why she wants to speak to me, anyway,' Belle said.

* * *

When Jane entered the room, despite the prison clothes and the guard, Belle saw just the same 'poor Jane'. But, when she sat down, that changed.

Jane looked around, made a pretence of spitting at Belle, then sat, legs sprawled under the table, arms folded. This was not 'poor, needy Jane'. This was the real person under the disguise she had perfected over the years. At last, Belle felt comfortable. She had been in a similar situation many times, albeit not with a murderer. Nevertheless, she was ready, now.

She matched the body language, sat back and smiled. 'Well, you had us all fooled, didn't you, me included.' She kept her tone light, and uninterested. 'You wanted this meeting. What do you want to say to me?'

'I've been speaking to the prison psychiatrist. She thinks it's a good idea to speak to you, as the person who put me here.'

'Do you think it's a good idea, Jane? I don't believe you're allowed to tell me anything new, or something that didn't come at your trial.'

'Nothing 'they' don't already know. You weren't at my trial. Why not?'

'I didn't want to hear it.'

In a sudden, rapid movement, Jane shot forward and put her hands on the table, palms down. 'You killed her,' she whispered.

The prison officer started to move forward, but Belle shook her head.

'It's OK. No, Jane, you killed her. She tried to kill me but I resisted and she fell onto her knife. But you put this ending in place, a long time ago. Teresa's death is at your door, not mine. Now you've got that off your chest, is that it? Do you have anything else, or can I go?'

Belle was considering Jane's posture and expressions, the small signs of anxiety: too much swallowing, a twitch of the mouth, flaring nostrils. She was on the brink.

'Last chance, Jane. Five … four … three … two … one.' She stood up.

'No! Sit.' Jane closed her eyes and put her head down. Belle sat, barely breathing, waiting. 'Alright, I suppose there's no point. You aren't going to change what you think about me. You've always despised me, haven't you?'

'No, Jane. The act you've been putting on irritated me and maybe I perceived, subconsciously, vague inconsistencies, but that's probably hindsight. I never consciously suspected there was anything other than what I saw in front of me. That's an interesting one. Why did you assume the persona of "poor Jane" when it's the polar opposite of who you really are?'

At the mention of 'who you really are' Jane sat up, smiling. This had been what she wanted.

'Teresa told you my mother sold me to deSouza when I was nineteen. I had begun to rebel, but she'd had control over me all my life and I was terrified of her. You really wouldn't understand that, so you'll have to accept it's true.'

Belle smiled back. *You have no idea how much I understand that, Jane Perry.*

'She made the arrangement through a dating company. We went out to South Africa for what was supposed to be a holiday. I was pretty much captive and the marriage took place in an office. He was a bestial man, and a paedophile. I was too old for him, but what he most wanted was to get into the UK. I'm not going into detail. Anyway, we had to stay in South Africa for six months after my mother went home. I managed to keep in touch with Teresa. Did they tell you she was sexually abused by her father from the age of six? And beaten, tortured, starved, humiliated. John Cormorant was a monster. Anyway, she got him to pay for a flight – not that he knew what the money was for – and she came out to Joburg. We met up, and we decided to kill deSouza. There was no other way out for me. I was horrified we had to do it, but Teresa was a stronger person than me, despite everything she'd gone through. You probably noticed that.' She paused and took a sip from a plastic cup of water.

'It was easy. She hired someone, who kidnapped him and his body was dumped on the side of the road. It was becoming lawless out there. It was easy to put it down to a kidnapping for money that had gone wrong. No-one questioned me too much. Teresa and I came home. My mother was angry. She soon got over it.'

'How and why?'

'He'd paid her ten thousand pounds for me. Pretty cheap, eh? She'd spent most of it on booze and drugs, plus a load of sessions at a beauty spa.' She stopped and laughed. 'Now that really was a waste of money. We gave her an overdose of vodka and pills one night. It was easy. We thought we were free. I went to work at the government office. No-one knew I'd been married. Then, we decided we needed to be free but with plenty of funds. So, we hit on the plan. I would marry John Cormorant then kill him. We were in the process of planning it, when bloody Angie Stephenson saw us, one night, in a bar in Cardiff. One kiss, that's all it took, one kiss.' She paused again, grimacing.

'She was going to tell everyone I was gay, a lesbian. Humiliate me, unless we paid her. She had a pretty big drug habit by then.'

But how does that fit in with Sue Jones' death?' Belle asked.

Jane looked puzzled. 'I don't understand what you mean?'

'I thought you'd started out on this killing spree because of Sue's death. Wait, are you telling me Sue's suicide played no part in the decision to kill Angie Stephenson?'

'None at all,' Jane replied, sitting back and folding her arms. 'I didn't know she was dead until a couple of months after it happened.'

Belle had to restrain herself, to call on every ounce of self-control she possessed not to reach across the table and grab Jane by the throat. 'So, let me see if I've got this right. You and Teresa decided that Angie Stephenson had to die because she knew you were gay and was trying to blackmail you? There was no element of revenge against your bullies?'

Jane nodded and started to reply, but Belle held up a hand.

'And the timing. It was entirely co-incidental?'

'Yes. It was only later, after Angie's death, that Teresa had the idea about revenge. I went out to South Africa at the start of January, after Sue died in December. I didn't hear about it until we came back.'

'So, let's be clear, when you killed Angie, it was nothing to do with the anniversary of the party?'

'That came later. The most important plan for us was for me to marry John Cormorant, then kill him. It was Teresa who realised the significance of the date. I didn't care too much about the others. She did. She hadn't been bothered by them so much. They must have sensed, even Kat Harris, that Teresa, or Hattie as she used to call herself sometimes, wasn't someone to be messed with. She thought up the plan for me. She really thought I was humiliated beyond bearing by what happened at that party, but, after deSouza, it was nothing to me.'

Belle put her hands down and gripped the sides of her chair. 'And after Angie, you married and killed John Cormorant.'

'Yes. I'd changed jobs by then, after Angie Stephenson died. I worked at the pharmacy at the hospital. It was easy to get the drugs that killed him. He had the start of a heart condition. I just made it happen sooner than it would have done. The idiot hadn't made a will. He kept boasting that Teresa would never see a penny of it, but he might leave me something. Fool! He just wanted a young wife for sex and housekeeping. He didn't like prostitutes, he was afraid of catching something. And I was a good cook and housekeeper.'

'You inherited everything from him?'

'Absolutely everything. We closed the businesses, liquidated it all. And we lived a great life. We travelled a lot. It was on a trip to Australia – we loved Australia. It's where we planned to go permanently – that Teresa thought up the plan to get rid of the others. It was a game to her. I went along with it. I liked it and it seemed only right they should suffer.'

Belle had had enough, but there was just one more question. 'Why did you talk about the strangeness of their deaths and disappearances at the reunion in September? Why draw attention to yourself? After all, with only Kat Harris to go, you were almost home and dry.'

Jane shook her head. 'Teresa was becoming more unstable. She hadn't been right for the past five years, I knew that. I had to get her away. We'd organised her death in 2010. We took Lizzie Maynard, killed her and used her body to say it was Teresa. Teresa had been taunting her, getting her ready. You didn't know Teresa had a period of thinking she was religious, did you? Her father's abuse had been especially bad. I told the police about the torture her father did to her. Even they didn't have strong enough stomachs. One of them threw up. Anyway, she must have said something when she was winding up Lizzie Maynard, who remembered, called her the 'wannabe nun'. The problem was, Belle, that she went to the reunion in September as Mary Conroy and began to talk about the Alpha Kat Crowd. As soon as I heard her, I took over. It had to come from me. If anyone, especially Kat Harris, took a really close look at the woman they thought was Mary Conroy, they'd realise something wasn't right.'

'But why did you send me the email to leave it alone? Ah, of course, you didn't. That was Teresa.'

Jane nodded. 'I couldn't stop her. We had to get away, but she was determined to get Kat Harris. I would have left the bitch alone. So, we waited.' Jane began to cry. 'I told her you were too tenacious, but she wouldn't listen.'

She was sobbing uncontrollably. Belle didn't care. She'd heard enough and signalled to the prison officer that she wanted to leave. He came forward and took Jane away. As she reached the door, she turned her head back. 'It's all your fault, Belle Harrington,' she said, in a whisper.

***

Once she had been escorted back outside, to where Posy was waiting in a nearby carpark, Belle stood for a few minutes to catch her breath and calm down.

'So, how was it?'

'Pointless,' Belle replied. 'Let's go home.'

Chapter 40

Revealed
3 Months Later

Belle sat on what had become her favoured bench at the top of the cliff where she came most days. It looked out on an uninterrupted view of the Channel. Breath came like smoke out of her mouth into the freezing air and rose towards the cloudless azure sky. She had lost track of how long she had been sitting there.

She was getting better, slowly. The prison visit had shaken her, more than she had expected. The flashbacks were lessening, and with the help of a good psychologist she was coping, but the nightmares continued. All because of that evil group of girls, who had made life such an unbearable misery for others, for their own entertainment.

Tears escaped, as usual, when she thought of Sue Jones. Such a waste of a young life. So utterly, utterly unfair. At least Bernie Moloney had felt and shown remorse for what had happened. But the others? Who knew? Kat Harris certainly hadn't and in the end had failed to save herself from Teresa Cormorant's revenge.

Belle was angrier at Jane than she was at Teresa. Teresa had been mentally disturbed, horribly abused since childhood and loved by no-one except Jane, the murderous narcissist.

Belle shook her head, suddenly aware that a walker had joined her on the bench. She started to get up, but a voice said, 'No need to go, Belle.'

Harry Teague was sitting with her. He smiled. 'I thought I'd find you up here. Peaceful it is, on a day like this. You'd think the world was a good place.'

'I don't want to talk, Harry.' She continued to stare out to sea.

'Not a problem. That's not why I'm here.'

'So why are you here? I don't need company. I just want to be alone.'

'I went to Cardiff, you know, to attend the trial. Bob Pugh was there.'

Belle's head shot round to look at him. 'You had no right to do that.'

'I didn't want to talk to him about you. Jane Perry is quite the actress, isn't she?'

Belle grimaced. 'I expect she was back to being "poor Jane".'

'Oh yes. But she didn't fool anyone this time. She's been jailed for life, but you know that. You've seen her, since. Her Barrister put a lot of emphasis on how her mother had mentally abused her, belittled her. Always called her plain Jane and stupid Jane, laughed at her openly in front of other people. He said people who had been abused as she had could never understand what it was like, nor understand what it was like to be gay, in those days. Which is probably true. Got him nowhere, though. Jane didn't seem interested.'

She nodded. 'Do you think Teresa was right? Were opinions so awful, so prejudiced, in the eighties?'

'Yes, they were. What would you have done, if you'd known that two of your school colleagues were in a gay relationship? What would have happened, do you think?'

Belle bit her lip. 'We were in a religious school. That religion was and is toxic. I expect they would have been removed, if not expelled. I would have been, I don't know, uncomfortable? What would I have done if I'd found out? Honestly, Harry, I can't bear to think what I would have done, how I would have treated them, back then. I feel ashamed to say that, to remember that morality, now.'

'We're a more tolerant society, in that respect, although I fear it's changing again. Much more hatred than there used to be, a few years ago. I don't know what's happening to us.'

'Me neither.'

They sat in silence for a few minutes, watching a couple of gulls swooping overhead.

Then he turned to her. 'But that's not what I'm here to talk about.'

She turned slowly to face him, taking a deep breath, staring, not speaking.

'Back in October, Rose told me why you came to St Foy. It was to look for a boy. I guessed, something from your past?'

Belle didn't move. 'I asked her not to say anything.'

'She was worried, she knew this was important. She wasn't here back in the nineteen seventies, but I was, as a boy. I know most of what goes on in this town. It's a small environment. People talk. She told me you asked her about a boy who died. Belle, no boy died here in the mid nineteen seventies. I would have known if he was a local boy, he would probably have been a pal. If he was a tourist, it would have been in the papers.'

She turned slowly to look at him. 'I know that, now.'

'Can I ask why it was important enough to bring you here? I really do want to help.'

She began to shake, her mind racing. If she didn't speak now, she might never have the chance again, to explain, to discover the truth.

Harry Teague is a good man. Trust him. Now or never.

Harry put a hand over hers. 'If it's something too troubling, Belle, I can be here whenever you want to speak.'

'I have lived my life believing I killed him.' There. It was out.

Harry paused. 'But now you know you didn't. Is that what you mean?'

She nodded. 'Yes. I need to know what really happened. If you were here, you may be my only chance to face this, at last, and find out. If I tell you the story, I want your promise you will never repeat it. The only other person to know is – was – my husband.'

He smiled and pointed at his chest. 'Me priest. Good secret keeper.'

'Right, but please don't interrupt. Let me say it all.' She drew in a long breath. 'I was born Virginia Arabella Somers. My father, Gerald, was fifty-nine when I was born. My mother, Gillian Penning, was nineteen. She was his secretary when she lured him into an affair and became pregnant. She wanted his money. Gillian was a monster.

'I loved my father and he loved me. We were on holiday, playing down at the cove. Dad went to get us an ice cream. I saw a boy on the rocks. He beckoned me over. I climbed up the rocks. He said he could jump into the sea. I told him not to be so silly, it was dangerous. He said I should jump with him. He took hold of my arm.' She paused, shuddering.

Harry steeled himself to not speak, let her take the time she needed and carry on.

'I don't remember what happened next. I turned away, as I thought. There was a scream and a splash and the boy was gone. I climbed back down to the beach and ran to my Dad, crying. He took me back to the car. Gillian saw her chance. She said she had seen everything and I had pushed the boy off the rocks into the sea. He had hit his head on the way down. She took me away, said my father was going to tell the police and I would be arrested and put in jail. I was just nine. I was traumatised and I believed her. She was my mother so it must have been true. She blackmailed my father into giving her money. She reinforced the story for years. Dad died soon after. He hadn't made a will and Gillian got everything. Throughout my childhood and teens I believed I deliberately killed that boy. She threatened me with it, always. Told me I was an evil child.

'My husband was the only person who stood up to her. Together, we checked for a death here, but couldn't find anything. Sam, my husband, told me she was a liar, but after believing it throughout my childhood, without evidence to the contrary, I couldn't let it go. In my head, I was a killer.'

She paused again. Harry sat on the edge of the seat, waiting.

'Two years ago, Sam died, of cancer. Gillian knew, she always knew where we were. She'd had a stroke and needed someone to look after her. She demanded I join her. She threatened to tell my workplace I had been a child killer, if I didn't agree.'

She stopped and turned to look at Harry. 'She couldn't have provided any evidence, but, you know, people will always say there's no smoke without fire. I realised, too, that I was still terrified of her. Crazy, for a fifty-something woman. Still, I gave up my job and went to be her carer. I won't tell you what she was like. Gillian was a vile woman. Anyway, she deteriorated and I had a nurse come in, when she had a second stroke. She was dying. A few days before she died, the nurse came to me and told me she was puzzled by something Gillian had said. She could still mutter out of one side of her mouth. She had told the nurse that I was stupid and gullible. That I believed everything she told me. That she had lied. She hadn't seen anything on the beach that day. It had been a way of leaving Gerald, taking me and using me as blackmail. Ironically, she hadn't left a will, either. I suppose she thought she could beat anything. So, I got everything. I was so confused, desperately angry. I didn't know what to do. My life had been based on a lie. I suspected it had also killed my father. I didn't know where to go. I bought the apartment in Newport, but it wasn't right. I was going downhill, on the brink of a breakdown. I suppose I knew I had to face what had really happened here back then. One day, when I hadn't slept for three days, I got in my car and drove. I found myself here. I knew then I had to find out, but I didn't know where to start or what to do. So, I rented the cottage. I've tried to find out, without help. I've been scared that if I said more, people might remember something and turn on me. So, here I am, Harry. Still without any idea of the truth.'

She stopped, put her head in her hands.

'I can help you.'

She looked up. 'Really? You can? You will? I need help, I know that.'

'I'll have to speak to people, but I won't bring you into it. Do you recall the boy's name?'

'Yes, it was Johnnie. He was older than me, maybe around eleven or twelve, tall, dark hair. That's all I remember.'

'Well, I'm not going to tell anyone what you've told me, including Rose. It will be up to you if you ever want to reveal this. In the meantime, I'll get back to you with anything I find. You are staying, aren't you?'

'Yes, for a few months more, at least. I have the cottage until the end of April. Then, we'll see.'

She smiled briefly and stood up. 'I am grateful, Harry. And relieved. It's like a burden off my shoulders. St Foy is growing on me.'

'Before you go, Dan Walker is back from his wanderings. You'll like Dan. He's an oddball. He'll fit in nicely with the Curiosity Club of St Foy.'

She left him sitting on the bench, staring out to sea. When she reached the beach, she took out her phone and called Bette's number.

'Bette, I've just heard. Your friend Dan is back. Shall we get together? Yes, four this afternoon is fine with me. See you all then.'